# SECRET OF THE OLD TOWER

## The MacKay Mysteries - Book 2

### Carol Amorosi

Gu Leor Publications

# ACKNOWLEDGEMENTS

Dedicated to my parents, who instilled in me the love of a good murder mystery.

My love and appreciation go out to my family, especially my husband, Dave, who always puts up with my craziness.

This could never have happened without my editors, Christina and Doris, and my cover designer, Emily.

And my heartfelt thanks to Michelle, Kate, Eileen, Alexa, Jess, and Amy, my fellow authors in the Pickle Jar, for their support.

# CHAPTER I

## DECEMBER 1768

HOME. WHERE IS HOME? Angus sighed deeply as he stared out at the snowy London lane. He itched to be doing something, to have a task to occupy his mind or at least keep him busy.

"Maybe my dinner party tomorrow night will cheer ye up," his uncle said hopefully, turning from his desk. "There might even be some young lasses there." He winked at Angus.

Angus turned back to stare out at the snow. He'd had mixed emotions about his return to London two months earlier. After five years of working with Charles Mason and Jeremiah Dixon in the American colonies, he'd been torn. Part of him wanted to stay with his new friends, and they had wanted him to remain. But how would he support himself? He had nothing to call his own. Angus sighed.

Plus, there was the excitement of working with Charles and Jeremiah at the Royal Observatory here in London. He had to admit that he was drawn to the challenge that opportunity presented. Ultimately, he felt he had no choice but to return to England.

Before his adventures in the wilderness, Angus lived in this house for six years. Why could he not consider it home now? He paced around the room, returning to the window, gazing out at the blinding white scene with the orderly row of brick houses set back from the lane. Angus felt trapped, and not just because of the snow, which was coming down harder now. Even if he could go out in this weather, where would he go?

"Ah, Lad, settle yourself," Lord John Shelton, his uncle, said, looking up again from his desk across the room. He removed his spectacles to peer at his nephew. "Ye are like a wild animal in a cage these days. Everything will work out for ye. Give it time."

"I suppose a caged animal is an apt description," Angus replied, half smiling. "I just find it difficult to be back here when part of me would rather be over there. The work was so exciting. And being cooped inside feels odd to me now."

"I understand," his uncle said kindly. This morning, Lord John was not wearing his powdered wig while working in his study. The light from the snow reflected through the window onto his uncle, and Angus noticed his hair was thinning on top.

"Have ye seen much of Mr. Mason or Mr. Dixon lately? How are they handling being back in town?" Lord John asked.

At the mention of his friends, Angus shook his head sadly. "Nay, I've not seen them since shortly after our arrival. They are busy with the Observatory report," he said as he leaned against the marble mantle.

Angus knew his uncle worried about him, and here he was, distracting him from his work. Crossing to the sofa, Angus lowered himself carefully onto the seat. Though he'd been back for a few months, sitting on the elegant furnishings felt strange, rigid, and uncomfortable.

"When they finish their report, Mr. Mason will return to his home in Gloucestershire to spend the holidays with his sons. As far as I know, Jeremiah will stay at the *Prince of Wales* in Leicester Fields. I know he is anxious to hear word from the Royal Observatory." Angus glanced at his uncle, hopefully. Surely that man's connections with the Society would carry some weight, but as yet, no opportunities had presented themselves. Lord John merely shook his head sadly, his gaze returning to his ledgers. Angus crossed to the window and watched the snow.

*A caged animal, aye, indeed. That is precisely how I feel.*

After two months, this inactivity weighed heavily on him. While involved with Charles Mason and Jeremiah Dixon on their survey in the colonies, there had been constant action. It was ground-breaking, a task never done before. For five years, he lived rough, often in the wilderness on the frontier, braving weather, wild animals, and native tribes. Occasionally, they were fortunate enough to stay in a cozy barn on someone's property, especially early in their work, when they were closer to settlers. His uncle's posh home, with its Chippendale furniture and damask draperies, was quite the opposite. It felt so foreign now.

John Shelton, his mother's brother, was well-placed in London. In fact, he was responsible for Angus being introduced to the surveyors when they hired him for their venture to the colonies. But now, Angus understood he had nothing to recommend himself, no formal education, no university degree. In private, he clung to the hope this lack would be overlooked, and they would see his sharp mind combined with the work they had accomplished on their task. The men successfully delineated the border between the colonies of Maryland and Pennsylvania. It was a revolutionary project, never attempted before, and Angus believed being a part of it would open doors for him on his return. But so far, those doors remained firmly closed.

Angus paced from the window to the marble fireplace and back. "Has Mr. Byrd returned yet? Is there any word?"

John Shelton shook his head without looking up from his ledgers. "Not yet. After the holidays, I expect."

Angus prayed that the elderly inventor would hire him again. Angus had worked for him before he left for the colonies. John Byrd had created the zenith sector that made the delineation possible. Along with his uncle, Mr. Byrd had recommended Angus as Mr. Mason and Mr. Dixon's assistant. Angus felt deeply indebted to both men for giving him a chance. He straightened his shoulders and tried to smile when his uncle rose. Lord John joined him at the window. He wiped condensation from the glass and looked out at the snow.

"Maybe my dinner party tomorrow night will cheer ye up," his uncle said again. The tall, auburn-haired young man was becoming very popular with the young ladies of the town, if not with their mothers. "And there will be many other events over the holidays. They should keep ye quite busy."

Angus smiled encouragingly at the kind older man, though he was not looking forward to the festivities or conversing with these ladies. He found London society dull and rather shallow, unlike his lively discussions with his friends in the colonies. Angus turned back to the window with a grimace, remembering Little Hawk's quick mind and their lively debates. He dreaded the upcoming parties. *I wish I could go back.*

The following afternoon, Angus stood in the bedroom and stared down at the clothing placed on his bed. He had no desire to attend this dinner. The formal wear laid out for him was so uncomfortable. The breeches, sized a bit small, were designed to show off a shapely leg, and the embroidered hose worn beneath them restricted movement. Even the casual daywear he had on at the moment was tightly fitted. His eyes were drawn to the clothes press where he had stored the coarse-woven linen hunting shirt and loose trousers he wore on his return. These had been his daily wear while he worked. When he returned, the housekeeper wanted to burn them, but Angus had stolen the clothing and hidden them away.

*Oh, to wear those again. I wonder what they would think if I wore them tonight?*

He chuckled as he briefly toyed with the idea. But ultimately, he decided that would embarrass Uncle John, and he had no desire to repay his kindness in that fashion.

Folded on the foot of the bed was the wool blanket Little Hawk had given him on his departure. Angus ran his fingers over it and thought again about his friends in Pennsylvania and felt a pang of sadness. He missed her and her brothers, Running Bear and Gray Wolf. The natives had been hired as their guides but became his friends.

And there was Liam and his family, whom he met aboard the ship on the passage to Philadelphia. They sold everything they had to come over and build a new life on a tiny farm. But Angus couldn't imagine himself as a farmer. He had an uncle there, too, from his father's side, whom he reconnected with after believing him dead. In his mind, they were the family he never had. Angus had written to each of them, but mail took months to travel back and forth. He pushed aside the memories with a sigh and reluctantly dressed for the dinner party.

Angus stood with Uncle John and his wife, Lady Anne, in the formal entry hall as they greeted their guests that evening. Angus tried to smile and be polite as the ladies batted their eyes at him over their fans.

*Funny how they all seem to be eligible for marriage.*

Often, he overheard their mothers as they pulled them away, telling the girls he was not wealthy enough for them and lacked a title. The last thing he needed to hear from them was a reminder he had no prospects. That fact haunted him daily as he sought employment.

Soon, all the guests had arrived and were mingling about sipping wine and sharing the latest gossip. Wanting to avoid the younger set as much as possible, Angus remained with his aunt and uncle as they chatted with their friends.

"Ye are free to mingle with the others, Lad," whispered his aunt under her breath to Angus. Lady Anne barely came up to Angus' shoulder and, with her blonde curls, appeared much younger than she was. She gestured toward a group of people closer to his age. Though he knew none of the guests she indicated, Angus reluctantly took the hint. He would have to mingle at some point. As he crossed the room, he grabbed a glass of wine from a silver tray, then joined the edges of the group. Angus watched the men try to be clever while the ladies flirted with their eyes. They giggled at something one man said.

*I hope dinner is served soon,* Angus thought. He dreaded making conversation with the sons and daughters of London society.

Though Angus had to admit some ladies were pretty, all the chatter was about upcoming parties and dances leading up to Christmas and New Year's Eve. *Don't they talk about anything else here?* Angus recalled the Hogmanay celebrations of his youth in Scotland and, more recently, the smaller festivals often held in a barn in the American wilderness. People provided whatever food and drink they could bring. Ale and cider flowed freely, and sometimes homemade wines were available. A musician or two would play lively tunes on a fiddle for dancing. The conversations were of more substance and often grew into heated debates. The parties in London were drastically different.

Angus cocked his head and tried to imagine these people debating the Stamp Act. What would they think of smugglers? Or seeing a wild bear? He shook his head. Then, Angus heard giggling nearby as he accepted an hors d'oeuvre from the elegantly arranged tray carried by a liveried footman.

"That's the man who spent time in the colonies," said a female voice. She pointed a gloved hand in his direction.

"Oooh, his hair coloring is so different," said another.

"Is he the Scotsman?" Another whispered.

Angus glanced across the group at the first speaker, wearing a deep blue gown trimmed with silver. She barely came up to his shoulder. Her long, dark hair was braided around her head. Leaning in, she whispered loudly to the others.

"Yes, he is. Though his hair is not like that flaming red of Andrew O'Connell," replied one lady. Wearing a pale pink gown, she fanned her face as she snuck a peek at him. "Have ye noticed? His eyes are so green!"

Angus pretended not to hear them as he sipped his wine and nibbled on the canape. His cheeks reddened; he loathed that he blushed so easily.

"Imagine spending time in the colonies! How daring!" The woman in blue gasped and brought her fan up to her face.

Angus turned away, not wanting to hear anything further. But he couldn't help overhearing them compare him to the other young men with their blonde hair and blue eyes or their dark hair and equally dark eyes. And their education and titles, things he did not have.

Then a flash of swirling bright green skirts caught his attention as a young woman stepped closer. She lifted her fan at his glance, hiding all but her blue eyes. Though her hair was swept back, a few long blonde curls hung over one shoulder, which she tossed about as she batted her eyes at him. He smiled politely back. She was pretty and taller than most.

But he recalled her mother was one of those he overheard in the entry hall warning her daughter against him.

"I do not believe we have been properly introduced, Sir," she said coyly, her blue eyes shining up at him. She curtsied and said, "Anna Smythe-Jones." She held her hand toward him and looked him boldly in the eye.

"Angus MacKay, ma'am," he took the offered hand and gave it the obligatory brush with his lips. He recognized the flicker in her eyes and fully understood that her mother's earlier censure had piqued Anna's curiosity—*forbidden fruit.*

Anna smiled. "I hear ye lived in the colonies," she said.

"Aye. I spent five years there." Angus waited for the line to follow, knowing she would ask whether he had met any natives. And sure enough, Anna obliged.

"Did ye see any Indians?" At his nod, she added, "Oh, how dangerous!" She stepped closer, her fan fluttering faster.

Angus felt the weight of the bear claw charm he wore under his starched formal shirt and replied, "Nay, the ones I met are not. And many speak English." He marked the expected disappointment in her eyes. He was used to this and hated their assumptions. Most people only wanted to hear stories of heathens and danger. Fortunately, the butler stepped out then and announced dinner was being served.

"Excuse me, Ma'am." Angus nodded to her and left to join his aunt and uncle.

Anna Smythe-Jones huffed off to join her friends.

Angus was pleased to find Lady Anne had seated him at a table with several older men; their wives sat together nearby, keeping close tabs on their daughters. He would be sure to thank her later.

His cousin, Rose, slipped into a seat nearby. While exceedingly wealthy, her husband was a self-absorbed snob, and Angus knew her marriage had not worked out as she had hoped. Rose spent more and more time here at her family's home. The couple began living separate lives when she gave birth to their third daughter. As his cousin took her seat, she winked at him and nodded, leading him to believe it might have been Rose who had placed him there. He smiled in return and nodded. With no surprise, Angus noted that her husband, Lord Henry, was nowhere to be seen.

"I'm sure you are relieved to be back in the real world," said the portly man to his left. Angus recognized his uncle's friend, Sir Charles Bellingham. The man took a swig from his wine and wiped his heavy mustache with his napkin as he waited expectantly for Angus to agree with his statement.

"Oh, things aren't so bad there, especially in the larger towns like Philadelphia," Angus replied, hopeful the men would understand. "It's not so different from towns here, though lacking the old buildings," Angus grinned. The other two men stopped chatting with each other and looked at him. Angus had only recently been introduced to Lord James Whitmore and Lord William Hawksworth.

"Well, I suppose Williamsburg was not *so* bad," Lord James, the gray-haired man across from Angus, offered. "I have dealings in Virginia and made the voyage to visit my interests. Though I believe once was enough." He chuckled at the others. "I hear ye made it out into the wilderness."

"Aye, we did. Much of our work was out there," Angus replied with relief, thinking he had finally found someone with whom he could converse. "I found it beautiful and exceedingly different from England. Out west are mountains that remind me of my youth in the highlands of Scotland." The other men seemed to listen intently. "The work was challenging, and Mr. Byrd's equipment was more accurate than anyone had predicted."

Sir Charles smiled at Angus and took up the subject. "I am pleased to hear John Byrd's equipment was successful. I believe he is up in Durham with his family for the holidays. He will likely return in the new year and resume work on his creations."

"I am glad to hear that," Angus said. "I've heard about his new device. They plan to use it for the observations of Venus in the spring." After hearing the stories from Mr. Mason and Mr. Dixon about the transit of Venus eight years before, Angus longed to be part of this project. Their tales of adventure stirred his blood, not to mention the opportunity to make a name for himself. This was his dream.

"Aye. Captain Cook has already set sail for Tahiti on HMS Endeavor," Sir Charles added.

Lord William, the remaining gentleman at the table, butted in, saying, "My friend, James here, did not see any Indians while in Virginia. But in five years, surely, ye saw some. What are they like? Were they frightening?"

Angus shook his head in resignation and shrugged. "Nay, the Indians we worked with were friendly and helpful. However, not all were so agreeable. A few of the Susquehannock were hired as our guides as we worked our way westward, and they translated for us when we met tribes who spoke no English." Angus noted the crestfallen looks on their faces;

maybe he had misjudged the situation. Like everyone else, they only wanted to hear stories of savages.

Angus was saved from any response as Lord John, seated at the head table, rose and welcomed his guests. The liveried footmen entered with steaming tureens of fish soup. The earlier conversation was forgotten. Angus quietly slurped his soup and listened politely to the men discuss their business. It seemed ridiculous to him how each gentleman he met felt the need to outdo the others with their talk of wealth and business. Angus remained silent as the servants brought out the next course of pigeons in white sauce with asparagus. By the time the footmen brought out the roast goose and savory pastries, Angus was no longer listening to the men's conversation. His thoughts drifted back to his friends in Pennsylvania and rabbit stew around a campfire.

Eventually, the long, tedious dinner ended, and the men rose while the ladies exited to the drawing room. The men pulled out their tobacco pouches, and Angus seized this chance to escape to the library at the earliest opportunity. But tonight, even that room he loved so much held little interest for him. The dinner had only reinforced the knowledge that he would never belong here.

# CHAPTER 2

SOON, THE HOLIDAYS WERE over, and peace settled over the household. Rose bustled into the library one January afternoon, bursting with news. She expected her cousin to look up and ask what was happening, but she received no response from Angus. Rose stood with her hands on her hips, puzzled. This was surprising, especially since there was no book in his lap. Instead, Angus was absorbed in what appeared to be a letter. It must be good news, as a shy smile curved the corners of his mouth. Rose had to know what was in it.

"Angus. Hello, Angus." She was positive he would want to know the news she'd just learned. It was what he had been waiting to hear.

Rose slowly approached, curious. She had never seen him so wholly absorbed—especially since she had rushed in, excited about her news, scarcely able to contain herself, knowing it was important. She paused, still several feet away, studying him for a moment. He sat at one end of the sofa, his right leg crossed over the other, completely riveted by the letter in his hands. Rose's curiosity to know grew rapidly. *Who is it from? What does it say?* She hated secrets.

Angus and Rose did not know of each other's existence until they were seventeen. When he first came to live with them, it was difficult for Rose to accept this new brother. She admitted that she'd been a bit spoiled being an only child. And she didn't enjoy sharing. Soon, however, they discovered they had much in common, despite his coarse manners and grating speech. Angus had admired her sharp mind and quick wit. And he had listened to what she had to say. Rose found his calm manner soothing whenever she was upset. Over time, the pair grew close. She helped him learn proper etiquette and speech.

Rose spent more time at her family home now as her disappointment in her choice of husband grew. When she gave birth to a third daughter, her husband started spending all his time with his unmarried friends at taverns and gambling establishments. At first, Lord Henry Willoughby had seemed so dashing and was incredibly wealthy. Rose knew Angus had not thought highly of him, but she figured Lord Henry brought that on himself as he mercilessly teased Angus about his background.

Her father's younger sister, Elizabeth, had run off with a dashing Scottish laird. As a child, starry-eyed Rose thought it was all so dreamy. But later, word reached them that Alasdair MacKay had been slain at the Battle of Culloden. When Elizabeth fled, Lord John had lost touch with his sister and knew nothing of her whereabouts. Later, Rose came to realize it was not so romantic after all.

Rose and Angus had often stayed up late after he moved in with them. He told her stories of his life before they met. During his childhood, the other boys were mean to him. None of the families trusted his mother's English heritage. Rose, English herself, did not understand this. She knew Angus had found peace in the nearby monastery, especially after the death of his wee sister and, shortly after, his mother.

During those late-night chats, Angus told her how he learned to read and write from the monks. They discovered he had a remarkable talent for mathematics. When his grandmother died, the sixteen-year-old considered himself a man and on his own. However, Father Donal had located his mother's family and convinced Angus to go to London for a proper education. Lord Shelton had agreed and welcomed him into the family.

Now Rose could not imagine her life without him. She tapped her foot impatiently and cleared her throat.

Angus looked up at Rose, suddenly realizing someone had entered the room. While he was sorry her marriage was not what she had hoped, Angus enjoyed having her around the house again. And now, Rose was bursting with news; that much was obvious. But as she was an avid gossip, Angus sighed. He knew it was probably of little import, but he resigned himself to listen.

Rose crossed the room and sat next to him on the Chintz sofa. "Is everything all right?" She nodded at the letter in his hand. He folded the paper. "I assume the news is good?" Angus knew she was prompting him to share.

"Oh, this? Aye, 'tis from a friend," he answered, not wanting to share his letter. At Rose's cocked eyebrow, he explained. "Little Hawk, one of our guides, has written to inquire about my safe return."

"Are ye sure that is all?" She teased him. "I have never seen ye smile like that afore."

To his shame, Angus felt the heat rise in his cheeks. "Aye. So, what brings ye bursting in on me?" He changed the subject, not willing to discuss it with her. Angus was unsure of his feelings toward Little Hawk and wasn't about to share. He missed her more than he had expected.

"Have ye not heard the news? John Byrd returned last night," she said, smiling at him. "He's back in his workshop today."

Angus turned to her, hoping her information was accurate. "Are ye sure? He was not due for another week!" Angus leaped to his feet.

"Aye. I just saw Sir Charles on my way here," she replied. "And he would know."

"He would." Angus nodded, stuffing his letter into his waistcoat pocket and approaching the door. "I must go see him." He reached for the doorknob but paused and, returning to Rose, stooped to give her a peck on the cheek. "Thank ye," Angus told her as he left.

"Good luck," he heard Rose say softly as he opened the door.

A gust of wind caught him in the face when he stepped outside, and Angus pulled the woolen scarf tighter around his neck. Another storm was brewing, and dark clouds hung on the horizon. Angus fought against the headwind along the snowy roads toward the Strand to Mr. Byrd's shop, *The Sea Quadrant,* in Court Gardens.

The bell over the door tinkled as Angus entered. The smells of the shop flooded his senses with memories. Even the aroma of burnt metal as it cooled in the molds smelled good as he stepped inside. John Byrd invented optical instruments and brass devices used to take measurements. He developed the zenith sector Charles Mason and Jeremiah Dixon used in their survey of the Pennsylvania-Maryland border. With its six-foot-long telescope, this instrument was small enough to transport to the new world, enabling the men to view the stars and pinpoint their precise location in the colonies.

Closing the door behind him against the wind, Angus took a moment to absorb the scene before him. Though it had been over five years since he worked here, nothing had changed; metal instruments lined the walls, highly polished glass lenses were laid out on a workbench, and a brass quadrant lay on another table waiting for the precise markings to be etched into it. A young man was languidly sweeping the floor.

The lad looked up when Angus entered. "May I help ye, sir," he asked.

Angus smirked at the term but thought maybe he did look the part. "Aye, I came to see Mr. Byrd. The name's Angus, Angus MacKay."

To his surprise, the blonde young man dropped his broom and hurried over to shake his hand. "I am so glad to meet ye," he stuttered. "Mr. Byrd has often mentioned ye."

"Oh?" Angus was startled. Charles Mason and Jeremiah Dixon were the men getting all the attention. Angus didn't think anyone outside his family knew he was part of the project. "What's your name?"

"Peter Taylor." He smiled up at Angus. "Mr. Byrd stepped out, but he will be back soon. Ye are welcome to have a seat and wait. No sense ye goin' back out in that wind. I know he'd be sorry to miss ye." He indicated a stool near the workbench.

"Thank ye," Angus replied as he sat. This lad seemed a good bit younger than himself when he worked for Mr. Byrd. He had been twenty-two then.

"How long have ye worked here?"

"Six months," the lad replied. "After David Browne moved on. He was here after ye." Shyly, he resumed sweeping the floors, ensuring the dust did not blow toward Angus. He peered up at him occasionally through the mop of hair that slipped over his forehead.

Angus, unused to the attention, studied the finely polished lenses on the table. Besides the cleverness of his inventions, John Byrd was renowned for the quality of his artistry. Angus resisted the temptation to touch the shiny glass objects.

So, his successor had been here for over four years. And it appeared Angus had just missed getting his old job back. Though watching Peter, he comprehended that would not have happened, anyway. Angus was too old to be sweeping floors and running errands. Seeing this youth in his old job made that clear. He had always assumed he could get his old position back. It gave him hope. Now he realized he wanted more than that.

But what would he do? His fondest desire was to work at the observatory in Greenwich. But deep inside, he now understood that was a long shot. Charles Mason had returned to his position as a clerk in Greenwich, but Jeremiah Dixon had not found employment there. Dixon was placing his hopes on the upcoming transit of Venus in the spring, though he was a licensed surveyor and had that to fall back on should he need it.

Angus felt his next step would be to find a place on the Venus expedition with Jeremiah. Maybe he could find out more about that from Mr. Byrd. What traits were they looking for so he could prove he was worthy? He took a deep breath. He needed to calm his thoughts and think rationally before he spoke to Mr. Byrd.

Those thoughts were interrupted as the door whooshed open, and a small, older man blew in, grabbing his white wig and situating it back on his head, hiding the few strands of gray he still retained. His eyes widened behind his spectacles when he closed the door and saw Angus before him. He rushed over and clasped Angus' hand.

"Angus, my lad! Ye've changed a bit. But I would know ye anywhere," Mr. Byrd gushed in greeting. "I believe ye have grown even taller." He laughed.

"Ah, 'tis good to see ye, Sir." Angus gripped his hand firmly.

"Ah, lad, I had hoped I would see ye soon," Mr. Byrd said, a wide grin splitting his face. He released Angus' hand, removed his coat and scarf, and peered up again.

"I want to hear all about your journey. Come, let's have tea in the office."

"That would be nice," Angus replied with a broad grin. As an assistant, he had never been invited into the office for tea. "Tell me about your work. I look forward to hearing about your latest projects."

Angus took a deep breath as they entered the long rectangular chamber running along the shop's length. While the workshop smelled of metalworking and solvents, the aroma of tea and books filled this room. One wall was lined with shelves overflowing with books that were bound, and others held together with string. Papers were piled randomly, and a stack of newspapers overflowed from a table in the corner. Angus remained just inside the doorway, taking it all in while Mr. Byrd set the kettle on the brazier. Most of the remaining space was occupied by a massive mahogany desk that could be used from either side. The older man asked Angus to sit in the red leather chair nearest the doorway, but Angus was initially hesitant.

"Sit, Lad." John Byrd said. He studied Angus while he waited for the water to heat. Angus sat quickly, feeling somehow as if he had passed a test. Maybe he did belong in this world with men of science.

"Ye've changed, more rugged-looking than the eager youth who used to sweep my floors," he said. "And more mature. I imagine ye've been through a great deal." The kettle whistled, and he turned to prepare the tea.

Angus pondered this. He did not feel any different. However, many of his beliefs had been challenged over time, and he learned so much.

"I would very much like to hear about your experiences," Mr. Byrd continued as he placed a cup in front of Angus. "I've seen Charles, so I have heard the technical side. And Jeremiah's highly entertaining version as well, but I am used to his embellishments. I would like to hear your version."

Angus grinned. He was all too familiar with Jeremiah's tall tales.

Then he began to tell his story, starting with their arrival in November 1763, describing the people he met and the sites he had seen as he told him about their work.

Angus spoke of his friend Liam and the Harlan family, with whom they often stayed. He told him about the Indians who were hired as their guides but soon were like their family. Angus talked about the similarities between their tribal culture and his own upbringing in the Scottish highlands. Unlike his uncle's associates, he knew Mr. Byrd would not ask if the Indians were dangerous. After working with him, Angus knew John Byrd was against slavery and held that all men were created equal.

Mr. Byrd was an appreciative audience and asked intelligent questions. He knew from Charles Mason how the new zenith sector had performed, so he asked about life in the colonial towns instead. He was especially interested in the wilderness. John Byrd seemed genuinely curious about the lives of people who gave up everything they had to start fresh over there.

"I must admit I am surprised to hear Philadelphia is so up-to-date," he said after Angus described the buildings. "I suppose I was misinformed thinking it was all log cabins and mud streets, except maybe in Boston."

Angus smiled. He'd thought the same thing before he arrived. "A common assumption, but Philadelphia has much of the same things to offer that you'd find here, though on a smaller scale. Even the clothing was not that different, though somewhat dated, as the fashions take a little time to travel across the sea."

Mr. Byrd chuckled. "I would imagine so."

"With all the timepieces ye design," Angus said excitedly, "ye'd appreciate the large clock Thomas Stretch built for the government house. It looks like a giant-sized hall clock, over forty feet tall."

"Forty feet, ye say?" Mr. Byrd gave a low whistle.

Angus sat up straighter in the chair, placing his hands on the desk in front of him. "I wasn't sure what to think initially, as we arrived in the middle of a massacre of the Conestoga tribe. While the Indians we worked with had traded with Europeans for generations, some tribes refused to abide by treaty agreements. 'Tis no wonder as some Europeans broke these treaties almost as soon as they wrote them." Angus paused and took a deep breath. "Like in Scotland, with my gran and the English. We lost our home. So, ye see, I understand them." He sipped his tea, which was growing cold. He'd never confided this to anyone before.

"And there were people from both colonies spying on our progress. None of us realized how important that border was to the folks living in the area. For over eighty years, it caused trouble, and the people were caught in the middle, with Pennsylvania and Maryland both demanding taxes." Angus smiled. "Though to be honest with ye, I enjoyed my time there. I was reluctant to come back when we finished. But I felt I had nowhere else to go."

Angus stared down at his hands. This was the first time he had even admitted this to himself. Maybe Little Hawk's letter affected him more than he knew. Her words touched him. But the man before him was someone he could confide in, who would understand.

"What will ye do now?" Mr. Byrd asked softly.

Angus looked across at him. He sipped the last swallow of cold tea. "I thought I might ask Jeremiah if he needs any help with surveying if he goes back to that. But I'd really like to be a part of the Transit of Venus project. Any suggestions?"

"Hmmm, let me think on it," he replied. And after a few moments, he said, "Maybe. I think they are still gathering assistants. I'll ask around."

Angus dreamed about being a part of that project, believing he could prove himself once and for all if he worked hard. He rose and shook hands with Mr. Byrd. "I'd like that very much. Let me know if ye hear anything."

Crossing back into the shop, Angus nodded at Peter. He bundled up against the biting wind and left the shop, heading toward his uncle's home feeling lighter than he had in the last few months.

Few people were about with the storm brewing. Angus kept his head tucked in, his chin on his chest as he fought against the headwind, now blowing in the opposite direction. He knew this route well, and peeking above his scarf was enough to ensure he didn't walk into anyone or anything. Most of the snow had been blown into the gardens that Angus passed as it drifted around the hedges and kept the brick pathway clear. Finally, he reached Shelton House. The hinge creaked as he pushed the heavy iron gate open. Angus stomped the snow from his feet before opening the massive oak door. Closing it softly behind him, he heard voices emanating from the drawing room. It was teatime.

Angus handed his heavy greatcoat to Mrs. Ward, the housekeeper, and placed his hat, gloves, and scarf on the table in the entry. Finally, he removed his boots so he wouldn't track ice and snow across the shiny floors. He slid his feet into nice warm slippers.

"Blustery day, eh? I've just served the tea," she told him as she took his coat. "It'll warm your bones."

Angus nodded at her. "Thank ye." He crossed the marble hallway and entered the large, formal drawing room. Before he left for the colonies, Lady Anne had tastefully decorated the room in sage green. The walls were now a soft, buttery yellow, with damask drapes of a slightly darker shade. The furniture was upholstered in a print of yellows and browns. As he entered the room, Angus decided he preferred the sage green décor. But at least Lady Anne had not replaced the Chippendale furniture. He felt it suited the space.

Lord John sat in a deep brown wing chair, staring into the fire with a dainty teacup in his hand and a plate of small cakes balanced on his knee. He glanced up as Angus entered and turned toward him.

"I bet I can guess where ye have been," he said, grinning. "How is John?"

"He looks much older than when I left but still as sharp and focused on his work as ever," Angus replied. "Though he claims I am more mature than I was." He chuckled.

Rose, seated beside her mother on the settee opposite the fire, laughed. "Mature? Ye?"

Angus winked at her as he poured a cup of tea.

"Ye are in fine spirits today, Angus," Lady Anne watched her nephew.

"Aye, being back in the shop brought back fine memories." He sat opposite his uncle's wing chair and stretched his long legs toward the fire. "Mr. Byrd has a new apprentice, so that option is closed."

Rose exclaimed, "Ye weren't planning to return there, not now. Not as an apprentice." She rose and placed Fiona, her infant daughter, into the bassinet nearby. The baby gurgled in her sleep.

"I realize that." Angus stared into the fire. "It is what I *will* do that is the question. John mentioned the upcoming transit of Venus." Pulling his eyes from the fire, he looked hopefully at his uncle. Lord Shelton was a member of the Royal Society and had connections with the members of the Royal Observatory in Greenwich.

His uncle shook his head. "Nay, I've not heard anything further, but this weather has prevented much communication back and forth the last few days. Don't give up hope, though. A task of this magnitude will require many people."

Angus knew his uncle had called on friends and put his name forward for consideration. He also realized he asked his uncle this whenever he left the house. He should know Lord John would tell him as soon as he knew anything.

Lady Anne looked at the men. "This happened a few years ago, right? Venus crossed the sun, and the Observatory tracked it, right?"

"Yes, dear," Lord John replied. "By comparing the data from different points around the globe, we can refine our measurements of the distance between the Earth and the sun. This was first attempted in 1639. Our friends, Mr. Mason and Mr. Dixon, made names for themselves eight years ago by calculating far superior data than anyone else. This spring will be the last transit in our lifetime."

"I would love to work with Charles and Jeremiah again. Do they know yet where they will be assigned?" Angus asked.

"Not that I've heard," his uncle replied. "I know Charles will be going. Since he is a clerk to the Astronomer Royal, he'll be on the list. I assume Jeremiah will be chosen as well."

Rose moved toward the tea cart. But before refreshing her cup, she placed three small cakes on a plate. "I'm sure ye will be needed on that venture," she said as she handed the plate to Angus.

"Let us hope," he said, taking the plate and crossing his fingers.

Later that evening, as the others remained in the dining room sipping coffee, Angus excused himself to his room upstairs. He listened to the wind screeching around the front corner of the house as he climbed. His room was at the back of the house and in the middle. He would not hear the storm. But would he be able to sleep? In the wilderness, he learned to differentiate the sounds he heard at night and could ascertain a threat from the usual sounds of the forest. Here in the house, though, it was too quiet. He suddenly wished he had a corner room.

With thoughts of the wilderness, his mind returned to the letter he had received from Little Hawk earlier. It had not been forgotten while nestled in his waistcoat pocket all day. He pulled his frock coat off, tossing it carelessly onto the back of the chair. As he sat on the bed, pulling the crumpled pages from his pocket, he wondered if she had received his message yet. On arrival in London, the first thing he did was let his friends in the colonies know he'd arrived safely. Angus sent letters to the Harlan family, the Bryans, Liam, Finlay, and Little Hawk.

When Rose interrupted him earlier, he had rushed through the letter, but now he would take his time. He carefully unfolded it, admiring her precise formation of the letters so different from his sloppy scrawl. But then, Angus rarely took his time when writing. Noticing the date, he was surprised to see it had taken almost four months to arrive. She had written it the day he left. As letters typically took around eight weeks, Angus wondered if the others had also written. He observed the crumpled envelope and picked it up. Where had it traveled all this time, and had anyone received his letters?

Angus sighed, then began to read.

*15 September 1768*

*My friend,*

*I watched your ship until it was out of sight today before moving from the wharf. My brothers and I will stay in Marcus Hook for the night as it grows late. Of course, Gray Wolf was hungry. I'm sure that does not surprise you. They send their greetings, but neither can be bothered to write.*

*This port has grown since the last time I was here. As ye know, I prefer to remain near our home and rarely go to Philadelphia with my brothers. There are so many people at the harbor. I feel a little unsettled by it all.*

*I hope you reached home safely and with no delays in your journey. We keep you in our thoughts, and I hope to hear from you as you return to your life in England. We leave for our village early tomorrow, but I wanted to send greetings before we go, hoping this will reach ye soon. Another ship leaves for England in 2 days. Give our greetings to Mr. Mason and Mr. Dixon when you next see them.*

*My daughter, Sun Blossom, wishes you well and asks about your return. Soars with Ravens sends her blessings on your future, which she claims will be filled with adventures.*

*Blessings to you, my friend,*

*Little Hawk.*

Angus read the letter four more times until he could recite it by heart. Once again, he was impressed with her command of English. He knew her brothers had often skipped out on their education, but she had enjoyed it. Memories bubbled to the surface, and Angus felt an ache in his heart. He had grown very close to the natives that guided them and considered Little Hawk and her brothers part of his family, and now her child Sun Blossom as well.

As was tradition, Little Hawk had been joined to a member of the Otter clan, uniting them with her own Raven clan. A matriarchal society dictated the man move into the longhouse of his wife. However, her mate, Lone Coyote, was unsatisfied with life as a trapper. After seeing Little Hawk give birth to a daughter, he felt he had fulfilled his duties and left to join a group of young warriors heading into the wilderness. He disappeared, and after three years, there had been no word of him.

Angus remembered his parents' love for each other, though he had been only six when his father died. This concept of a union was difficult for him to understand. Still, Little Hawk had taken the warrior's departure in stride and focused on raising her daughter and helping her mother prepare the medicines that kept their tribe healthy. Angus had attended Sun Blossom's naming ceremony, and his heart wrenched again at leaving his friends behind.

Angus had grown hesitant as the men had prepared to leave the colonies. Charles Mason eagerly looked forward to seeing his sons again after five years. Jeremiah Dixon had enjoyed their adventures and thrown himself into the work, but he also looked forward to returning to London. But what options had Angus had? The question had filled his mind as the work neared completion. Even then, Angus understood returning to life in London would be difficult. He hadn't fit in there even before he left. And he still did not feel at home here.

The candle flickered, bringing Angus back to the present; it had burned to a stub. As he stared at the flame, he thought again that he should have remained in the colonies. But what would he do there? He only had the small sum of money he earned on the survey. The contract with the Commissioners had met his needs, so he put aside a little. But it wasn't enough. Besides, his head had been full of dreams about coming back here to work at the Observatory. But opportunities there hadn't materialized yet.

Angus placed the letter on the small desk in his room, smoothing out the crumpled pages. He would write to Little Hawk. Maybe that would make him feel better. He opened the drawer and pulled out a sheet of paper, which made him smile. The creamy, smooth paper was a plus side of returning to his uncle's home. After leaving Philadelphia and heading west, they'd saved every scrap for their calculations. He had written on whatever he could find in the wilderness, a piece of wood here and there. One time he covered a stone with numbers. Ink was not a problem, as it could be made from local plants. But the writing leads had worn down early in their work.

Pulling up the chair, Angus sat at the desk. Since his return, he spent very little time in this room, preferring the library, and now he noticed there was no ink in the jar. He rose to fill it but did not feel like returning below.

Angus moved to the bed and sat down. He thought about the transit of Venus. He needed to focus on that. It was the door to his future. Though it seemed his uncle had exhausted his connections. Angus decided to write a note to Charles Mason, who should be back at the Observatory by now. He would also seek out Jeremiah Dixon. And Angus would get in touch with Mr. Byrd again soon, but he did not want to pester the man. Subconsciously, his hand stroked the wool blanket at the foot of the bed. Little Hawk had given it to him. No, he decided. He would write to her now. He hopped up and descended the stairs to the library.

The wind howled outside. No one was around, and Angus filled the jar with ink and quietly slipped back upstairs to his room. He lit a new candle from the stub as he sat at the desk and picked up the quill.

*My friend,*

*Your letter arrived today and was most welcome. It was good to hear from you. As it took four months to reach me, I am in hope my letters to you have arrived in a more timely fashion and that you have received my brief note that I arrived safely in London.*

*I kept the holidays with my aunt and uncle, though there were many parties here during this season. I will admit to you, who knows me so well, that I did not enjoy myself.*

*Mr. Byrd, the inventor who designed the zenith sector, returned to London from holidays in the north with his family. I passed an enjoyable afternoon with him today. A kinder gentleman I have never known. My future is uncertain at the moment, but I hope to assist with the Transit of Venus project as the planet crosses the sun in the spring. Many hands will be required during the observations.*

*I have not seen Charles or Jeremiah of late, but I will gladly give them your regards when I do. Please give mine to my friends over there. And a special hug to Sun Blossom.*

*I think fondly of you all,*

*Angus*

*10 January 1769*

Angus sat back in the chair. He had not expected a letter to affect him so strongly. He set it off to the side for the ink to dry and pulled out a clean sheet to write to Charles Mason.

# CHAPTER 3

JANUARY DRAGGED BY SLOWLY, seemingly endless. The storms became less intense by the end of the month, though snow still blanketed the ground in white. Angus alternated between Mr. Byrd's shop and Lord John's impressive library, its walls covered from floor to ceiling with bookcases. Angus was slowly but steadily working his way through his uncle's collection. After Mr. Byrd's return, Angus visited almost daily, hoping for news.

Jeremiah Dixon was there one morning waiting for Mr. Byrd when Angus arrived. He rushed across to shake his friend's hand before removing his greatcoat.

"Jeremiah, 'tis good to see ye!"

"Aye, and ye as well." Jeremiah warmly clasped his hand. "I hope your holidays were pleasant. How is your family?"

"Fine, thank ye," Angus responded. "How are ye?"

"Cold. And tired of it. Charles is back at the Observatory. I visited him there last week. And I've been to the theatre a few times. Ye should join me sometime."

"Maybe I shall. Charles is well?" Angus asked. He wasn't sure he would enjoy attending with Jeremiah. Angus knew he usually escorted a young lady.

"Aye, he's well and hard at work as ye would expect, though nothing is available yet for me." Jeremiah shrugged his broad shoulders. "And ye? Enjoying London society?" He winked.

"Not really," Angus replied. "I find it rather dull. Will ye be working on the transit of Venus?"

"I imagine so, but there has been no word yet. If not, I will head north to Mr. Burton to check his workload. I may resume surveying in Durham."

This was not what Angus wanted to hear, and he said flatly. "If that happens, and ye require help, please keep me in mind."

"Ye know I will, Angus. Ye'll be the first one I ask."

Mr. Byrd returned, and Jeremiah followed him into the office. Angus started to follow them but realized Mr. Byrd had expected to meet with Jeremiah. Angus was in the way. He no longer worked there, nor was a position available in the shop. He had no reason to be hanging around. A bit embarrassed at his behavior, he decided to limit his visits to once a week. Angus chose Wednesdays for no reason other than it was in the middle and broke up the days.

After breakfast one morning, Mrs. Ward handed him a letter that had just arrived. Angus recognized Liam's block lettering and eagerly escaped to the library to read it.

*My friend,*

*Autumn has been quiet here, and I hope to hear you have arrived in London safely by now. It has been 8 weeks since ye left. I am sure you will be working soon at the observatory and making a name for yourself. Maire delivered our new son last month, and we have named him Angus, after our friend. I hope that pleases you. Niamh and Cara are delighted with their new brother. Michael and Patrick couldn't care less about this new arrival. Maire is well and was soon on her feet again. Can you believe Michael is 10 years old? The boys are a big help to me, and we are expanding the farm.*

*Send our love to Mr. Mason and Mr. Dixon as you see them. And it would please me to hear from you when you can.*


*Your friend,*


*Liam*


*15 November 1768*


Rose entered the library just as he finished, and Angus swooped her up in a big hug. He was happy for his friend and glad to hear the news of their growing family.

"They named their wee son after me!" He gestured at the letter.

Startled at his actions, Rose snatched the letter and read it for herself.

"Liam? That's your Irish friend, right?"

Angus nodded and snatched his letter back. "This one took ten weeks to arrive, much quicker than my last letter. So hopefully, by now, he's received my letter letting him know I arrived here safely." Undoubtedly, one of his letters had made it through. They were posted shortly after this one from Liam. He pulled on his cloak.

"I would think so," Rose said. "Are ye heading to the *Sea Quadrant* today?"

"Aye. I'll be back this afternoon." Angus stuck the letter in his pocket and left for the shop.

This particular Wednesday, the sun was peeking out over the tops of the bare trees lining his way. The sight lifted his spirits and gave him hope. Maybe today there would be news. Once again, he expected he would be part of the transit of the Venus expedition. Word trickled in from Greenwich now that the weather had improved. Angus had run into Jeremiah Dixon exiting the Drury Lane Theatre a week before with a young blonde on his arm. The woman stared up at Jeremiah and laughed. Angus decided not to intrude on the couple, but Dixon saw him and said hello. He introduced his friend as Lady Jane Seaforth, and after a brief chat, Angus continued on his way. He knew if Jeremiah had heard anything, he would have told him. Today, as he walked toward *The Sea Quadrant*, Angus hoped he might run into Jeremiah at the shop. Charles Mason had not yet answered his letter.

No one greeted him when Angus entered the shop, even though the bell over the door tinkled, announcing his arrival.

"Hello?" he called out. The shop appeared empty. Where was Peter? Mr. Byrd never left his shop open when no one was there. Angus called out again and wondered about the silence until he heard a slight cough. It came from the office. Angus crossed the shop and tapped on the wooden door, which stood slightly ajar.

"Enter," croaked a voice from inside.

Angus entered as Mr. Byrd coughed again and looked up to see who was there. Seeing Angus, he smiled and gestured at the chair opposite. "I did not hear ye come in."

Angus removed his cloak and hung it on the peg inside the door before taking a seat. "I was beginning to be concerned. Where is Peter?"

"Ah, he is off delivering some lenses. I am looking over *The Method of Constructing Mural Quadrants.*" He gestured at the booklet on the desk in front of him. "I feel it could be improved upon. I rushed this to publication last year at the commissioner's insistence, though I was not content with it." He cleared his throat.

When he worked in the shop, Angus remembered the Astronomer Royal hounding the inventor to write about his gadgets years ago. Mr. Byrd never wanted to take the time to bother. "That cough doesn't sound good. Shall I put the kettle on?"

John Byrd nodded. "That would be nice. Add a wee bit of honey and lemon to the tea, please. I find it soothing on my throat. The winter dampness wears on me now."

"Aye, my gran swore by that, though she always poured in a bit of the whisky," Angus said, smiling kindly at the old man.

When the steaming cups of tea were ready, Angus placed one in front of Mr. Byrd and returned to the other chair. "Is there something particular ye didn't like in your work?"

"Well, I'm not so sure. I just felt rushed through it, thought I'd take a new look."

"I could take a look if ye'd like, see if I notice anything," Angus offered. He winked at Mr. Byrd, "I have a bit more experience using a quadrant now." Five years of assisting Charles Mason and Jeremiah Dixon had provided the opportunity to experiment with several new instruments.

"Aye, lad, that ye have. I'd be pleased if ye would. A fresh set of eyes might be just what I need. Take this copy home with ye and give it a look." He nodded at Angus as he slid the booklet across the desk.

Suddenly, the outer door slammed open, banging against the wall. Footsteps stormed in and then stopped.

"Byrd! John? Are ye here?" A deep baritone voice called out. "Where are ye?"

Angus rose, looking across at Mr. Byrd. "That sounds like Jeremiah," he said as he crossed to the door.

Angus stopped short as Jeremiah swooped through the workspace toward the office. His long legs closed the gap quickly, his trademark red frock coat billowing around him. Jeremiah Dixon cast an imposing figure at well over six feet tall, even had he been dressed in more subdued attire.

"Jeremiah, what is going on?" Angus noticed the set jaw on the man's face.

"Is Byrd here?" he thundered as he scowled and brushed past Angus on his way into the office where John Byrd was just rising from his seat. Angus hurried to close the door to the street left ajar by Jeremiah's arrival. He then followed him to the office but remained in the doorway.

"What do ye know of this?" Jeremiah raged at Mr. Byrd.

"Of what?" Mr. Byrd responded.

"The transit. What else?"

"I don't know what ye are talking about; I received no word yet from Greenwich," Mr. Byrd said with a cough, slowly sinking back into his seat. He glanced at Angus in the doorway. Jeremiah was angry, and it had to do with the transit. Angus felt the blood drain from his face. His knees felt weak.

Jeremiah took a deep breath as if to calm himself. Angus saw his shoulders sag as he placed his hand on the back of the chair where Angus sat before the interruption.

"The decision has been made at last. Charles and I are to be split up. We will not be working together. He is going to Ireland, and I am going to Norway. Under William Bayley, no less!" Finishing his outburst, he collapsed into the chair. "Got anything stronger than tea?"

John Byrd looked at him momentarily before reaching down and opening the bottom drawer of his desk. He pulled out a bottle of whisky and a small glass and slid them across to Jeremiah. Then, he reached back down, withdrew two more glasses, and looked up at Angus.

"I did not know," he said softly, looking back and forth between them. He pointed to a small chair in the corner and gestured for Angus to move it over and join them.

Jeremiah threw back the shot and poured himself another. Then he poured a glass for Angus. "You know as well as I that Charles and I are the best men for the job. How many times do we have to prove ourselves to these men? University education be damned. And well they know it."

"Well, maybe that is why they made that decision," said Mr. Byrd after considering the news. "Maybe ye and Charles can instruct the younger members of your teams; to share the knowledge, as it were." He sounded hopeful to Angus, who took heart in those words. He hoped to be one of those younger members.

Jeremiah scoffed. "Ridiculous. We've been a team since the first time eight years ago." He bolted back the second shot. "But I am serving as a *junior* under Bayley!"

Angus' hand shook as he reached to accept the whisky Jeremiah poured for him. Who would he be paired with? Or would he go at all? Angus was afraid to ask.

It was then Jeremiah fixed his gaze on him for the first time. Angus stared him in the eye, the question on his mind evident.

"I'm sorry, I do not know, Angus. I only received word about Charles and myself. Keep your chin up. It's still early days."

"Lord John may have received word," Mr. Byrd offered.

Angus downed the whisky and rose. "Aye. Maybe I should return home and see." Full of hope, he pulled his cloak about him and wordlessly left the office. Peter returned as Angus crossed the shop to go, barely noticing the young man as he held the door for him. It closed quietly behind him as he stepped out onto the cobblestones.

The skies were gray now as the heavy storm clouds rolled into the town, and suddenly Angus dreaded going home. Halfway there, he remembered his copy of Byrd's book lying forgotten on the desk.

Angus' initial stride slowed as he drew closer to home. He had exited the workshop in a panic, but now, his steps grew smaller. Soon, Shelton House loomed in front of him. He opened the gate, thankful the footman had oiled the squeaky hinge. He would attempt to slip in and up the stairs without notice. After the long wait, he was suddenly afraid of speaking with Uncle John, afraid of the answer.

Angus closed the front door with barely a click and removed his cloak. Suddenly he heard a sneering laugh from the drawing-room. The door stood open.

"What? Ye thought they'd consider him for a position?" the voice exclaimed. "Gracious, he could barely speak the King's English when he arrived."

Lord Henry, Rose's husband, was here. He was the last man Angus wanted to see. Angus well remembered his arrival here. But that was many years ago, and there was no trace of his Scottish dialect in his speech now. Outwardly, he looked the part of the gentleman he knew he was not. For a moment, he considered slipping past the doorway and up the stairs but realized he would be seen. There was no hope for it. He might as well get it over with; the last shred of hope drained from him, and his shoulders sagged.

Lord John stood across the room near his son-in-law, who leaned against the marble mantle. His uncle was scowling. Setting tea cups on a tray, Lady Anne paused, a delicate cup in her hand. Rose was seated in a wing chair, trying to settle Fiona. But the first thing Angus saw as he entered was the smug face of Lord Henry Willoughby.

However, seeing Angus enter, the smile drifted slowly into a frown of disappointment.

"Oh, ye have heard the news," Lord Henry stated flatly. He was of average height, but though he had just turned thirty, soft living, combined with evenings gambling in the tavern, was taking its toll on him. His face lacked the color of one who spent time outdoors, and he had developed a bit of a paunch, surprising for one his age.

The hall clock chimed three, and Lord Henry straightened. "Ah, 'tis later than I thought. I should go. I must be at my club." As an afterthought, he turned to his wife. "I assume ye will remain here?"

"Aye." Rose glared at her husband, who shrugged in response and left.

At that moment, Angus understood Lord Henry had wanted to be the one to tell him.

Lady Anne rushed to her nephew's side. "I am so sorry, Angus." She placed her hand on his arm. "Did ye hear the news from Mr. Byrd?"

"Nay, all I heard was from Mr. Dixon that he and Mr. Mason were not to work together this time." He looked accusingly at his uncle.

"Well, that is more than I knew. I've only just returned from Fleet Street to find Lord Henry gloating in my drawing-room." Lord John looked dismayed. "But I shall confirm it. Ye can't take that man's word." Glancing at his daughter, he added, "Sorry, Rose."

"No need for that. I understand. But at least ye denied him the satisfaction of being the one to tell ye," she said to her cousin. "I am sorry for ye, Angus. But I enjoyed seeing ye wipe the smile from his face. Let's hope there is good news yet to come when Papa receives official word from Greenwich."

Angus tilted his head at her, though his lips did not smile as he collapsed onto the settee. The delicate legs creaked, and he looked up at his aunt.

"Don't worry," she said. "They are sturdier than they look."

Rose peered into the bassinet, where Fiona slept soundly. Then, moving to the cupboard in the corner, she withdrew four glasses and placed them on a silver tray. Rose pulled the bottle of brandy from the shelf above and filled each glass. "I think we could all use this," she stated as she passed them around.

Lord John swallowed his drink in one gulp and placed his glass on the mantle. Rose and Lady Anne politely sipped theirs. Angus held the amber liquid up to the light from the fire and gazed through it.

"Martha Bryan gave me port in a tin cup," he remembered fondly. "She thought it calmed my nerves after finding a dead body," Angus remembered how shaken up he'd been at finding a member of their survey team murdered. He downed the glass in two swallows.

"How awful for ye," Rose exclaimed. "I think I prefer brandy," she added as she sipped.

"I suppose this is it for me, aye, Uncle?" He looked hopefully at him.

"We don't know yet." Lord John crossed to the bar and filled his glass. Turning, he held up the bottle to see if anyone else wanted more. They shook their heads, and Lord John returned to the fire and sat in the wing chair. "I don't want to get your hopes up. It's too late to go there today, but I will check in the morning and see if 'tis true. Who did they pair with Jeremiah and Charles?"

"Mr. Dixon didn't mention who was going with Charles, but William Bayley will lead Jeremiah's team. I am not familiar with that name."

"He's leading? Not Jeremiah?" Lord John asked, surprised at the news. "Bayley is a good enough mathematician, but to lead the team? I know little about the man, though Maskelyne took him on as his assistant, so he must have some qualifications." He turned away from his nephew, but not before Angus caught the expression on his uncle's face. Angus immediately understood that if they could put this man in charge of Jeremiah, what were his chances?

While he was at his club the next day, Lord John learned Angus was not selected. Many sons of the Royal Society members had suddenly decided the expedition would be great fun, and they were chosen, though few were qualified. For the next three days, Angus did not leave Shelton House, alternating between his room above at night and the library below during the day. He scarcely even looked out of the windows though the weather improved, and there was more bright sunshine than dark clouds. Angus never noticed as he wallowed in self-pity. Entering his room that night, he saw the envelope still lying on the desk. He knew he ought to write to Liam, if for no other reason than to congratulate him on the birth of his son.

*Greetings, my friend,*

*I read your letter with pleasure. I'm sure I do not deserve such an honor as to have him named after me. I don't think it is as much of a name as I had hoped it would be. You are a dear friend. Things have not worked out as I desired, and I realize I do not belong here. I know that now. But I left Philadelphia with such dreams of a different return home, and it seems now that my work in Pennsylvania was in vain. There is nothing for me here as I had hoped. I am not sure what my future holds. Maybe I should have considered starting a new life over there as you have done. But I felt unqualified to take on the challenge. I am glad it is going well for you. Give my love to Maire and the children and such of our acquaintance as you may encounter.*

*Yours truly,*

*Angus*

*27 January 1769*

Angus sealed the letter in an envelope and set aside the writing tablet. Then, picking it up again, he considered writing to Little Hawk. However, Angus quickly reconsidered. How could he tell *her* he had failed? Little Hawk was so strong and self-assured. She knew who she was and had her life planned out ahead of her.

Once again, setting the tablet aside, he picked up the book beside him. Stuck between the pages was an accounting of his assets. He arrived in London as a young man, barely more than a youth, with nothing but the shirt on his back and his grandfather's ring. Now, he possessed another family heirloom, a brooch, a sizeable cloak pin that once belonged to the Templar Order. However, that was not to be sold but held in trust. The small amount he earned on the survey might buy him passage to the colonies but certainly was not enough to set him up in the new world. He briefly considered selling himself as an indentured servant. Surely seven years would pass quickly, and he'd be free again.

Mrs. Ward brought in a tray with cold meat and cheese as Angus slouched on the sofa in the library the next day. It was a lazy Saturday afternoon, though one day blurred into the next for Angus. An open book lay across his lap, but he sat staring into the fire.

"I've laid some mail for ye on the table by the door," she said as she set the tray on the side table. She remained unsure that Angus heard her until he pulled his gaze from the fire and looked up at her.

"Thank ye," he replied, eventually noticing her as she turned to go. Though she closed the door softly behind her, the movement was enough to blow a small card onto the floor where it lay neglected. A message was scribbled on the back: *Meet me for supper at the Prince of Wales at 6.00.* It was signed by Jeremiah. But the card remained on the floor unnoticed.

Family members came and went, and Angus tried to be polite, but he just was not in the mood for idle chat. After Lord John had received word from Greenwich that the positions were filled, they avoided any mention of the project.

Rose and her girls remained at Shelton House. Little Annie climbed into his lap and tried to make him smile.

The following morning, Angus rose at dawn and drank his tea. He was in the library staring at a book on his lap when the door burst open, and Jeremiah Dixon stormed in unannounced. Mrs. Ward hurried behind him, her hands out to accept his cloak and hat. Handing them to her, Jeremiah approached Angus.

"And where were ye last night?" he asked.

Angus pulled his gaze from the fire and asked, "last night?"

"Aye, did ye not receive my card? I invited ye to supper."

"What card?"

Jeremiah dropped one of his gloves and bent to retrieve it, grabbing a small piece of paper on the floor near the leg of the sideboard. He handed it to Angus.

"Well, I was prepared to give ye a piece o' my mind, but it appears ye didn't see this. So I won't hold it against ye," Jeremiah said. He looked from the stack of books on the floor to the untouched tray on the table next to Angus. A look of concern crossed his face. "Have ye been out o' this room lately?"

"Aye. I sleep upstairs." Angus turned to look at him when Jeremiah sat in the wing chair. "Jeremiah, what is to become of me?"

Years of working closely together, depending on each other in the unknown, created a bond among the men. Angus felt he could speak of such things to his friend, things he would not say to his family. He knew Jeremiah understood his situation better than most. Though from a wealthy northern family, his father had refused to allow him to attend a university. Unlike Charles Mason's family, the Dixons could easily afford it. A younger son, Jeremiah, had no desire to work in the family's mining business and had secretly apprenticed to a surveyor, ultimately earning his license. When his father found out, he had disowned him. Jeremiah found solace for the time in a bottle. He had confessed this to Angus one evening around the fire.

"Well, when I saw yer name missing on the list, I knew exactly how ye must feel. I came to see how ye were, especially when ye didn't join me last night."

Angus winced as he heard the words spoken aloud. Everyone else had tiptoed around the subject, but in true fashion, Jeremiah laid it on the line and spoke the words.

"And 'tis time to stop sulking and face the problem. 'Tis why I invited ye to supper."

"But, I-" Angus started to argue that he was not sulking.

Jeremiah cut him off. "Aye. I know I have a lot of room to talk there, but I believe I can help ye." Before Angus could say anything further, he forged ahead. "I have some time before I head to Norway. I still can't believe I am heading there. But I suppose in the land where the sun never sets, I will have the best view." He grinned.

Angus agreed. "Though I imagine that even in June, it will be cold there. I heard from Mr. Byrd that ye and Bayley are to be equals and will be sent to different locations in the country."

"Ah, I wasn't sure how to tell ye," Jeremiah said and had the decency to look repentant.

Angus ignored this, "so, what did ye have in mind for me?"

"Well, I have a couple of months yet, and I thought I would return to Bishop Auckland and resurrect my surveying business. Would ye like to accompany me? I'm not sure, but I may need it to fall back on when this task is complete. I want to be prepared just in case."

Angus hesitated, wondering if the offer was made out of pity. But after consideration, he realized it was made in friendship and said, "aye, I would like that very much. When do ye leave?" *What choice do I have?* He thought to himself.

"There are a few details I need to resolve here. Tuesday?"

"I'll be ready."

# CHAPTER 4

WITH THE PROSPECT OF a journey to distract him, Angus joined the others for a late brunch after Jeremiah departed that morning. Lord John and his wife exchanged glances when he entered, but neither said anything. Both looked happy that Angus had joined them. Angus greeted his aunt and uncle, but he wanted to think over his sudden decision, so he did not tell them of his intentions until that afternoon at tea. It was Lady Anne that broached the subject.

"Mrs. Ward mentioned that Mr. Dixon called earlier. Did ye receive him?" she asked.

"Aye, I did. Jeremiah invited me to accompany him north to his home near Bishop Auckland. He wishes to resume his survey business in the future." There was a glint in his eyes that had been missing for some time. "I hope it leads to something for me when he returns from Norway. I will need to get my license somehow afore I can find a proper position. But accompanying him north will be something for me to do."

"That will be nice and far better than staying around here," Lord John told him.

"Oh, yes!" Rose exclaimed. "Ye need something to do, though I shall miss ye. So will Annie and Mary. So don't be gone too long." She indicated her daughters having their tea in the kitchen with Mrs. Ward.

Mary, dark-headed with brown eyes, was five and named after Lord Henry's mother. On the other hand, Annie looked like Rose's mother, with curly blonde hair and bright blue eyes. She would be three soon. The third daughter, Fiona, Rose named after Angus' sister, who died of a fever when they were children. "Do ye know how long ye will be away?" Rose asked.

Angus shook his head. "I will miss them, too. I've grown rather fond of your girls," he replied. He ruffled Annie's soft curls when she entered. "I don't know how long, maybe two months. Jeremiah will need to return to prepare for his trip to Norway."

Lord John pondered their route as he sat back and sipped his tea. "I imagine it will be at least four days by coach. But to my mind, that is preferable to long days in the saddle."

"Aye, 'tis true, Uncle. I spent several long days on a horse the last few years." Angus looked forward to the journey. He joked with his uncle as he recalled how saddle-sore he became on their extended trips. "However, the process was slow-moving; we used wagons or on were foot most of the time."

Lord John stroked his chin. "I'm thinking London, Northampton, Nottingham, York, and on to Bishop Auckland. It will make for some long days, but I shall see that ye have the fare to ride inside the coach."

"Oh! I have heard stories of people that rode outside falling off," Lady Anne exclaimed. Her eyes were wide as she turned to Angus.

"Oh, Mother, I don't think that really happens," Rose told her. But none of them knew for sure, as the Sheltons owned private carriages. However, only Lord John traveled very far from London. Other than the occasional visits to the seaside, the ladies stayed close to their social circles in the town.

Angus woke up Monday morning eager to pack, though his possessions were few. The only valuable items he possessed were the Templar brooch and the ring that belonged to his grandfather, which were kept safely under lock and key with the Shelton valuables. He would leave them behind. Angus had heard stories of footpads on the road. The items were safer here. He always wore the bear claw around his neck, which had more sentimental than monetary value.

Angus laid two pairs of breeches, two pairs of hose, and two clean shirts on the bed. He wondered if that would be enough and decided that he could wear one set while the other was being washed and dried. And with what Angus wore the next day, he would have a spare shirt and hose. The breeches were black, and the waistcoats contained green to match his frock coat. He added his best shirt and breeches at the last minute. When he closed the door of the clothespress, he spied the trunk and grabbed his loose trousers from it. With Jeremiah, one never knew what to expect. He rolled the items carefully and placed them in a leather bag.

When he finished, the sun shone through the window, and he was overcome with a desire to be outside. Angus burst from the room and ran down the stairs.

Rose was putting Fiona back into her cradle when a thundering noise emanated from the hallway. She looked up, eyes wide. The two older girls sat by the fire, playing with their dolls. They looked at their mother, startled, as Angus barged into the room.

"In the colonies, children spend time outdoors," he explained to Rose. "When they have a chance, they play." He held out his hands to the girls.

Jumping to their feet, Annie and Mary begged, "oh, please, Mummy?"

Moments later, Rose found herself seated on a wooden swing in the garden, holding Fiona bundled against the chilly day. Though Rose had to admit sitting in the sun, it was warmer than she expected here in the walled garden.

Angus played a game of hiding and seeking with Mary and Annie, though his size and red hair made it difficult to find places to hide in the garden. It was still winter, and nothing was in bloom. But her girls were happy. It looked like fun, she thought wistfully.

Lady Anne came through the gate at that moment, hooking the clasp on her cape. She smiled at Rose, "let me take the little one. Ye have some fun." Rose eagerly handed the baby to her mother. Hitching up her skirts, she ran to join them.

After two hours of running and hiding, the merry group went inside, where Mrs. Ward had cups of warm cocoa in the kitchen. As they hung their cloaks on the pegs in the hallway, Rose turned to Angus.

"Thank ye," she said. "That was fun. I can't remember the last time I did anything like that." She hoped her cousin wouldn't be gone for too long.

"I'll return soon. Race ye to the kitchen," Angus challenged her and ran in that direction. Rolling her eyes, Rose followed.

Too excited to sleep that night, Angus stared at the moonlight shining across the bed and onto the floor. He disliked closing the drapes almost as much as he hated the silence. Eventually, he drifted off and woke early the following day.

When Jeremiah arrived at Shelton House, Angus was ready. He was finishing his eggs and coffee when Mrs. Ward ushered Mr. Dixon into the dining room.

"Ah, Jeremiah," Lord John said as he swallowed his bite of toast. "Join us, please."

Jeremiah declined, shaking his head. "No, thank ye. I've got a hired carriage in the lane. 'Tis a kind offer, but I ate before leaving the inn. We should be going."

Angus rose and hugged his aunt and uncle before grabbing his great coat, hat, scarf, gloves, and leather bag.

"Do ye have everything?" Lady Anne asked him.

"Aye. I will only be gone a short while. Give my love to Rose when ye see her. I must have worn her out yesterday." He grinned. Rose had gone home, but they knew she slept in whenever the girls allowed it. Angus turned toward the door and followed Jeremiah to the waiting carriage.

"It will be a long day, but we should reach Northampton this evening," Jeremiah told him en route to the depot where the coaches arrived and departed from the city. "I suggest we pay the extra two shillings and ride inside. That will at least be warmer and out of the weather."

"Aye. I agree," Angus responded. "Uncle John insisted on giving me the fare for the journey. Besides, it looks like rain." He pointed at the horizon.

Everyone heading north opted to pay the extra shillings, and the coach was full. Pressed up against the side of the coach, Angus was glad he sat on the end of the bench where he could lean against the side wall. With Jeremiah opposite, they could stretch their long legs and not disturb anyone else. A young girl, bouncing blonde curls like Annie's peeping out below her cap, rode beside him on her mother's lap. Shortly after they departed, she relaxed against her mother and slept.

This coach was the express and would make only two stops to change horses between London and Northampton. The passengers disembarked in St Albans to stretch their legs and relieve themselves. Only a few ended their journey there. The next stop was Bletchley, where they changed horses again.

"When we get to Northampton, would ye prefer to find a room in the inn? Or are ye fine with shared spaces above the tavern?" Jeremiah asked Angus as they walked around the town, shaking out their stiff muscles.

Angus looked wide-eyed at him. "After the places we've slept? The tavern would be heaven!" He chuckled at Jeremiah. "I can't believe ye asked that. Besides, it'll save some coin."

"Well, I wasn't sure if ye'd grown soft living in Shelton House," Jeremiah teased. "Truthfully, I could do with saving a bit as well. The Society initially paid for Charles and me to have rooms at the *Prince of Wales*, but the last few weeks have been out of my pocket. We made good money overall on the survey, but I need to find a source of income after I return from Norway. My pockets are not so deep, either. 'Tis why we are heading north today."

"Aye, I understand. I spent so little of my earnings in the colonies that I have a small sum put by, but that is for my future, whatever that will be. I don't want to stay at Shelton House forever, living off my uncle. A trade of any kind would be welcome at this point."

Angus noticed the slight smile on Jeremiah's face, little more than a slight curling of his lips upward. And there was a glimmer in his eyes. Angus wondered what his friend was thinking. "I want to thank ye for inviting me along. It has already improved my temperament immensely. I began to feel I was drowning; I was completely at a loss and lacked motivation for anything."

"Aye. I've been down that road," Jeremiah acknowledged as the men climbed back aboard the coach. Two men had joined for this final stretch. Angus nodded at them as he sat.

He knew the story. George Dixon was a wealthy mine owner who intended his sons to be involved in the family business. But Jeremiah had different ideas for his future. He studied mathematics and surveying and discovered an aptitude for both. In his youth, he often snuck off to learn the surveying trade in Durham until his father had found out and cut him off. Young Jeremiah had fallen into drunkenness, ultimately leading his father to have him cast out of the Society of Friends. Thomas Burton, the local surveyor, and John Byrd, who had worked in Bishop Auckland, had rescued the lad and were responsible for his selection to accompany Charles Mason on the 1761 Transit of Venus. Some, including Jeremiah himself, felt the quality of these two unknown men's work embarrassed the Royal Society's members, and they sent them off to the colonies to get them out of the way.

"I know. If anyone understood that feeling, it'd be ye." Angus listened to the pouring rain and hoped something would come of this trip north. He would enjoy working with Jeremiah again.

The coach arrived in Northampton in the driving rain on Tuesday evening. They grabbed their bags and hurried into a tavern near the coaching station. Angus and Jeremiah shook the water off on the covered porch before they entered. Both ordered ale and venison stew. It was served with biscuits and was thick and filling. While the biscuits were dry, dipping them in the stew made them edible and tasty.

While they ate, they arranged for two straw mattresses on the floor upstairs, along with several other men passing through town. The two men from the coach were also making sleeping arrangements. Finished with his pint of ale, Angus rose and stretched.

"I'm done in," he said.

Jeremiah agreed, and the pair made their way upstairs, where Jeremiah chose a mattress furthest from the door. He was exhausted and sleeping soundly within minutes, despite the other men's snoring. Angus stretched out in his greatcoat on the straw padding, with his bag as a pillow, and slept soundly through the night.

The following day was a repeat of the previous one. The men grabbed biscuits and ham from the tavern. They downed cups of coffee and grabbed seats against the wall once again. As before, they would stop twice to change horses before reaching Nottingham for the night. At least the day was sunny, and Angus could see glimpses of the surrounding countryside from the window. The leather flaps covering them had been secured against the rain most of the previous day. The coach on this leg, though also crowded, was more comfortable, being one of the newer models with a steel spring suspension. It glided along smoothly and was capable of incredible speeds. The latest models claimed they could go from Liverpool to London in only three days. Angus and Jeremiah were fascinated with the new technology, and the coachman was happy to show it off. The men crawled beneath the carriage to inspect this new design.

It was not yet dark when they disembarked at their final stop that evening. After arranging for two straw mattresses in the loft of the coaching inn, they walked around the town. As they walked toward Nottingham Castle, Jeremiah grabbed Angus by the arm and pulled him down a side street.

"Come, I've something to show ye," he said excitedly.

Startled, Angus followed him up Castle Rock, past the grand estate the Duke of Newcastle built on the grounds of the old medieval castle. Then, veering down a lane below the cliffs, Jeremiah stopped before a small sign reading *The Pilgrim Pub.*

"It looks old," Angus said, staring at the building jutting from the rock below the castle. He'd never been to Nottingham before.

"Aye, 'tis rumored the knights of the crusades stopped here on their way to the holy land," Jeremiah explained. They entered what appeared to be a small, rather ordinary building from the outside.

However, inside, Angus gasped. "It is cut into the very stone of the cliffs." He was filled with wonder as they ordered two pints and joined others around a large table. Angus studied the walls cut into the stone, enlarging the interior space.

"If those stories were true, this tavern has been here since the 12th century," a man seated next to Angus claimed.

Compared to structures in the colonies, this was ancient, but there were older ones in Scotland. Later, after a few pints too many, Angus and Jeremiah staggered back to the coaching inn, where they slept like babies until morning.

To their great delight, they continued with the new coach the following day. Many passengers had alighted at the stops, but new passengers took their place, and the coach remained full. The final stop was York, and Angus fervently hoped the weather would hold and they would arrive early. He had heard stories of York Minster and wished to visit it. His luck held, and they arrived earlier than expected because of the excellent weather and shorter stops en route.

Angus nearly ran up the steps to the walk atop the old walls. The cathedral towered over the city and was visible from everywhere. Walking toward the massive structure, Angus studied the architecture he knew dated from the early 1200s. Once inside, Angus strained his neck, staring at the graceful arches high above and the elegant tracery in the windows. He was astonished they could build to such heights so long ago. Having grown up near Durham's cathedral, even Jeremiah was suitably impressed.

After an hour, they pulled themselves away. As they returned to the coaching inn, they wended their way through a quirky street of half-timber buildings, whose upper stories stretched over the walkways. Jewelry shops and tea rooms lined their way down the cobblestone streets. They paused in front of a bakeshop before entering and buying buns dripping in a sugary glaze to eat on their journey down the lane. Finishing the sticky treat, they stopped for a pint to wash it down.

"Long ago, this was the old flesh market where the butchers displayed their meat on shambles or shelves," the tavern keeper told them. He placed their pints before them on the bar. Angus decided he preferred the pretty pastries on those shelves now to slabs of meat and turned to say so to Jeremiah. But his friend stared into his beer, looking a million miles away.

"Are ye alright?"

Jeremiah nodded, but as the evening wore on, he seemed less interested in the delights of the town. Angus felt Jeremiah's anxiety growing as they stretched out on their mattresses among the other men that evening, and he worried about his friend. Was he nervous about seeing his family? Jeremiah had not returned since he had left almost ten years before. When Angus tried to broach the subject, Jeremiah merely answered that he was tired. Angus suspected otherwise.

The coach departed for the final stretch early the next day. Although the distance was shorter, the express to Durham did not pass through Bishop Auckland, forcing them to take the local coach. The roads were rutted from the recent rains, which created an uncomfortable, rough ride.

Angus stared out of the window most of the day as they passed through mile after mile of rolling hills and flat river basins. The first portion of their journey followed the River Ouse. Angus caught glimpses of it flowing along as they traversed the smoother ground in this stretch. The coachmen changed horses in Thirsk and Darnton while passengers disembarked, and new ones climbed aboard.

Angus eagerly jumped out of the carriage to stretch his legs. Thirsk, though small, was a market charter town over five hundred years old, and its market square was still well-defined. Jeremiah stepped from the coach and joined him. He'd been quiet, though an impish expression appeared on his face whenever he spoke of Thomas Burton, the local surveyor. Angus was curious to meet the man.

"One more stop, and we'll be there," Jeremiah smiled at Angus. "I'm sure ye will be happy to finish traveling."

"Aye, that I will. But ye seem anxious about our arrival." Angus watched Jeremiah's face as he said this.

"Is it that obvious?" Jeremiah shrugged his broad shoulders. "I suppose I don't know what to expect. Oh, don't worry, Mr. Burton will welcome us. And his wife will take charge, a force of nature that woman. Well, she was." He paused, as if remembering. "But I've not been home in almost ten years, nor have I kept in touch with my family. I cut those ties long ago. But now, Mr. Burton writes that my mother is ailing. He tells me that my brother, George, will accept me back into the family, but I am unsure of his terms. I will not have anything to do with the mines."

In the five years they had been friends, this was the most emotional, Angus had seen Jeremiah. On the survey, he had been very professional in his work; however, he had been a fun-loving joker when he wasn't working, unlike Charles Mason, who often brooded and took everything seriously.

Horses changed, the men sat down, and the carriage continued, stopping in Darnton. Angus explored the old market and went into St. Cuthbert's Church. Jeremiah paced around the market while Angus explored. Jeremiah sighed more frequently as they rode and seemed more distressed the further they traveled. Though Angus felt more relaxed as they went, he was concerned about his friend. The ungracious thought that this might affect his own future crossed Angus' mind, and he pushed it aside.

The stagecoach rolled into Bishop Auckland later than planned because of bad weather on their final leg, but their journey was completed. Angus was relieved that he would not need to climb aboard a coach in the morning.

"This way." Jeremiah gestured to him. "The Burtons will be expecting us, though I did not know when I wrote to them which day we would arrive."

Jeremiah led the way to a sprawling stone house consisting of two levels. A long, low addition extended from one side with a wide door in the middle, with windows on each side.

"The office." Jeremiah pointed at the extension. A narrow front door was centered in the middle of the main house, with two windows on each side and the corresponding ones above in perfect symmetry. The shutters were painted white, visible in the gathering gloom.

Jeremiah pounded on the door, and a short, slightly overweight woman answered. Her hair was pulled back under her cap, but Angus suspected it was gray, judging by the wrinkles on her face, which lit up as she saw who was at the door.

"Jerry, my lad." She threw her arms open, and Jeremiah stepped into her embrace. His face lit up, and he smiled from ear to ear. Angus grinned at the term *lad,* as Jeremiah had celebrated his thirty-fifth birthday just before they left the colonies.

"Thomas," she called, "he's here!"

A thin man whose clothing hung loosely on him approached behind her. He also greeted Jeremiah with a hearty embrace. "Jerry! It has been too long. I know ye've written, but ye stayed away for ten years!"

Jeremiah's face paled. Changing the subject, he said, "this is Angus MacKay, who was such a help to us in the colonies. The one I mentioned to ye." Though he dropped his voice at the end, Angus overheard him.

*What was that all about?*

Jeremiah stepped out of the way, "Angus, Thomas, and Martha Burton." Angus shook their hands. The couple greeted him warmly.

"Ye must come in. I'm sure ye both are tired and hungry. Drop your bags by the door and come eat." Mrs. Burton led the men into a large kitchen, where a pot hung over the fire. We just ate, but there is plenty of stew left."

Mr. Burton gestured for the men to sit. He poured pints of ale and joined them at the table. "Well, it will take months for ye to fill me in on your adventures, Jerry, but I'd love to hear all about them."

"Jerry?" Angus cocked an eyebrow at Jeremiah, who blushed.

"Only these two call me that. When I was old enough to slip away from home, they were my substitute parents until my father found out and forbade it. Though I continued sneaking down here anyway, I ran away after a few years." He smiled fondly at the older couple.

"He always was the defiant one. And I see ye still wear that red coat." Mr. Burton laughed. The sound filled the room, dispelling all the tension of the previous day.

Mrs. Burton brought steaming bowls of stew and a loaf of dark bread to the table. The men listened while they ate. Mr. Burton related the local news, including word of Jeremiah's family. Following their father's death, his brother, George, had taken measures to improve the living conditions of the miners, but there was still a long way to go. Jeremiah's mother had recovered after a long illness, though she remained frail.

"Ye must go visit her." Mrs. Burton encouraged Jeremiah, and he grudgingly agreed, admitting he knew he would have to pay a call.

"Jerry wrote to me often while ye were in the colonies," Mr. Burton told Angus. "I understand ye also have an aptitude for mathematics."

"Well, figuring does come easy to me." His face reddened at the compliment.

"He also tells me that ye learned the surveying trade over the years."

"Well, I did try to help."

"Help? Ye did as much as any of the local surveyors. For one, Joel Bailey was quite impressed with how quickly ye understood the process." Jeremiah added.

Angus blushed again, unused to praise. "Well, it makes perfect sense to me, and I enjoyed it. I miss the work."

Jeremiah exchanged a glance with Mr. Burton. "Shall I tell him? Or ye?"

Angus looked warily back and forth between the two men, trying to understand their unspoken words.

Mr. Burton sat up a bit straighter. "Jerry wants to help ye after all ye did for them. He feels ye did more than was required as an assistant. He asked me to test ye on various topics associated with surveying and teach ye about measuring metes and bounds. This process defines plots of land, which differs from what ye did over there. If ye pass my exam and I feel ye are qualified, we will count the time served under Jerry as your apprenticeship and issue ye a surveyor's license."

Angus was stunned. He tried to form words, but nothing came. This was a complete surprise. Angus glanced across the table at Jeremiah, seeing the wide grin splitting his face.

"Do ye know how hard these last four days have been? I almost blurted out the news several times. But I wanted to include Thomas in the announcement. What do ye say, lad?"

"I'm speechless. I dinna ken how to thank ye." In his excitement, Angus' dialect slipped into his speech.

Mr. Burton laughed. "A Scot. I guessed by your name. There are many here as the border between the two countries went back and forth for centuries. My brother, James, is a tailor up in Durham town who took over our pa's business. Pa had a bit o' the Gaelic in his speech, though just a word here or there."

"Welcome to County Durham, Angus." Mrs. Burton rose. "I am sure the two o' ye need some rest now, so I shall show ye upstairs where ye can stow your bags and get a decent night's sleep in a real bed."

Jeremiah and Angus followed as she led the way. Angus was still full of wonder at this development. Could he do this? He considered all the possibilities open to him once he had his license. Too excited to sleep at first, Angus listened to the snoring from the other bed. He thought back on how much he enjoyed learning from Charles and Jeremiah. Mr. Burton would be another man to learn from, and Angus promised to do his best. Soon, he drifted off.

# CHAPTER 5

Angus awoke to the cock crowing and the church bells ringing. Eager to get started, he jumped out of bed. It was Saturday, but he hoped they would not wait until Monday to begin his training. Jeremiah snored softly in the other bed. Angus dressed quietly, not wishing to disturb his friend. He knew Jeremiah had not slept well the last few nights.

Angus closed the door softly and tiptoed down the hall, unsure if anyone else was up yet. He crept down the stairs into the kitchen. No one was there, but the fire in the massive flagstone hearth fire was lit. As he stood by the table, Mrs. Burton entered through the back door; her apron pulled up in one hand, a brick of butter in the other. Nestled in the fabric of her apron were a dozen fresh eggs.

"Ah, good morning," she greeted him as she entered. "The tea will be ready soon. I hope ye slept well. Or do ye prefer coffee?"

"Oh, tea is fine, ma'am. I slept like a baby," he replied. "I didn't think I would with all the excitement. But it was nice to sleep in a real bed."

"Thomas should be down soon. He's usually an early riser," she said as she placed the eggs in a ceramic bowl on the table. "Do ye like pancakes?" she asked.

"Aye, ma'am, thank ye." His stomach growled.

Within moments, she placed a steaming cup of tea and three large pancakes on the table before him, then handed him a jar of marmalade and a bowl containing fresh butter. Mrs. Burton returned to the griddle over the fire and ladled more batter onto it.

"I assume ye haven't always lived in London," she said as the two chatted amiably.

"Nay, I was born just south of Inverness," he told her. "I was seventeen when I moved to London. I lost my pa when I was six at the Battle of Culloden. After that, mam, Gran, my sister, and I moved about among our relations. I was ten when my mam died and sixteen when Gran died." He paused, idly stirring his tea. "That was when Father Donal learned of my mam's family in London. She was English, ye see. Because o' that, the other lads didn't trust me. When Gran died, I thought I was old enough to be a man on my own, but Father Donal convinced me I could get a better education in the city. My uncle was kind enough to take me in."

"A common story. Quite a few here arrived here from the north in the aftermath o' that battle. I hear life has been tough for those that remained." She stacked pancakes on another plate as her husband entered. "Come to think of it, yer story of hiding from life with the monks isn't that different from Jerry's. Though he hid here with us." She chuckled.

"And I'm no monk." Mr. Burton gave his wife a peck on the cheek before taking his seat opposite Angus. "G' morning," he greeted Angus and dug into his pancakes.

Breakfast was soon finished, and Mrs. Burton had refilled their teacups when Mr. Burton turned to Angus. "Well, lad, it's raining something fierce out there, so we won't do much today." He must have noticed Angus's crestfallen expression, for he continued. "Don't fret, lad. We'll spend the day getting to know each other so I can get a sense o' how much ye already know about the business."

"Aye, that will be fine, sir," Angus said, relieved.

"Ye'll soon see that we are not so formal here. It's not necessary to call me sir. Ye can call me Mr. Burton if that is more comfortable for ye. And as ye see fit, Thomas is fine as well."

"Thank ye, si—I mean, Mr. Burton."

"Well, bring your tea and come with me into the office. Ye can tell me about the work ye did with Jerry and Mr. Mason."

The men bid Mrs. Burton good morning and passed through the connecting door from the kitchen into the office.

"That is certainly convenient," Angus said as they entered.

Mr. Burton stepped back to allow Angus to take in the long, narrow space Jeremiah had pointed out the night before. The office was divided into three sections. In the middle, closest to the main entrance, was a desk with two chairs and a side table laden with papers. Near the end, where they entered from the kitchen, was a large table over eight feet long. Pinned to the top were maps of the local area. Other maps hung from the walls above it. This was where they plotted the boundary points of the properties Mr. Burton surveyed. The far corner was used to store equipment. Shelves lined the walls, and pegs with instruments hung nearby.

Mr. Burton led Angus toward the door leading in from the street. He pulled the curtain over the window as he explained, "I often spend Saturdays getting the paperwork done. My neighbors will drop in if they see me sitting here. So, tell me your story." He gestured to the other chair and seated himself behind the large desk.

Angus took a seat. "Where would ye like me to start?"

"Well, I'm most interested in how ye met Jerry and your role on the survey. That way, I can gauge your training better."

Angus spoke for the next hour while Mr. Burton sat back in his chair and listened.

"Ye already know I have no formal education," Angus began. "When the Society was looking for an assistant for Mr. Mason and Mr. Dixon, I was not chosen initially, but the young man they had selected could not perform the task. A competition was held to select his replacement."

"Oh?" Mr. Burton asked. "A competition, ye say?"

"Well, honestly, I think Mr. Byrd was behind it." Angus blushed. "I was assisting him in his workshop then."

"I would not be surprised if he was. I know John Byrd well. He's from here, ye know."

"Aye, I know. 'Tis how he met Jeremiah," Angus replied. Mr. Burton nodded.

Angus returned to the topic at hand and explained to Mr. Burton the purpose of their expedition and the procedures used, from the calculations based on Charles Mason's observations of the stars through Jeremiah Dixon's measurements on the ground. Throughout the tale, Mr. Burton was thoughtful and questioned Angus about their methods and equipment.

When Angus stopped speaking, Mr. Burton sat pondering for a moment. Angus shifted in his seat, wishing he would say something.

"Well, short of learning metes and bounds, I am not sure there is much left to teach ye. And with five years under Jeremiah and Charles, I'd say ye'd done your time." He rose and gestured for Angus to follow him to the long table.

"So, what do ye know of metes and bounds?" he asked Angus.

"Well, it defines a piece o' land," Angus said simply. "But back in Scotland, we would say a parcel o' land went from a specific tree to a certain rock or maybe a bend in the river. We might even name the adjacent property owner. But I know now that it can be precisely determined with that equipment you have." He pointed toward the corner.

Mr. Burton grinned. "Aye. That is exactly right." He leaned over his table and pointed at lines on the map. "The metes are the precise measurements from point to point using distance and angle, or bearing, like what ye did in Pennsylvania." Looking up, he studied Angus as if making sure he understood. Apparently satisfied, he continued. "The bounds, more properly called beating the bounds, are the physical markers written out in words. For example, a stone wall or a tree, as ye mentioned. When there is no physical feature, we place a marker."

"We did that as well," Angus told him. "We placed milestones along the route with a more prominent marble marker every five miles."

"Very well, ye seem to have good basic knowledge. I can work with ye to gain experience measuring and identifying the metes. Bounds are pretty simple, a written description in words."

Mr. Burton crossed the shop and pointed at several chains neatly coiled on a shelf. "I suppose ye are familiar with Gunter's chains."

Angus nodded; this had been one of his primary tasks on the survey. Once Jeremiah took his sightings with his transit and marked the path, the measurements were taken using the chains. "After a while, I led the chain crew, often pacing the distance next to them. It freed Jeremiah up for more critical tasks."

"Good." Mr. Burton smiled, then indicated long poles suspended from the ceiling. "I don't suppose that ye used rods on a survey of that sort." He glanced at Angus for confirmation.

"Nay, we didn't." He hoped to learn more about them.

Mr. Burton explained, "we use the chains too, but depending on the parcel, the rods are easier. A rod is sixteen and a half feet long or a one-quarter chain. They're good for smaller plots and tighter spaces."

"Nay, we never used those as we were working with long distances, measuring miles at a time." Angus grinned.

Jeremiah entered and paused in the doorway, yawning as he listened to them. He sipped his tea, and after a few moments, he crossed the room to join them. "Looks like ye are getting along well."

They spent the rest of the rainy Saturday afternoon in the office telling tales of their adventures in the wilds of America. Angus felt right at home with the two men. But there were also moments he realized how much he had yet to learn.

After a time, Mr. Burton entertained Angus with stories of Jeremiah's youthful exploits, to that man's great embarrassment.

Before they rose, Mr. Burton turned to Jeremiah and then to Angus. "I will take ye on, lad. I have some time now and a small job that would be perfect for getting ye started. I will pay the normal wage for any work ye do. We have a large undertaking laying out an expansion for the town, and I'd love to have ye stay and join me on that project. But I must warn ye there will be very little local work once that project is complete. And several licensed surveyors will be looking for work when we finish. I hate the thought that I won't be able to keep ye on if ye prove worthy, but I want to let yet know from the start there most likely won't be any work here when we finish."

Angus leaped from his seat in his excitement. "I understand, sir. And I accept your terms. I have no ties and am free to find work anywhere." Angus couldn't believe it. This was the answer to his prayers. He would become a surveyor; Angus knew he could find work once he was licensed.

He eagerly gripped each man's hand. Plus, Mr. Burton was going to pay him!

Monday dawned clear and sunny with a tease of spring in the air, though it was early February. The air was crisp, and Angus shivered as he loaded the freshly split firewood into the rack. Back inside, he warmed his hands by the hearth.

"I've decided to go to Cockfield and see the family," Jeremiah told them. "I might as well get this over with rather than fretting about it. Depending on how well things go with my brother, I will either be back tomorrow or spend a few days with Mother."

Mr. and Mrs. Burton looked at him encouragingly. "Ye'll be fine. Your brother is not your father," Mrs. Burton said. "He is making improvements in the mines. There have been fewer accidents recently."

But Angus knew how his friend had fretted over this visit on their way north and studied his face. He could see Jeremiah had accepted that he needed to visit his mother."I still don't agree with how the miners are treated, but I want to see my mother." Jeremiah sat back in his chair. Knowing he dreaded this visit, Angus patted him on the shoulder in encouragement.

After seeing him off, Angus and Mr. Burton loaded their equipment onto a small cart and headed to a plot on the outskirts of the town.

"Mrs. Smith, the widow, wants to portion off part of her parcel of land to her son. It's a tiny plot, but it will be an ideal job for ye to start."

Mr. Burton explained the purpose of the survey and the process they would use. Though the corners of the property had been defined previously, they measured them again for Angus' benefit. They returned to the office late in the day, so Mr. Burton tasked Angus with writing the descriptions in the morning.

Angus was feeling confident when he rose the following day. He sipped his tea as he pulled out his notes and began scribbling. *Beginning at the Northwest (NW) corner of Section 6 in Township 5 North, Range 8 West, going 3000 ft. south and 1160 ft. east to corner One (1), then go 600 ft. east to corner Two, where lies the previous marker (2), then 1,500 ft. south to corner Three at the large oak (3), then 600 ft. west to corner Four (4), then 1,500 ft. north back to corner one.*

Once completed, he drew a rough sketch, labeling the angles and measurements in his neatest handwriting. And before supper that evening, he handed his work to Mr. Burton.

"Well, ye are the easiest apprentice I have taught. But I might have expected it after five years with Jerry."

"Thank ye, sir," Angus replied. When Mr. Burton turned and walked toward his desk, Angus gave a little skip before following him. "It is work I enjoy, and the mathematics of it makes sense to me. It's all a matter of distance, elevation, and angles. Ye use the same principles I learned on the border survey."

"Aye, I understand, but there are many that don't. I see people like John Byrd and his inventions or the beautiful silver pieces Mr. Kelly creates. They are like magicians to me. So, I suppose some think what we do is magic, too."

Mr. Burton rose from his chair and unrolled a large paper spool on the table. "We'll get that written up for Mrs. Smith and deliver a copy; then ye can work with me on the projected plan of expansion for the town. The others will join us starting Wednesday. It's a major project and will keep ye busy."

"That will be great; I look forward to it." Angus smiled at the older man. He gave another little skip as he left the office.

* * *

Jeremiah remained with his family for ten days before returning to the Burton home. "I've made amends with my brothers," he told Angus that night, "especially George. He's the eldest. I talked a lot with my mother. She was surprisingly interested in my travels and my work."

"That's wonderful. I am glad it worked out well for ye. I thought as much when ye didn't come back immediately," Angus said. He thought of his own family. He'd written, telling them of his news, but it was too soon for a reply. One of these days, he should write to Liam and Little Hawk, but he was too busy.

Jeremiah joined the men on the town project. The rest of February flew by, one day blending into the next. The weather in early March was pleasant most days, and they did more work outside, completing the fieldwork by mid-month. In the evenings, Mr. Burton lit a fire in the office's wood stove, and the men analyzed their calculations and plotted them on the maps spread across the large table.

The following week brought heavy rains drumming on the roof and wind rattling the shutters. After three days cooped up in the office, Jeremiah announced it was time to depart. He had preparations to make in Greenwich before leaving for Norway.

"I must go soon, maybe in a couple o' days. Will ye stay, Angus?" he asked. "Or return south?"

Before Angus could answer, Mr. Burton rose from the table and crossed to his desk. He picked up a rolled parchment.

"I had planned to make more of a celebration of this, but as Jerry plans to leave us soon, I suppose this is as good a time as any." He gestured for the other two to stand. Angus noticed the broad smile on Jeremiah's face as he stepped next to Mr. Burton.

Jeremiah held his hand toward Angus as Mr. Burton handed him the paper tied with a red ribbon. Angus shook Jeremiah's hand as he took the parchment.

"We decided ye deserve this, Angus. Welcome to the Society of Surveyors. This is your license. Use it well." Mr. Burton's smile spread across his face.

Angus' mouth dropped open. Stumbling over what to say, he shook their hands and accepted the certificate. Carefully, he untied the ribbon and unrolled the document, which bore a red wax seal signed by Jeremiah Dixon and Thomas Burton.

"I don't know what to say," he stammered. "Thank ye both." There were tears in his eyes as he looked at the other men. He smoothed the document on the table, staring at his name inscribed in large letters across the top. His voice quivered as he thanked the men again.

Jeremiah departed for London, but Angus chose to stay and help Mr. Burton finish the work on the town project. Their measurements were completed, except for a few points they needed to revisit. However, there was still much to do on the maps, and the descriptions needed to be written.

"Please, give my regards and best wishes to my family for me," Angus said. "And tell them I am well. I wish to pursue surveying, but I don't feel London is where I want to be. I am not sure where I will go, but I will write and let them know my decision. There is plenty of work to finish here. Oh, and my regards to Mr. Byrd, too. I will write and tell him the news."

Jeremiah assured Angus he would pay a call on his family. "But be sure to keep in touch as ye can. I am sure Mr. Byrd would appreciate news from ye. I leave ye in good hands here."

After Jeremiah's departure, Mr. Burton and his men spent the next few weeks completing the new town plan. They celebrated its completion at the *Wild Hart Tavern*, which Mrs. Burton claimed was 'just a good staggering distance' from their home.

Several pints later, while he enjoyed the companionship of the other men, Angus heard voices in the next room singing an old Gaelic song. He recognized it from his childhood. Though he thought nothing of it then, the tune stuck in his head over the next two days. Angus even hummed it as he helped organize the office.

"That's a nice tune," Mrs. Burton said as she brought them tea.

"I learned it as a child but never gave it any thought until I heard it the other night."

The men sat down to drink their tea. Angus bit into a scone.

" I told ye afore Jerry left that I couldn't offer ye a permanent place here. I want ye to know I still feel bad about that, especially since ye chose to stay and finish the project." Mr. Burton told him. "But County Durham seems to be a hotbed of surveyors just now, and there are more people here than there is work for them."

"I understand. Ye've been honest with me," Angus acknowledged. "I've met many of them on the job and at the tavern the other night."

"Many were there to celebrate completing the town plan, but I don't know what most of them will do now." Mr. Burton shrugged. "I am happy to write a recommendation for ye when ye decide where to go. Have ye changed your mind about returning to London?"

Angus suddenly realized what he must do. "I think it's time I returned home to Baile na Croise, my hometown." At Mr. Burton's blank look, Angus translated, "Crosstown in English. I think it's time I went home. My cousin, Rose, mentioned it afore I left Shelton House. And that tune they played the other night; I think it was a sign."

Angus counted what he had left of the pounds his uncle gave him for the journey. Not expecting his life to change as it had, Angus had not brought his savings. The money he earned in the colonies was for his future. It was all he had. And until today, he had not known what that future would be. He returned the coins to his pouch; if he were thrifty with his spending, Angus could travel a reasonable distance north, though he would have to look for employment as soon as he arrived. Well, he'd lived rough before. His gaze fell on the certificate on the desk, and he decided to write Little Hawk to share his news; at least it was good news this time. She had also asked him if he would visit his homeland when he left the colonies.

*My friend,*

*It has been long since I have written, and for that, my deepest apologies. I was not in a good place in my mind. However, my fortunes have recently changed, and I am taking your advice. I plan to travel north to my homeland to see what opportunities may be available there. I have been in the north with Jeremiah for the past two months. Owing to his influence with his former teacher here in Durham, I have earned my surveyor's certificate and hope to find employment in the field. I feel like dreams really can come true. I do not know how long it will take for this letter to reach ye now that I am away from the city. Today is the 3rd of April. The day I begin my new life.*

*I think of you often and send my regards to your family.*

*Your friend,*

*Angus*

"I don't know how to thank ye. I have learned so much, and ye have given me a fresh start," Angus thanked Thomas profusely. "And I will put this to good use." He jingled the bag of coins Mr. Burton had paid him for his work. Angus shook the man's hand.

"Ye earned it, lad." Thomas clasped his hand. "All the best to ye. Let us know where ye land."

"And to ye, thank ye for all your hospitality." He turned and hugged Mrs. Burton.

They wished him well as they said goodbye at the Durham depot. Angus would travel four days to Kingussie, the nearest town to his former home. Unless an opportunity presented itself along the way, he would head there. The manor house had been severely damaged when the English soldiers marched through after the battle at Culloden. And as far as he knew, he had no relations living there anymore. Like himself, they had scattered.

After studying the maps, he chose the route to Gretna, which proceeded to Edinburgh the following morning. Angus could get further each day by coach with the change of horses than riding one himself. He debated staying in Edinburgh for a few days before continuing onto Kingussie via Dunkeld.

Traveling in the Scottish coach was less crowded, but the roads were not as smooth. Angus arrived in Gretna on the first night in a coach full of young couples sneaking across the border where the age limit for marriage was lower. In the morning, the coach to Edinburgh was only half full, and Angus had room to stretch his legs. However, as he neared the city, Angus decided to continue north. It was important for him to make peace with his past. Afterward, he would return to Edinburgh if nothing presented itself near home. Angus had few companions on the next stretch, primarily those traveling from one village to another.

Angus arranged for a straw mattress on the floor at each stop. Paying for space on a bed would be too dear, even with the money Mr. Burton had paid him. He would have to purchase a horse for the last leg up into the hills. On the fourth day, the coach pulled into Kingussie late in the evening. Paying for space at *The Coachman* tavern, Angus collapsed onto the mattress and slept soundly for the first night since leaving Durham.

As he expected, no coaches ran toward Crosstown, so Angus was forced to purchase a horse and sought to find one at a reasonable price. "Besides, if I stay in the area, I will need one." He justified the purchase.

Angus stood at the paddock rail, watching the four horses trotting around. An older-looking black plodded heavily along. A white mare looked like she might be in foal, so he'd pass on that one. He looked once again at the other two.

"I'll take him," Angus told the man at the stable as he studied the large gray before him.

The stable master nodded. "His name is Luath, for his speed. He's young and a bit frisky but not too difficult for someone your size to control."

Angus handed over the coins and mounted for his ride eastward. Baile na Croise, or Crosstown as it was now known, lay to the east in the shadows cast by the peaks of Ben MacDuibh. As he left the town behind, he glanced up uneasily at the remains of Ruthven Barracks on the rise above the River Spey. A chill ran up his spine.

Initially the home of the Lords of Badenoch, the castle had been converted into a fortified structure for the English soldiers. As a child, Angus had been fascinated by the stories of the Wolf of Badenoch, who wreaked havoc on the local area. Following the decisive battle in April 1746, Jacobite soldiers had fled to the site awaiting word from Prince Charles. When word came from his officers to disband and make their way home as best they could, they destroyed the structure before leaving. It still lay in ruins.

Angus became confused, continuing east into the hills toward his former home. The terrain was not as he remembered it twelve years earlier. Suddenly filled with emotion from that time, he nearly fell off when a scream startled Luath. It sounded like a man filled with terror, but Angus wasn't sure which direction it emanated from, as it echoed off the hills. He sat still for a few moments, scratching the horse's neck to calm him. He listened for another scream before resuming his way along the path. All was quiet.

Just ahead, the stark, gray bluff of the headlands arose before him, and Angus realized where he was. Around the next bend was An Dùn Dubh, the old black fort, as folk called it. The broch was on clan land near his former home. He had bypassed the village, which was now behind him.

Though still out of view, his family's manor sat on a rise further to the north.

The broch was a crumbling ancient tower believed to be haunted, and Angus remembered scampering along what remained of the ruin's walls. It stood between the village of Crosstown and the manor house. Angus turned Luath toward the tower. However, as they neared the clearing where the ruin stood, Luath shied and would go no further. Angus spied something blue on the ground. At the base of the structure was a pile of stones; a man lay spread-eagled on the top.

# CHAPTER 6

Angus cautiously slid from the saddle and tied the reins to a nearby tree. He crept slowly toward the unmoving body on the ground, his eyes scanning the area as he moved. The man sprawled awkwardly on stones that appeared to have fallen from above. Shielding his eyes from the sun, Angus peered up the wall and saw where the loosened blocks had previously rested. The coloring of the edge was darker than the sun-bleached stones around them. The man must have fallen when the stones gave way. But what was he doing up there?

The double wall rose almost to its original three-level height on one side, but as it curved around, much of the side where Angus stood was missing. Centuries before, these round structures dotted the landscape. In his youth, the tower was often used for storing grain rather than for defensive purposes. He remembered nights as a young boy when he would follow his cousins from the nearby village. They sat in the dark, listening to stories of ghosts and mythical creatures. He shivered as he recalled the eerie howling sounds and the screams of the ban-sìth, the fairies. His scientific mind now told him it was the wind, but the other side, which believed in things like second-sight, told him otherwise. Angus shook his head. Did he still believe in fairies?

"What happened to ye?" he asked the man, looking at the crumpled figure. It took only a glance to see that his neck was broken. Despite knowing what he would find, Angus kneeled beside the man, listened for any sign of breathing, and then checked for a pulse. Was this the scream he had heard earlier? The man was still warm but definitely dead.

He rocked back on his heels as two men suddenly rode up fast, their horses ridden hard, breathing heavily.

"Who are ye?"

"What have ye done?"

The two men shouted at Angus as they slid from their mounts. Angus rose to face them.

"Why, that's Dougal Og! What have ye done?" the man asked again as he stepped closer and looked at the body on the ground.

"Nothing," Angus protested. "I just arrived. But I heard the scream several minutes afore that."

"I dinna ken who ye are, but few strangers pass through here," a third man approached on foot from beyond the broch. "I find that mighty suspicious."

Angus rose, "I had nothing to do with this." He felt the blood drain from his face as memories of being accused of murder by a short, fat sheriff in Pennsylvania put him on edge. The other two men had arrived from the direction of the manor house, not the village, so Angus took a chance.

"We should inform the Laird at Taigh-Croise," he told them; it was his former home, House of the Cross. He hoped there was a laird there these days. At his mention of the name, the men exchanged a glance. Angus realized his supposition was correct. Someone had claimed the manor in his absence.

A man whom Angus noticed was taller than himself kneeled near the body. The man peered up at Angus, shading his eyes from the sunlight filtering into the clearing around the ruined tower. His green eyes studied Angus before he turned back to the others.

"Dougal Og is dead. We should inform the *laird.*" He returned to his feet, addressing the others as he rose. Angus was puzzled by the emphasis the man placed on the title. He started to question him as he stepped away from the body but paused. The man seemed familiar to Angus until he saw his distinct limp. Angus didn't remember that.

"Well, I say we take this one with us to see the laird," the dark-haired man who arrived on foot insisted. Clad in a frock coat of higher quality than the other two, he seemed in charge. He crossed his arms over his chest and stood well back from the body on the ground. Angus had initially thought he might be the laird based on his clothing, but apparently, he was not. Angus grew concerned.

The stocky blonde holding the reins agreed. "Geordie is just over the ridge with his horse and cart. We were on our way to meet him when we heard the scream. I'll ride over and fetch him. We can take Dougal back with us in the cart. We canna leave him here."

"What about him in the meantime?" The dark-haired man insisted Angus be detained.

Angus gritted his teeth, trying to hold his temper, knowing he was outnumbered. He would go with them, but only on his terms. He searched his mind, trying to find a way out of this situation.

"Well," said the man with the limp, staring intently at Angus. Tall and lean, Angus felt he should recognize him. The man continued, "I dunno. I think it is fairly obvious the man fell, Callum. I don't think he'll be a problem. Ye best be on the way, Archie. Go fetch Geordie and his wagon."

But the man called Callum argued with him and insisted Angus' hands be bound.

"Do what ye will. I am going for Geordie," Archie, the blonde, said, mounting his horse and speeding away.

Angus weighed his options as the man rode off. Could he escape? Even down to two, Angus chose not to argue, though he would not let Callum bind his hands. He tried to control the panic rising in his chest and again denied having anything to do with the man's death. "I don't even know the man," Angus told them. But now he had two of their names, plus Dougal, the deceased.

Callum insisted it would be better to wait inside the tower when Archie left. "That way, we keep him contained if he tries anything."

There was only one way in and out. The man with the limp shrugged and agreed. "We can leave his hands free," he said.

When Callum grabbed his arm to force him inside, Angus shrugged free and ducked through the low doorway on his own.

The taller man kept sneaking surreptitious glances at Angus. He seemed irritated with Callum and remained on the opposite side of the room from him once inside. Angus watched him scowl at the other man.

Angus paced. He didn't want to stand around waiting. Angus wanted to talk to the laird and explain his recent arrival on the coach the night before. It looked like an accident to him, and he felt pretty confident the laird would see the sense of it and not turn him over to the English soldiers. His uncle spent seven years in an English prison after the rebellion. Were the British still the law around here these days? Memories of the short, drunk sheriff in Pennsylvania filled his mind. Murder was a hanging offense.

*Dougal.* Suddenly, he remembered the man. Was this the son of his grandfather's steward? He'd be much older now. *Don't panic.* Angus felt his heart pounding in his chest as he paced. He'd been gone a long time, over twelve years. When he neared the door, Callum hurried over to stand in front of it. The man thought he was trying to escape; Angus couldn't resist testing him. He grinned at Callum and ran up the stairs instead.

Angus turned and saw the other man trying not to smile. Hmm, there seemed to be no love lost between those two. Could Angus use this to his advantage?

Initially, the old Pictish tower consisted of three levels, with a viewing platform around the top. A narrow staircase between the outer double walls led to the upper floors. The inner wooden structure, as well as the roof above, had long since deteriorated. The upper levels had been missing when Angus was a child. Only the ground floor, used for storage, had been covered; now, even that was gone. For their safety, the people who built the broch did not include windows. The only access was through a tiny door that even women had to duck to enter.

Angus could sense Callum's eyes boring into his back as he slowly climbed. He ignored him as he moved carefully, cautious of the crumbling stonework. The last thing Angus wanted to do was fall. Eventually, he reached the point where the wall had broken away, presumably where Dougal had fallen. Footprints in the dust ran up and down the stairs. Examining them, Angus saw they appeared to be smaller. *So, the local youth still sneak up here at night.* If the stones were that weak, should he warn the laird? Though he knew that would not stop the boys.

Carefully, he placed a hand on the remaining portion of the wall and leaned out over the stones. The wall was three feet thick, and though the remaining segment felt solid, Angus was leery of putting much weight on it. He spied a sliver of blue fabric caught on the edge. Leaning carefully against the stones, Angus retrieved the cloth and examined it. He stared down at the body; it matched the blue of the dead man's cloak. He had been up here. This was indeed where he fell.

Angus sat down on the stairs and considered this for a moment. *Why was the man up there? What was he doing?* They called him Dougal Og. So, this was the son of Dougal Mòr, his grandfather's steward. Why would he step out onto the old wall? Angus was not sure how the stones had fallen. The wall did not seem weak. Did Dougal jump? Or did he have help?

*Ok, now ye are letting your imagination take over. Just because ye found another dead body does not mean he was murdered.*

Still, Angus looked around for signs of a struggle. But there were too many footprints in the dust to be sure. Angus clenched his fist, angry that the man Callum thought he was responsible. He remained seated on the stairs until he heard the cart arrive. Angus wondered if he would feel the same if the roles were reversed, and he found a stranger kneeling over a dead man. The more he thought about it, he hoped he, at least, would not jump to conclusions without evidence.

But Angus found the fact that there was a laird encouraging. Maybe he would be more sensible. He wondered who it was and if he might know the man from before. Or did strangers live here now? Perhaps he could convince the laird to listen to him.

A gust of wind tickled the back of his neck as he rose. He studied the wall again. A nagging feeling lingered at the edges of his mind. Angus started down the stairs, stopped, and looked back at the structure. Something was not right.

When the cart stopped, Angus descended the stairs to help. But Callum stepped in front of him. "They'll take care of it," the man told him. He snapped the rope between his hands.

"That is unnecessary. I will come with ye willingly. There is no need to bind my hands," Angus told them. "Take me to speak with the laird."

"I don't know if we should trust him, but we'll leave his hands free. Grab his horse, and we'll escort him back," said Callum. "And get mine too. It's on the far side of the clearing. I was on my way to pay a call on the laird when I heard the scream."

Archie paused and glanced at Callum before crossing to the tree. He untied Angus' horse and fetched Callum's mount. Returning with them, he took the reins of his own horse from the tall man who had checked the body. "Ye are limping more today, Hamish. I'll take these horses if ye'd like to ride."

"Thank ye, but I'll be fine," the man said. *Hamish*. Angus finally had the third man's name. It was a common name in the clan, yet there was something about him. Angus tried to remember. He could think of several boys of that name. But none of them had a limp.

Geordie jumped down from the cart and stood looking at the body; his gaze then drifted upward to where the stones were missing. Callum remained back, gesturing to Archie to help Geordie load the body. "While I keep an eye on *him*." He pointed to Angus.

While the men loaded Dougal's body into the cart, Angus tried to search the ground around the rubble but was thwarted each time by Callum. "Ye ain't sneaking off."

"I am not. I'm just looking. I'll go with ye to see the laird and then be about my business." Angus repeated his request. He was in no position to fight or attempt to escape. He still believed his best course of action was to plead his case to the laird. A chill went through him. What if he didn't believe him? Angus was beginning to regret his decision to press on and come here. Maybe he should have remained in Edinburgh and sought work there.

Eventually, Hamish climbed into the cart with Geordie while Archie led the other horses to Angus' left. Callum walked to his right. They entered the gate leading to the old manor house about thirty minutes later. When his old home came into view, Angus felt the rush of grief from losing his family, first his father and grandfather, and later his mother and sister. And finally, Gran. He blinked back tears. He had not expected returning to affect him so powerfully, creating a hollow in the pit of his stomach.

Catriona stared at the stranger. Her hands rested solidly on her hips, a fire in her light green eyes. Her fiery red hair streamed loosely down her back.

"Who are ye? And what do ye want with the laird?" She glared at him. Something about this man unsettled her. She had heard the group arrive, but Hamish had merely mentioned someone had requested to see her. The man before her in the forecourt towered over Archie and Callum and stood nearly the same height as Hamish. She took in the burnished red hair. *Were his eyes green?* She looked back and forth between this man and her cousin. Hamish's hair was light brown, but he had the same green eyes. Who was this stranger?

Callum shoved past the visitor and joined her, "Dougal Og is dead, ma'am. We found him lying beneath the old tower. And this man was standing over the body. Archie went for Geordie and his wagon to fetch him back here." He indicated the cart left just inside the gate.

Catriona paled at the mention of Dougal's death. Her hands trembled, and she pulled them inside her cloak. Last week the seer had warned her of danger ahead, which would come in an unexpected form. Morag had told her to trust her instincts. Was this what she meant?

"Who are ye?" Catriona asked. Her instincts screamed at her; there was something about this man. She needed to be wary.

"Name's Angus. Angus MacKay," he responded warily to her. "I'd like to speak to the laird, please." He looked around at the faces of the growing circle of people.

"I grew up here," he told her. "May I please speak with the laird?"

"Well, I've been here all my life, and I dinna remember ye." She studied his face. She noticed that Hamish, at her side, paled and winced at the name. She recognized it, too but dismissed it. It was common enough in this area. Just another MacKay. But why did this one, with his proper speech, cause her such unease?

She turned to Hamish. "What happened?"

"I believe he fell from the upper wall," he replied. "There was a pile of stones beneath him as if it gave way on him."

Catriona looked back and forth between Hamish and Callum, then at the stranger. "What was he doing up there?"

"Hmph," grunted Callum. "Is it a coincidence to find this man standing over the body?" He stepped closer to Catriona.

She looked from Hamish to Callum and back. "Is this true?"

Hamish shrugged and shifted again, shuffling his feet as if he didn't want to agree with Callum. She saw Angus study him more closely. Then Hamish looked up, and the two men stared at each other. Catriona half expected them to break into a fight, judging from the tension flaring between them. Then Hamish smiled.

As he followed the man through the gate when they arrived, Angus saw only his noticeable limp and stiff left leg. Now, however, he looked at his face. The man was only a few years older than himself, and Angus felt he knew him. *But who is he?*

Angus broke his stare first, looking back and forth between the man and the woman before him. Then he looked again at the man. A flashback of hiding in the caves up in the hills, watching the Redcoats burning his home below, filled his mind.

Angus did not know who the red-haired woman who stared at him was, but he felt he knew the man. On entering the grounds, he noticed the repair work on the manor house. Someone was rebuilding it. Was this Hamish's doing? Or hers? The men seemed to defer to her, not to Hamish. The laird's wife, maybe?

Hamish smiled. "Angus? Not that scrawny wee lad that hid out with the monks?" he asked, tilting his head slightly.

Memories flooded back. *Of course. Hamish.* This was the only one of his many cousins who had been friendly to him. After the defeat at Culloden when Angus lost his father, the rest of the family had not wanted him and his English mother around. But this one lad had stood up for him. Hamish was the one who took him to the tower the first time to hear the ghost stories and later to search for the sìth, the wee fairies he claimed lived in the ruins.

"Aye, 'tis me. Hamish! I should've known ye." Angus stepped closer, holding out his hand. Hamish took a few moments, casting a wary glance at Catriona before he reached out and grasped the offered hand warmly. His other arm came around, clasping Angus firmly by the shoulder.

"Now I remember. Ye seemed familiar, but ye've changed." Angus smiled.

"So have ye. This is Catriona. She manages the place now." He turned to her, "Catriona, yer cousin, Angus. We grew up together."

So, he had another cousin, though he did not remember her. Angus extended his hand as he took in her long red hair, the green eyes and noticed her height. They were definitely related.

"Cousin? Who were yer parents?" he wondered aloud. She seemed a few years younger than himself.

"My mother was Eileen MacKay. I never knew my pa. Mam told me he was killed at Culloden along with the others. I guess that includes your pa, too?" The end of her statement rose in a question. Reluctantly, she gripped his hand in a firm handshake and stated almost defiantly, "I run the place now. It belonged to my pa's family. My mam spent her entire life making this place provide for the people. It was the death of her, and I run it now."

Angus didn't know who her father was. But the bloodline was evident. The wary look in her eye told him she knew who he was and feared he had come to claim the manor and assume his rightful place. Angus' grandfather had been the laird before he was killed. With the death of his own father, Angus was next in line. But she was the laird now, it seemed. It had never been his intention to resume that life when he returned. He needed to make sure she understood that fact. He'd better tread carefully.

Catriona ordered two nearby men to help Geordie and Archie with Dougal's remains. She had to inform his family—arrangements needed to be made for the wake.

Afterward, she turned to Angus and Hamish. "Well, ye might as well come inside to discuss this privately. At least I can show ye proper Highland hospitality." She dismissed the people gathered in the courtyard and led the way into the hall.

Callum started to follow them, but Angus heard Catriona dismiss him. "Thank ye for your help, Callum. I promise ye this isn't over, but 'tis family business. I will send word if I need your help."

Callum remained in the courtyard as the others scattered.

# CHAPTER 7

A s Catriona led him into the large entry hall, Angus wondered about the woman before him. He hoped he could trust her, especially if Hamish believed him. Angus was happy to see his cousin again and wondered what happened to him to cause the limp. Angus took a deep breath and tried to relax, but he was suspicious of Catriona. He needed to convince her he was innocent. But at least she had sent Callum away.

The stone walls of the entryway were open to the floor above. A gallery with a wooden railing ran along one side—the staircase with its ornately carved banister curved gracefully up the side wall to the upper floor. Amazingly, the wooden handrail had survived the fire. Angus remembered family portraits once lined the walls, but those were long gone. As his eyes drifted upward, he saw someone had replaced the roof. Memories of the old, vaulted roof in flames that fateful day came surging back. Angus quickly looked back down at the floor.

All the furnishings were taken or destroyed when the soldiers left. A round oaken table once dominated the entry hall, and six pairs of crossed swords had hung on the wall below the gallery. Clan members had grabbed the blades as they left for the battle. Now, the walls were barren, devoid of any decoration.

Though he was only six, Angus' father had left him in charge of his mam, wee sister, and Gran. For many years, a sense of failure haunted him as each died. Little Hawk finally convinced him that none of it was his fault. She had pointed out how far he had come since then. Angus clung to her words and touched the bear claw under his shirt.

The manor was constructed in 1700 by extending a 13th-century stone keep belonging to an early McKay ancestor who had been granted the land for service to the clan chieftain. That square structure formed the central part of the hall and included the vestibule. The entry's ceiling had been removed to open up the gallery above, but the three upper floors of the old keep were retained. Wings were added later, with public areas on one side and space for the family in the wing on the other.

Catriona led them past the staircase, through an archway into the smaller of the two dining rooms. The fire was lit, and papers were strewn on a small table along the far wall. Next door, the larger dining room was used in the past for large gatherings and formal dinners. Like the portraits in the hall, those days were long gone. The once elegant space no longer served that function, nor were dances or parties held in the great hall upstairs. At a glance, it appeared Catriona used only the ground floor and had turned this room into her workspace. He would sneak a peek upstairs later, he decided.

Catriona bid the men sit at the oak table surrounded by four simple chairs to the right of the large fireplace. She stepped toward a small doorway in the corner and bid Elspeth, who appeared to be the cook, to serve food and drink for her guests. Shortly afterward, a young girl of perhaps fourteen entered with a pewter jug and three glasses. She poured the cider and left. A moment later, a young lad with light brown hair came through the door carrying a tray with three empty plates, a basket of bread, and a platter containing an assortment of cold meats and cheese. He quickly ducked back through the door.

"I'm afraid this is the best I can do for ye on short notice," Catriona told Angus.

"Dinna fash, it is a feast to me," he told her.

Catriona and Hamish both stared open-mouthed at Angus.

He laughed. "I havena lived in London long enough to lose my bur completely!"

"Aye, but ye sure have developed pretty speech and manners."

While Hamish teased him, Angus still felt the tension in the room and saw Catriona's smile did not quite reach her eyes. Once again, he wondered why he didn't stay in Edinburgh.

Catriona gave the men a few minutes to reacquaint themselves with each other. But she sensed a wariness in them as they sized the other up. She wasn't sure they immediately trusted each other. Her senses were on full alert; Catriona could not understand why, but Angus made her nervous. It wasn't fear, she realized but was tinged with anger. She now knew who he was. Had he come back to claim his inheritance? As the only surviving son of the laird, it was his by right. But her mother was the one who remained behind, who worked to rebuild. Eileen cared for the people, even allowing homeless folks to live in the buildings on the property, even inside the manor house itself.

Over the years, they had worked together to rebuild this structure and the homes in the village. It was no longer the seat of a clan chieftain but a farm that provided for the people. And while most of the ground level was liveable now, the upstairs sat empty. There had only been enough resources to replace the roof. And now that the people had returned to their homes in the nearby village, no one lived upstairs.

As her unofficial steward, Hamish had a suite of rooms down the hall where he slept. And Elspeth, left homeless when her husband died, had taken over cooking for Eileen and Catriona. She slept in a small room off the kitchen at the back of the house. The children who served the food were her son and daughter and lived with her. Gone were the days of the laird of the manor, the representative of the clan chief.

Catriona spent most of her time in this room, which was once the family's dining room. She ate in here and managed the farm from her desk in the corner. The formal dining room next door now held bags of grain, temporarily stored there until the spring planting. A small room on the opposite side of the entry hall contained her bed, a clothes press, and a trunk for the few items she owned. While she lived simply, she was happy.

And now this man arrived to take it all away. How was she going to handle this? Catriona would keep an eye on him, that was for sure. She had men that could help with that. And she would get to the bottom of Dougal Og's death. Did Angus have anything to do with that? She gritted her teeth. As Catriona listened to him talk to Hamish about his exploits in the colonies, she scolded herself. He had made no claims. Yet. But the seer had warned her danger would arrive in a form she would not expect. Well, she certainly had not expected the arrival of the laird's son.

"It sounds odd to hear ye refer to it as Crosstown," Angus said to Hamish as he described the village.

"Aye, it still sits wrong on my tongue," he replied. "At first, we struggled to maintain our language. And many of us speak Gaelic amongst ourselves and try to keep it alive for the bairns. We want our children to know our history. But there are punishments for being overheard speaking it, and they can be severe. So we speak in English whenever there are soldiers or strangers around." He looked at Angus; they'd been speaking English.

Angus understood the implication and said, "Are things still that bad here?"

"Well, ye have been away," Catriona said sternly. "Besides, what would ye care? Ye and your English mother left. Ye lived with others and abandoned your people."

Angus was taken aback, surprised at her tone. "But I lived in the area. For sixteen years. After the battle, we moved about in the hills. Do ye think the people here trusted my mother? Neither the locals nor the Sassenach wanted anything to do with us."

Hamish jumped in nervously, eyeing them as he answered Angus' earlier question. "There are many rules still in effect since ye left. We still canna wear the kilt, play the pipes, or speak our language." When Angus' attention returned to him, he continued, "Though the soldiers are not so interested as time passes, the younger ones dinna even remember why, nor care, as long as they get paid. They used to come looking for a reason to punish us, but they mostly leave us alone these days. We avoid the more obvious infractions, like wearing the kilt or playing the pipes, though I do wear this." Hamish turned back the lapel of his frock coat to reveal a small swatch of the Mackay tartan.

Angus grinned. "I, too, have my token." He reached inside his shirt and pulled out the bear claw. "One of the Indians gave this to me for good luck after the village seer predicted danger."

Catriona startled in her chair, sending a spoon clattering across the stone floor. She fumbled a bit as she retrieved it.

Angus misinterpreted her reaction, "Oh, dinna fret. Those Indians were our friends." He tucked the token inside his shirt and sat back, sipping his cider. "This is delicious. Is it made here?" Catriona settled in her chair, but Angus noticed she eyed him suspiciously.

"Aye, we have an orchard just beyond the rise that Catriona's mother started," Hamish told him. "Best apples around."

"It has grown to several acres since then," Catriona added. Angus guessed she was showing him how well she was managing the estate. Then she sat up. "So, how did ye come upon Dougal Og? What were ye doing at the broch?"

"I'm hoping to find work as a surveyor in Edinburgh," Angus told her. "But afore I start, I had a hankering to see the old house. Maybe I shouldn't have come. I'm sorry about Dougal. I remember him. And his father."

"I wonder what he was doing up there," Hamish commented. "I didn't know the walls had grown so weak."

Catriona glanced at the window. "It's growing darker. I suppose we should make up a bed for ye soon. There's a small space off Hamish's room."

"Thank ye," Angus replied. *A room off Hamish's,* so she wanted an eye kept on him.

Angus stretched out his long legs toward the fire. "Ye know, I never fully realized it afore, but the story of the Indians is not so different from yours."

Hamish looked puzzled. "How do ye mean?"

"Ye talk about the loss of your culture and your language. It is the same with the Indians. The Europeans come over and push them further away from their homeland. They write treaties and then immediately break them. Then they punish the local people for their beliefs and traditions." Until that moment, Angus had not seen how similar their stories were. In the colonies, he recognized some similarities between tribes and clans. But he had not seen the bigger picture.

Catriona leaned forward, placing her elbows on the table. "Why did ye return?" she asked, looking him boldly in the eye.

"The work was finished. I had nowhere else to go," Angus replied honestly. Her question sounded like a challenge. *She thinks I came to recover my heritage.* "I admit I had little money and no skills. Though I do now. So if ye think I am here to stake my claim to any inheritance, ye are wrong."

"I dinna believe in coincidences," she began. "And it bothers me that ye show up here unexpectedly, and one of my men is murdered."

"We dinna ken that, Catriona," Hamish said. "He fell from the broch."

"What was he doing up there?" she fired back at him.

"I dinna ken, but it doesn't mean he was murdered."

"Aye, I believe he was," Angus broke in. A startled silence followed.

Catriona shot him a look that said, 'Aha, got ye' as she sat back confidently. Angus shrugged it off; he needed to explain.

"Oh?" asked Hamish.

"The angle is all wrong." That earlier nagging doubt had suddenly sparked an idea in his mind. "If he fell, the body should have been closer to the base of the wall. It was too far away, meaning he either jumped or was pushed. Had he any reason to take his own life?"

Hamish and Catriona shook their heads.

"I'd like to take another look, if possible." Angus turned to Catriona for permission.

"Do ye have experience in these matters?" she asked. Angus nodded, and she continued, "Ye seem innocent enough, and that statement that ye think it was murder, would the murderer admit it? Wouldn't he claim Dougal fell? On the other hand, it seems too coincidental that ye appear just at that moment. So, I reserve judgment. We'll look in the morning and see if we notice anything. It hasn't rained in a few days, so there may be traces. But I'll keep an eye on ye until I have something I can see."

Angus was shown to a chamber down the hall adjacent to Hamish's room. To his dismay, Catriona stationed one of her men outside, guarding the door. Angus tried telling himself he would do the same thing in her situation; having been accused of murder in Pennsylvania, this was becoming all too familiar. He tossed and turned through the night. Would they ever trust him? Deep down, he realized that he did not belong here anymore. By morning, Angus had decided. He would clear his name and depart. This was no longer home. *Ye canna go back.*

Angus was awake and dressed when Hamish knocked on his door the following morning.

"I am awake," Angus said as Hamish unlocked the door.

Hamish stepped inside. "I want to apologize for Catriona last night. Dougal Og's death shook her more than she wants to admit."

"I understand. I imagine my appearance has as well. Ye or I would do the same in her position. But how do I convince her I am not here to take over? Even if I stay in Scotland, it would not be here." He gestured at the room around him. " I am passionate about becoming a surveyor. I learned so much with Mr. Mason and Mr. Dixon. And I am thankful to Mr. Burton in Durham. Now that I have my license, *that* is what I wish to pursue." Angus watched the mixture of emotions wash across Hamish's face, a sigh of relief followed by a look of sadness.

"I know ye talked about it a bit last night, but sometime, I'd like to learn more about what ye do." He blushed. "I never understood ye sneaking off to the monks. But now, I kind of regret not going with ye. Learning to read later on is hard." He clapped Angus on the shoulder, "let's go eat."

Catriona was already in the dining hall, seated at the table, chatting with Elspeth, the cook. The women stopped talking when they entered. Hamish suspected they were talking about Angus.

"It's about time ye were awake," Catriona said as they sat. "Elspeth has eggs and tea ready."

The cook retreated to the kitchen and returned with the breakfast, thick slices of bread, and small bowls containing butter and jam. "The wild berries have been abundant lately," she said as she placed the food on the table.

"Oh, I love those!" Angus told her, eagerly scooping a spoonful of the jam onto a slice of bread. Hamish dug in as well.

"So, I imagine ye are hoping to prove your innocence today?" Catriona asked Angus precisely as he took a large bite of bread. He could only nod at her in agreement.

Hamish noticed she was on the attack this morning.

Swallowing and washing it down with a gulp of hot tea, Angus said, "aye. I hope to. And then, I'll be on my way."

"I'd like to know what happened. Dougal Og was a big help to me as well as being a friend." Catriona stared into her teacup.

Hamish looked back and forth between them as he ate in silence. Then, scooping a bite of egg onto a piece of bread lathered in butter, he said, "I believe Angus."

And he found he believed him. He knew this man from a young child into a youth, though Angus had spent much of his time down the hill with the monks by then, something Hamish never understood. Angus was only a few years younger than himself, but Hamish had been more interested in lasses at that age. But he remembered that lad, bright and eager to please, though often quiet. Murder just didn't fit with his memories. And he'd been close to Dougal Mòr, his grandfather's steward. Why would he kill his son? It did not make sense to him.

As he ate, he looked at the pair and was struck by their resemblance to two ginger cats sizing each other up, claws out, preparing for a fight. That is precisely what they reminded him of, though he hoped they would get past their differences. He would not admit it to anyone, but he recently discovered he was in love with Catriona, likely he had been for several years now; the feelings developed far beyond friendship. But she kept her distance from all men, not wanting to become involved with anyone. He understood her fear of losing control of the home she and her mother built. But he would never take that away from her but continue to assist in any way he could. He would be her right hand. But Hamish needed time to prove that to her.

More than that, however, he hoped his impressions of Angus were correct, and he did not wish to remain. Hamish needed no more competition than from those already after her. Thinking of Sergeant Wolfe and Callum Campbell, he felt he could handle them. But Angus?

Breakfast finished, and the tea consumed, the threesome rose to leave. They pulled cloaks around themselves as they stepped outside. The sun was up, and the sky was a vivid blue. While April was warming up, the brisk wind whipped around them as they crossed to the stable.

No one said anything as they rode toward the broch. Angus was itching to find something, some small piece of evidence. It did not matter what it was as long as it did not implicate him. As he had just arrived, and nobody knew he was coming, it was not likely anything would be planted. But he was still worried. No evidence pointed to him in Pennsylvania, yet that incompetent sheriff had tried to arrest him.

Catriona rode in front astride her horse; her skirts hitched over her knee. When she mounted, it surprised Angus. He was used to Little Hawk riding this way, but other than the natives, all the women he knew rode in carriages or side-saddle. They turned down the narrow track. Hamish brought up the rear.

Angus' thoughts turned to the task ahead. He suspected Catriona felt he was responsible for the tragedy or was trying to convince herself it was true. Otherwise, it meant she would have to look closer at the people around her. Angus knew how she felt.

The dead man was older than himself, though Angus was unsure how old he was. He had been the son of his grandfather's steward when Angus was a child.

"Did Dougal have any family?" Angus asked as they approached the tower.

"His wife died a few years back, and they had no bairns," Hamish answered. "He had a nephew, though, who has a family. His sister's son. But he lived alone and didna go out much if the weather was poor."

"Trying to work on the theory he killed himself?" Catriona turned in the saddle to glance back at him.

"Nay. Just curious. I remember him when his father worked for my family," Angus told her. "Back then, I would not have thought him the type to take his own life. A religious man, as I recall. I would often see him down at the abbey."

"Aye, he was." Hamish nodded.

Reaching the site, they dismounted. Catriona stood by her horse for a few moments before approaching the rocks. Angus could see the dark blood stain from where they stood, and he allowed her time to compose herself before approaching. Of course, she would be upset by his violent death. She knew this man. When she sighed and stepped forward, Angus crossed to where he could view the angle from the side.

Unfortunately, he could not see the stain on the rocks where Dougal had landed from where he stood. He picked up a rock and placed it in the middle of the blood stain. Returning to the side, he sighted up the tower where the stones once sat and then down to the rock he placed on top. He tried to visualize the angle.

Hamish remained quietly by the horses. Catriona crossed to the fallen stones and kneeled on the ground, crossing herself as she mumbled a prayer. Angus looked up and down the tower, then back and forth along the bottom. He was so absorbed he didn't notice Hamish join him.

"Can ye explain what ye are doing?" Hamish asked curiously. "I do not know what ye are about, placing that stone and looking up and down."

"I'm trying to work out the angle," Angus remembered trying to explain this to his friends in the colonies. He paused from his mental calculations to explain. It helped to draw it out. He fetched a stick and smoothed out a patch of dirt near his feet. He drew a line. "This is the tower." He drew another line at the end, perpendicular to the first. "This is the ground." He drew an X on each line. "This is where Dougal Og landed, and the stones fell from up there." He pointed at each X.

"Aye," Hamish said. "I am with ye so far."

Catriona joined them, watching Angus sketch in the dirt.

"Wait." Angus had an idea and picked up two stones. Holding one in his palm, he tipped it just enough for it to fall. It landed not far from his foot. The other, he gave a slight nudge. That stone landed several inches further away from the previous one. "See how that one is close to the wall, and the other is not?"

They nodded. Then Catriona moved to where Angus had been studying the angle. "Ye are right. The body is too far from the wall." Suddenly, she picked up two stones about the size of small cannonballs and ducked into the structure. Shortly after, she appeared in the gap and placed both stones on the edge.

Angus recognized what she was doing. She was bright; she would work this out on her own. As he watched, Catriona barely touched the first stone and watched it fall, landing close to the tower's base. She pushed the other one, which landed several feet away from the wall.

"Well, that sure puts things in a different light. Dougal did not fall." She called down to them, tilting her head as she studied Angus. "Are ye going to push the idea that he jumped?"

Angus gritted his teeth in frustration. "Nay. I don't believe he did. But who killed him? I have been away too long to venture a guess." Angus looked at each of them.

"Well, ye could have pushed him." Catriona accused.

"So, I ran up there and pushed a man I hadn't seen since childhood off the tower. Then I ran back down to kneel over him when the others arrived? For what purpose? I only arrived in the area the night before. "

Angus stomped away to examine the ground around the fallen blocks and shook his head. "We stirred things up too much yesterday. And there are too many footprints on the stairs to recognize a particular set."

"Aye, the lads still come here for ghost stories as we did," Hamish said. "Their rite of passage. It's no wonder there are so many footprints."

"Not just the lads," Catriona told them. Hamish cocked an eyebrow at her. She grinned.

Angus worked his way outward from where they stood, thankful he had learned so much about tracking from Gray Wolf, one of the native guides he had befriended in the colonies. But the ground had been heavily trampled, and the wagon wheels had obliterated the footprints near the body. He kept searching, hoping to find something. The rocks tumbled down a steep incline to one side of the doorway, so exploring there was no use. He focused on the opposite side, where a narrow track disappeared into the forest. There were far fewer footprints here. Angus followed them back until he reached the hard-packed rocky ground, where the marks in the loose soil disappeared.

There was only one set that caught his attention. They ran from the hardened earth to the clearing and back again, disappearing under the wagon tracks and hoofprints. Someone had either left the tower and then returned or, more likely, vice versa. Angus bet that someone had come to the ruin and returned by the way they came after killing Dougal.

"Look at this set," he said as he gestured to the others. "They appear to be more recent than the rest and are on top of the other marks, wiping out parts of the ones beneath."

"They look recent and run in both directions, coming and going," Hamish said as he stared down at them.

Angus kneeled. He reached out and touched the set heading from the clearing.

"Whoever it was, they don't walk evenly on their feet. This man has a distinct limp." Though he did not want to believe it, Angus stared wide-eyed at Hamish. The youth he knew would never have done something like this.

"Nay! 'Twas not me," Hamish protested. His face paled as he shook his head vigorously. "They aren't the same size." But as he placed his foot beside the nearest imprint, he looked at Angus in horror. They matched exactly. "No! It couldna be."

"Nay, 'twas not." Catriona stepped next to Hamish. "There is one man here it could not be: Hamish. We spent all of yesterday on the ledgers until he left with Archie to fetch Geordie and his wagon to haul some grain for me."

"Aye. We were on our way there when we heard the scream." He glared at Angus. "How could ye even think it was me?"

"I didn't, and I don't believe it was ye. But it was someone else with a limp or somebody wanting everyone to think it was ye." Angus rose and patted Hamish on the shoulder. Though it was twelve years since he had seen his cousin, he believed a man's character didn't change that much.

Catriona studied the prints. "Hamish, just so we can say we ruled ye out as a possibility, come stand in these and show us they are not yours."

Hamish obliged again, and to his shock and dismay, not only were they the same size, but the prints were a perfect match to the boots he wore. "Nay!" He shouted. His face was pale. "Ye ken it wasna me, Catriona. And Archie will back me as well."

"I believe ye, Hamish," she replied, taking his hand. "Ye are the person I trust most in the entire world. We'll sort this out."

"Have ye another pair, Hamish?" Angus asked.

His friend nodded. "Aye. Wait, I wasna wearing this pair yesterday."

Angus continued, "Two men were murdered in the colonies while I was there, and a cantankerous sheriff liked nothing more than to accuse me. Fortunately, we proved him wrong, and I was cleared. Somehow, I will do the same for ye."

"Thank ye, Angus. I guess this clears ye also," Hamish said. "And thank ye too, Catriona. I'm glad to know ye have faith in me." He stared down at the ground. "Who would do this to me? And why?"

"The first thing that comes to my mind is getting ye out of the way," Angus nodded at Catriona. "Have ye any suitors?"

"None that I am interested in," Catriona answered. Angus watched Hamish glance away.

# CHAPTER 8

"So, THE ONE CALLED Callum that was with ye when we found the body? He doesn't live here?" Angus asked. At first, he had thought Callum was the laird with his elegant clothes and stately bearing. But Angus didn't believe he was a MacKay with his dark coloring and diminutive stature.

"Callum Campbell? Nay!" Catriona exclaimed. "Thank goodness."

"Nay," Hamish explained. "He owns a large estate outside Kingussie on the Spey River." He tilted his head toward Catriona. "But he spends a good bit o' time up here." Angus did not miss the scowl on Hamish's face.

*Ah, so that's the way of it, then.* "I wondered why he left and hadn't joined us when we went inside. He seemed in charge at the tower. I assumed he lived here."

Hamish fairly growled, "Nay, but he's always here." He blushed and glanced at Catriona, who walked beside him toward their horses.

Catriona stood up straighter, placing her hands on her hips. "It seems that way sometimes. Take the new year. He has his own manor, yet he showed up here for Hogmanay."

"For *your* celebrations?" Angus asked.

"He claimed none of us fair-haired MacKays could be the First Footer," Hamish spat.

"I hope he offered a nice gift." Angus smiled grimly. He remembered Hogmanay from his youth. The first person to cross the threshold in the new year should always be a dark-haired man bearing gifts to ensure good luck. Gran had explained this harkened back to the Viking invasions, where the sight of a blonde man never meant good news.

"I suppose we should head home," Catriona said. "I don't know if there is anything else to see here." She turned to Angus. "Is there?"

"Nay, we've worked out that Dougal didn't fall, but who pushed him? I just don't know." Angus mounted his horse.

"And someone is trying to frame me," Hamish added. "I've no desire to swing from the gallows for this." He shuddered. "Ye do believe it wasn't me?"

"Aye, Hamish," Catriona looked kindly at him. "I know ye are not to blame." She looked up at Angus before quietly asking, "So, do ye think he jumped?"

"Not if he's still the man I remember," Angus said softly. "Even if his life was not what he had hoped, he was a religious man. He'd not take his own life."

The others agreed and rode back to the manor in silence, each absorbed in their thoughts. At one point, Angus thought he heard someone moving through the trees, paralleling their route. It was a mere whisper of a sound, and neither Hamish nor Catriona seemed to notice. Further on, he swore he heard the sound again like gentle hoofbeats on soft earth. He paused to listen, but the others continued.

"Did ye hear that?"

"Hear what?" Catriona asked. Hamish shook his head. However, their faces paled slightly as Catriona shook her head.

"Twice now, I've thought I heard someone over there," he pointed to the left. The others agreed they hadn't heard anything.

"Maybe a critter," Hamish said.

Angus knew this was not an animal. He'd lived too long in the wilderness. And he'd witnessed the exchange between them; there was something they were not telling him. They'd agreed he wasn't responsible for Dougal's death, but Angus felt they still did not fully trust him.

Soon, they reached the cleared lands around the manor, and Angus heard nothing more. However, he was sure someone had been tracking them. But for how long? And were they present while they were at the ruin? Why are they so secretive?

These thoughts plagued Angus as they rode into the stable and dismounted. Needing time to think, he sliced an apple and fed the pieces to Luath after brushing his coat and filling his water pail. This was no longer his home, and he didn't know if he could trust anyone. There were many people he did not recognize, so he had no idea who had a motive. Why would someone kill Dougal Og? And why did it appear they were trying to frame Hamish?

Angus entered Catriona's office. It was unrecognizable from the family dining room he remembered. But then, everything was different now. He had lived briefly in the ruined house with Mam and Gran, but it was no longer that grand estate. Now it was a working farm. His family had been shunted among other family members, most likely because of Gran's influence. After the battle, people didn't trust his English mother.

Angus tapped on the doorframe as he entered. Catriona was staring into a cup but glanced up at him and gestured for him to join her.

"Do ye have any thoughts on the matter?" Angus asked her as he pulled up a chair.

"Nay, none of my people would do this."

Angus was slightly taken aback at her use of the possessive but realized they were hers now. He needed to remember that. She was in charge these days.

"Any more coffee?" he asked her. This might be a good time to ask some questions.

Catriona gave him a strained smile, "if ye think I'm drinking coffee, ye've been away too long." She turned to the sideboard behind her and grabbed another mug and a bottle of whisky. Tilting her head at him in inquiry, she poured a healthy shot into a cup when he gave a slight nod in thanks.

"When I found the bodies in Pennsylvania, Mrs. Bryan gave me port." He threw back the amber liquid. "I find this more satisfying."

"Well, 'tis in your blood," Hamish said as he entered the room. He grabbed another mug before joining them at the table.

"So ye both are sure ye heard nothing in the trees on the way back?" Angus asked them again, watching their reactions.

"Why? Do ye think Am Fear Liath Mòr has come down from the mountain?" Hamish teased him.

"The great gray man?" Angus almost choked on his drink. "I never believed the stories of the mountain being haunted." He paused at Hamish's glance. "Oh, alright, for a time, I did. But later, I realized her stories of a man eating the young was Gran's method of keepin' me off the peaks of Ben MacDuibh."

"I've been there," Catriona scoffed. "But I didna hear anything. Purely stories for the children."

"I've heard tales from those who claim to have seen him, though most only admit to hearing rustling and footsteps."

It seemed Hamish believed in the creature. But what were they not telling him? He decided to be patient and see what he could get from Hamish when Catriona was not around.

Catriona groaned as she saw Sergeant Wolfe lead his men along the lane toward the manor. Word of the events at Crosstown reached the soldiers at the garrison the next day, and it wasn't long before a unit approached in the afternoon. With the clan's warning system always on high alert, the village and the manor knew of their arrival well before they reached the gate.

Catriona detested Sergeant Wolfe, who was always flirting with her. His demeanor was as greasy as his longish blonde hair. Catriona would not trust him to tell her the sky was blue. Wolfe asked her to dine with him whenever he saw her, ever persistent and never happy when she declined. She was relieved when Hamish hurried to her side as the sergeant and his men approached. Catriona and her people toed the line, giving the English soldiers no cause to harass them as they did other folks.

"What can I do for ye, *gentlemen*?" she asked. "Ye are a bit away from home."

"I never mind paying ye a visit, Ma'am," Sergeant Wolfe said as he slid from his tall white horse. He held out his hand, and Catriona politely grasped it and shook it, releasing it quickly before he could draw her hand to his lips as he often tried.

Frowning, he said, "But we are here on official business this time. Word came in of a suspicious death here." He cocked an eyebrow and held out his arm for her. "Care to step inside and fill me in on the details over a wee dram?"

Catriona cringed; the last thing she wanted was to go inside with him. These were her people, her problem, and she would deal with it without his help.

Hamish stepped forward. "I can fill him in on what happened for ye," he said to Catriona. "I know ye are busy just now."

She smiled up at him. "Thank ye, Hamish. I have a few moments to talk to the sergeant, but please join us." She saw the scowl on Sergeant Wolfe's face. She'd make this as quick as possible, but be careful not to upset him. He could cause trouble for her people if he desired. She detested the man.

"It is nothing suspicious. One of my men fell from the old tower. It shouldn't take much of your time." She informed the sergeant, hoping he'd leave soon.

"Take all the time ye need, Ma'am. I am at your service." He bowed his head and followed her inside.

Catriona was surprised to see Angus sitting at the table writing when they entered. He'd explained to her how Charles Mason wrote daily in his journal, mainly about their work, but he also noted events of interest. As the survey team had turned westward toward the mountains, Angus had started his own and found it a pleasant habit. Catriona scoffed at the idea. Where would she find the time?

"Pardon me," he said to her as he looked up. "I'll be out o' yer way."

"Nay, stay. Ye should be present." She believed him about the murder. If she put the pieces together in her mind, Angus didn't fit. But that didn't mean she trusted him. She wanted him to leave. If he wanted to clear his name, it might be better to let him stay and then be on his way.

She saw Hamish pause and look at her. Angus looked surprised at her words as well. "The sergeant may need to ask ye some questions. Ye might as well do it now and save him having to return."

Once again, Sergeant Wolfe scowled. "I don't believe we've been introduced," he responded flatly. Angus looked from Catriona to the soldier before him and instantly disliked the man. *Sergeant.* Angus quickly assessed the state of affairs.

"Angus MacKay. I'm a cousin up from London on a visit," he said in perfect English as he straightened his waistcoat and held out his hand.

Catriona was relieved to see how quickly Angus took in the situation and adjusted to his posh London manners. She did not want to explain to the soldiers that he was the true heir to the manor. Once the men left, they needed to have a long talk. Catriona noted the puzzled expression on Hamish's face.

The sergeant took Angus' hand and shook it as he deferred to what he perceived as the other man's station. The sergeant removed his hat and tipped his head to Angus. Catriona gritted her teeth at this exchange, unsure what Angus was up to, but decided to follow along as he played the gentleman.

The change in the sergeant's demeanor was evident to all, and Hamish grinned at Angus as he turned to grab the whiskey from the sideboard. Catriona almost choked as she heard Hamish mutter, "Like flies to honey."

Once they were seated, Sergeant Wolfe turned to Angus. Catriona felt Hamish give her hand a quick pat under the table.

"So, the Lady believes ye know something o' this?" He asked.

"Well, I arrived soon after it happened, but it appears Dougal was on the stairs inside the old ruin when a section of the wall fell away. He must have been leaning against it and tumbled to his death. Ye know how these old structures like that can crumble." He gave the sergeant a knowing glance. Catriona exhaled softly. Angus understood her desire to get rid of the sergeant.

"Well, uh, I suppose." Sergeant Wolfe tried to slide his chair closer to Catriona, who rose quickly. Keeping her face from breaking out in a wide grin was challenging. Angus was playing this man perfectly. She half expected him to invite the man out to the tower to take a look for himself. And right on cue, Angus did just that.

Catriona's head snapped back to Angus, who nodded slightly.

"I can take ye there if ye like," Angus offered.

Sergeant Wolfe looked hopefully at Catriona.

"I suppose I can take time to join ye, Sergeant, but there isn't much to see," she said. She stole a glance at Angus. Catriona understood he was doing this for her, but he was playing a dangerous game. "Ye should come too," she said to Hamish, who nodded.

Catriona took the lead when they finished their whisky and, with no further reason to delay, led them to the tower.

Angus understood from the first moment that Catriona wanted this man out of her hair. He also knew it was better if the soldiers didn't know he was the true heir, the oldest surviving male descendant. However, Angus had no intention of claiming it from Catriona. He could see how much it meant to her. She was happy here, while Angus knew he could never settle down and be a farmer. So, he played the London gentleman he did not wish to be and chatted amiably about absolutely nothing as they rode.

"So ye see, it was a shock to my nerves to ride up and find a dead body sprawled afore me," he exclaimed. He faked a shiver.

"How are ye related to them?" the sergeant asked. He slowed to move alongside Catriona's horse.

"Distant relations on my father's side," Angus twisted the truth. "My mother is related to Lord John Shelton in London. I'm sure ye heard his name afore."

"Uh, aye, of course," the man stammered, leading Angus to believe he had never heard the name but was impressed by the title.

"I was heading to Edinburgh, to the palace of Holyrood, when the idea struck me to see if I could find these relations. I'll head home as soon as I can politely leave them." Angus peered sidelong at Sergeant Wolfe and was pleased to see him swallow the bait. Ha! Angus realized the sergeant was glad he was not staying around. So, she had two suitors, at least: Callum Campbell and Sergeant Wolfe. He felt a moment of pity for Catriona but realized she could easily handle this wolf. Now, he understood how carefully she had to tread to keep the peace between the locals and the soldiers. Angus didn't envy her that task.

Soon, they reached the site, and Angus held his breath. He avoided glancing at Catriona and Hamish. Catriona pointed out the blood on the ground and the pile of stones that had obviously fallen from above. One man was even savvy enough to notice the difference in their color. Angus tapped a rock with his foot, trying to appear casual. Fortunately, no one realized how far the blood was from the structure's base nor understood the significance of the rock Angus had placed on the pile. Treating it like a cairn, both soldiers picked up stones and stacked them next to the one Angus had placed. Even the sergeant added one to the pile and smiled at Catriona.

"Well, it looks like he fell," Sergeant Wolfe said.

"Aye. 'Tis a sad story all the same. If ye follow the trail off to the west, it will take ye back to the fort and is much shorter than heading back past the house." Hamish directed them.

Sergeant Wolfe hemmed and hawed a few minutes, staring at Angus. He could not come up with a reason to stay, and eventually, he spun his horse toward his men, who were already heading in the direction Hamish indicated. The sergeant shook Angus' hand and rode away, but not before giving Angus a hard stare.

Angus waited until the men were out of sight before he relaxed. But he couldn't shake the look the sergeant gave him. Angus knew he wasn't finished with him. He felt a tickle in the hairs on the back of his neck, a warning sign, according to Gran. He wiped his hand on his leg.

Catriona snickered at his side as they walked to their horses.

"I think he bought it," she said with a smile. "I hope that will be the end."

"Now, we need to figure out who did it."

Catriona's expression turned serious. Hamish stepped up next to her. Angus noticed him studying him. "Ye really are quite the gentleman."

Angus scowled and mounted. It was a role he was loath to play.

Catriona's task that day was sorting the bags of grain to prepare for planting. She focused on what needed to be done. Organizing the bags helped distract her from the fact that a murder had occurred. The omens looked good that there would not be another significant frost this year, and they could begin tilling the ground. After sending Hamish and Geordie to the upper fields with a cartload of bags to stow in the shed until Beltane, she re-entered the barn and counted out the next load.

Unfortunately, when she moved the top bags to the side, she noticed rats had eaten the bottom row.

"Curses on ye wee beasties!" She hollered at them. What good were the cats she allowed to spend the winter in here?

Callum entered the barn at that moment. "Can I help ye, milady? What distresses ye?"

Catriona scowled at him as she shifted the bags to determine how much grain was lost. He rushed to help her move the bag, but she shrugged him off. "Rats. They've gotten into the bags on the bottom layer."

Callum ran his fingers through the dark curls hanging over his shoulders and stood straighter. "Ye shouldn't be doing this heavy work. Let me get one of my men to finish it for ye while we relax with a wee dram." He reached out his hand to take hers.

"I dinna need your help," she scowled back at him. "I am perfectly capable of inspecting the damage."

Callum's attitude that she always needed his help infuriated her. Her mother, Eileen, had completed most of the restoration work so far and was the driving force behind making the land work for them. But some men, including Callum, did not believe women could do the job. Catriona had improved on what her mother had started in the three years since her death. She was proud of her farm, which was beginning to provide for the people so that no one went hungry or came up short. And everyone had a roof over their head. Like her mother, Catriona expected everyone to pull their weight and contribute, and the system was working. She did not need men like Callum to run things.

"Well, I thought I would offer." Callum affronted. "I was hoping to meet Geordie. Have ye seen him?"

"He's helping Hamish up in the high fields. They should be back soon." Catriona was surprised. She didn't consider those two men friends. Callum was educated and thought highly of himself, whereas

Geordie, though helpful and eager to please, could neither read nor write. And he scarcely had a coin to his name. What would Callum want with him? Dougal had told her Callum had asked him to intercede on his behalf for her hand. Was that why Callum was at the tower? To meet Dougal? He had said he was coming to visit *her*. With Dougal's death, was he now going to approach Geordie? That was a laugh.

"Can I give Geordie a message for ye?" She asked as she dropped a bag between them. It suddenly occurred to her that she and Callum were alone. She edged over to the next stack, putting it between them.

Callum moved closer. "Ye deserve better than this. I can offer ye plenty. Ye know that." When she stepped away, he persisted. "I've money, a nice home in the town, and my estate." He pointed to a rat-eaten bag and said, "I can offer ye a better life than this."

"I'm quite happy here," she replied. She'd turned Callum down twice already. Why wouldn't leave her be?

"With Hamish? His leg keeps him from being much help to ye. Ye deserve dancing and dinner parties. I can offer ye that." He grabbed her arm tightly as she stepped away. "Or do ye prefer that fool from London?"

At that moment, Catriona caught sight of Angus entering the building behind Callum. "Well, that fool, as ye say, thinks ye ought to remove your hands from the lady," Angus said.

Callum spun around. "What's it to ye?"

"Well, true, it isn't my business. But it is hers."

Catriona seized the opportunity to slip free of Callum's grasp. "I think ye should leave."

"If that's what ye wish, I was only trying to help." Callum straightened his frock coat and strutted from the barn; his jaw clenched tightly.

"Ye all right?" Angus asked Catriona.

"I'm fine. Thank ye." She sighed. "I wish he'd leave me alone."

"Well, I am glad I came in when I did."

"Ye've probably made an enemy." Catriona stepped closer and rested her hand on his arm. "And thank ye for helping with Sergeant Wolfe, too. I didn't want him to get involved, at least not yet." She caught his eye and continued. "We have much to work out between us yet, Angus, but I want ye to know I don't think ye were responsible for Dougal's death."

As she spoke, she thought she saw Hamish turn and slip back out of the door.

As Angus ate supper with Catriona later that evening, they spied Hamish trying to slip past the dining room. Catriona rose to catch up to him.

"Hamish! Where were ye? I was worried when ye didn't return with Geordie. Ye missed supper."

"We finished up on the hill, and I decided to go for a pint. No big deal." He swayed as he glared at Angus and turned to go.

"Hamish? Is everything all right?" Still seated at the table, Angus wondered why Hamish was upset with him.

Before Hamish could answer, Catriona ordered him to join them. "I am not happy with drunken behavior, as ye know."

Hamish squirmed a little as he sat in the chair. "Aye, ma'am."

"Ma'am? What is wrong with ye?"

"I saw ye two in the barn earlier, having a cozy chat. And well, I just decided I'd be intruding, so I left."

Angus realized Hamish was jealous. "Nay, Hamish! Catriona was only thanking me for intruding and helping her with Callum. That's all."

"He was here... again?" Hamish squinted at Catriona, who nodded in response.

"Oh, Hamish..." She leaned over and hugged him. "What would I do without ye?"

Returning to her seat, she spoke again. "Hamish knows this already, but strange things have happened around here, even before Dougal's death. I know we ignored ye when ye heard the sounds in the woods, but I don't know what is going on. But things have gone missing. Or sometimes I walk into this room, and I can tell someone has been in here."

"Or hear people following ye through the woods?" Angus asked grimly. Why was she telling him now? Why not before?

"Aye," Hamish said. "I've heard them." He looked at Catriona with a puzzled expression on his face. "Ye trust him?" He indicated Angus.

Catriona smiled sheepishly. She took Hamish's hand in hers. "Maybe. But I would like Angus to stay on a bit longer until we figure out what happened. I can't help but think Dougal's death is somehow related."

"What can I do?" Angus had already told them he would help with Dougal's death, but the rest? This was not part of his plans to leave soon. "Besides, I didn't think ye trusted me."

Catriona looked him squarely in the eye. "I'm not sure that I do, to be honest. Not fully, anyway. I don't know why ye are here or what ye want. But ye are a fresh set of eyes and ears. And your actions today in helping me with Sergeant Wolfe meant a lot. And with Callum. Not to mention how candid ye were that Dougal didn't fall to his death. I'm willing to take a chance on ye remaining a spell. I'm sorry I kept secrets from ye, but maybe ye were drawn here for a reason. Will ye stay and help us?"

"I suppose I could do that," Angus turned, "but only if Hamish agrees."

Hamish nodded and smiled as he stuck out his hand to Angus.

# CHAPTER 9

WITH NO FAMILY LEFT to host Dougal's wake, Catriona offered to hold it at the manor and sent the bell ringer through the village announcing the time and location. She had hoped to have the manner of his death resolved before this, but the required five days of mourning had passed with no resolution. Dougal's death had been an accident, as far as anyone else knew. Catriona told the men she planned to keep it that way. Hamish rode to the next town to hire the keeners, who would chant laments.

The following afternoon, the procession made their way through the village and entered the gates just before sunset. Two keeners lamented the loss of the worthy gentleman as they moved along the path. They sang of his many deeds and the quality of his life. As they recounted his ancestry, the other MacKays joined them. Dougal Og was wrapped in linen and laid on a stout piece of wood carried by four men. Hamish held one of the front corners. A simple flower lay upon his breast. A clump of soil representing his return to the earth from which he came lay on one side. On the other, salt represented his eternal soul.

Once they entered the old dining hall, the men placed the body on the dais at the far end. Angus remembered hiding under the finely carved dining table that used to sit there. Catriona slipped coins to the keeners as their lament finished. The wake celebrating the life of the deceased would begin.

Once the village ladies heard the bell ringer's announcement, they began baking, and cakes and other sweets sat between platters of cold meats and cheeses on wooden planks stretched across barrels. Benches of similar construction were placed about the room for those who wished to sit. Several men had set up a table for whisky, beer, and cider in one corner.

"Do come in." Catriona stood at the door, greeting each person as they arrived. Hamish and Angus stood with her. Angus shuffled his feet now and then, feeling out of place among the locals. After speaking with Catriona, an elderly man clasped Angus' hand in a surprisingly firm grip. The man squinted up at him and squeezed his hand tighter.

"I'd know ye anywhere," he said, looking up at Angus. "Ye are the image of your da. Ye even have his height. He was a good man."

"Aye, he was," Angus replied.

"Sorry to hear about Dougal Og," the man continued.

"As am I," Angus responded.

Angus glanced at the dais. Both father and son bore the same name, which was common in those parts. True to highland custom, they were known by nicknames. The steward was Big Dougal, for his size, despite his gentleness. His son was Dougal Og, the younger.

Callum, often called Callum Dubh with his dark hair and countenance, stood by himself, glaring at Hamish and Angus at Catriona's side. Angus wondered if this man truly loved Catriona or only desired her property. But why would Callum want her small farm? He and Hamish would keep her safe through the evening.

The musician tuned his fiddle, and everyone turned to toast Dougal Og on the dais. Hamish and Catriona led the first dance before everyone formed two lines for a rousing reel. Angus spun as he cast off and headed down the line; his partner, a petite redhead who giggled uncontrollably, kept pace with him down the opposite side. They met at the end and danced their way up the middle. Unlike the formal dinners at Shelton House, Angus was enjoying himself.

Suddenly, there was a hush over the room, and Angus turned to see Sergeant Wolfe strut through the door and head immediately to Catriona. *What is he doing here?* Angus caught Hamish's eye, and both made their way toward her.

"I heard about the wake and thought I would pay my respects, ma'am," the sergeant said as he held out his hand. He smiled at her as she took his hand and quickly released it. "If you need anything, you only have to ask."

"Thank ye for your kindness," she replied.

Noticing that Hamish had reached her side, Angus moved toward the men at the bar. He could hear them from there. He picked up a mug of ale and took a sip.

"It's a bit odd for an English soldier to show up at a Scottish wake, isn't it?" Hamish asked, stepping closer to Catriona.

"I'm here to support Miss MacKay," Sergeant Wolfe replied. "We could be friends." He held out his hand to Hamish. But his smile barely curved his lips. It did not seem genuine to Angus, who watched.

One man sipped his whisky and leaned closer to Angus. "What's that soldier doing here? He seems to spend more time lurking around here than in the town where he belongs.""Really? Here? Doing what?" Angus turned to the man. Other men joined them.

"Watching, mostly." He pointed to the men around the table. "We think he wants to marry the mistress, to take over her lands." He hemmed and hawed a bit.

Another stepped forward, saying boldly, "Are ye here to claim your heritage?"

Noticing the circle of men closing in, Angus felt surrounded; his palms curled into a fist. While the words were a simple question, they seemed like a challenge. The men seemed concerned that was precisely what he planned.

"Nay," Angus reassured them. "I promise, I have no plans to take this from her." The tension left the group as they released a collective breath.

"Well, that's good then," said the first man. Another handed him a whisky.

Hours later, Angus felt somewhat lightheaded between the dances and the whisky. He watched as the first rays of the sun appeared on the horizon. It was time for the men to take the body to the gravesite for burial. Prayers would be said for his soul the next time the priest passed through the community.

Angus rubbed his eyes, wondering if he should follow them to the graveyard. He chose not to go, not wanting to become too close to the villagers. People were already beginning to comment about his presence. And he had no plans to stay.

With the wake depleting the stores of fresh meat, Angus was pleased when Hamish invited him to go hunting. He hoped this meant his old friend was beginning to trust him again. Angus and Hamish rode side by side through the gorse of the scrubby moorland beneath the heights of Ben MacDuibh the following morning. Armed with shotguns, they hunted game birds through the uncultivated lands. Hamish checked the traps for hares and small game. Though they saw several deer, the penalties for killing them were high. Soldiers often patrolled here.

"Ye know, from this angle, Ben MacDuibh's peak does look like a pig. I never noticed it from the manor," Angus said. Local folk still referred to the mountain as the black pig, from the Gaelic, a' mhuc-dhubh.

"Aye, but the only pig around here is that sergeant. Ye wait and see. He'll be along soon. Every time I hunt, it never fails." Right on cue, three men appeared on the horizon.

"I told ye he would show up," Hamish growled as the men came over the hill opposite. "We still can't hunt deer or own muskets or rifles, but the soldiers have grown more lenient about using these fowling pieces for small game." He explained to Angus. "Folk must eat."

Angus looked up to see Sergeant Wolfe and two deputies riding toward them. Hamish dismounted and opened his saddlebags, placing the shotgun on the ground before him. Realizing this must happen frequently, Angus followed suit.

"After ye check their bags, scour the area to make sure they don't have a deer lying in hiding somewhere," Sergeant Wolfe ordered his men.

"C'mon, we go through this dance every time," Hamish said to the sergeant.

"Aye, and I'll continue until I catch ye," Sergeant Wolfe retorted. "And one o' these days, I will. Ye be mindful o' that."

"If I don't shoot 'em, ye will ne'er catch me," Hamish said.

They watched the deputies empty the saddlebags scattering the contents on the ground. They did not pick anything up and return it to the bags, leaving everything strewn in the grass. Once they finished searching their belongings, the men fanned out across the moorlands, looking for a deer carcass. The farther they went, the deeper the scowl on Sergeant Wolfe's face. Eventually, he called his men back.

"I'll get ye yet, MacKay." Sergeant Wolfe mounted his horse, giving Hamish a snarl. Then he glanced at Angus. "And ye, related to Lord Shelton. Ha! Thought ye'd play me for a fool? I'll be keeping an eye on ye as well." His lips curled in a scowl.

Before he rode off, Sergeant Wolfe turned to Hamish. "Give my greetings to the lovely Catriona, if ye would." He raced after his men as Hamish grumbled, "The hell I will."

"I didn't realize things were still so bad here," Angus said as he repacked his bag. He ran his hands through the scrubby grass to grab everything he had inside. Angus grimaced as a thorn poked into his thumb and rose, placing the pouches back on his horse. He turned to see Hamish frowning at the retreating horsemen.

"Aye, 'tis bad enough. But things used to be worse. There were times we werena even allowed the shotguns. Fishing and trapping were all that we could do to feed our people. That man has it in for me, though. No one around here gets harassed as much as me. I wouldn't put it past him to blame me for Dougal's death." He looked at Angus. Someone was blaming him; the thought dawned on both men.

"Jealous?"

"Me? Nay, why?"

"Nay, I was referring to yon sergeant. I think he has an eye on our lovely cousin." Angus watched Hamish smile.

"Well, I'll keep her safe from the likes o' him." Hamish grimaced as he swung his leg up over the horse.

So that was the way of things, Angus noted as he mounted. The men turned toward home with only three small rabbits dangling from Hamish's saddle. However, his statement about the sergeant blaming him stuck in Angus' mind. Would the sergeant blame Hamish for the murder in order to pursue Catriona?

Angus slept fretfully a few nights later and rose early in the morning. Feeling anxious, he got up and dressed. Since Catriona had asked him to stay on and help, there was no longer a guard on his door. He wasn't sure if she fully trusted him, but their relationship had improved. Angus' gaze was drawn to the window as he put on his shoes. The sunrise glowed pinks and yellows, and he watched the golden orb appear over the horizon. He felt the pull to be outside, wanting to be free.

The sun had cleared the trees when Angus exited through the back door. Turning to his left, he walked around the side of the house. Angus knew Catriona's mam, Eileen, had replaced the house's roof. But besides the stable, Angus had not yet explored the outbuildings since someone was always watching him. He hoped Catriona would not misinterpret his actions; he was merely curious. Only a few structures remained, but those like the old carriage house now held farm implements. A horse-drawn plow sat in one corner. Angus remembered seeing two tall, broad-shouldered draught horses in the stable.

Next to that was a small blacksmith's shed. The forge, with its bellows, sat under an awning in front. A burly smith was stoking the fire to prepare for the day's work. The man was of average height, his blonde hair pulled back with a strip of leather. But it was his arms that caught Angus' attention. They were large and muscular and reminded him of the forearms and paws of a giant bear chasing him and Gray Wolf in western Maryland. The pair had barely escaped into a barn, barring the door, until the bear wandered away, presumably returning to her cubs.

Angus greeted the man and introduced himself. "Morning, the name's Angus." He held out his hand.

The blacksmith grunted at him, "Iain." He turned back to the fire and picked up a plowshare he was making.

Not a friendly sort, Angus decided. Behind the main house, a portion of the old stables remained; the short leg of the former L-shaped structure had not been rebuilt after the fire. Only a handful of horses occupied it now, two of which were those draft horses who pulled the plows in the fields.

Angus grabbed some apples from the barrel near the door as he entered. As he moved along the aisle, he sliced off pieces and fed them to the horses. Luath, his horse, stood at the far end. The tall gray knickered at him as he approached.

After sharing an apple with Luath, Angus decided a ride would do them good. He pulled the horse blanket off the peg on the wall. The horse danced about and raised its head up and down. Its name, meaning fast in Gaelic, suited the spirited beast. Angus quickly saddled him, and the pair set off across the dewy morning grass and through the gate.

Angus rode, ambling down one path and then another with no particular destination. He hoped to find evidence in the woods of whoever had followed them that day. And out here, he was away from the others. Angus wanted to leave. He did not feel comfortable here and had few good memories from his childhood. And the sooner he solved the murder, the sooner he could begin his new life. Even the beautiful morning had not shaken off the unease he felt.

He told Luath about his former home and how the soldiers came and destroyed everything. Once the soldiers departed, his mother and gran had returned with the two children. Only one portion of the manor's roof survived the fire. Angus remembered his mother's tears as she stood in the great hall, the rain pouring into the wide-open space. Gone were the beautiful chandeliers. Bits of painted wall plaster lay in melted clumps in the puddles. Their belongings were gone, and most of the furniture was taken or consumed by fire.

Angus remembered tossing a ball to his wee sister, Fiona, to entertain her while Gran helped his mother find straw and blankets for their bedding. They would sleep in the two covered chambers on the ground floor. The family had lived there for several months before briefly moving in with Gran's brother. That man's son was Duncan, Hamish's father. Then they moved again.

Memories filled Angus' head while he rode until he noticed the old tower before him, the hillside rising beyond it. He stared at the hills and the cave. No wonder Angus felt so ill at ease today. It was April 16th, twenty-three years after the Battle of Culloden, when his life changed.

Angus couldn't resist. His eyes were drawn upward above the ruined tower. He forced himself to look away, but his gaze returned. Growing up, he ignored the pull of the cave, not wanting to face the memories. But as he grew older and understood the events that struck the village that fateful day, he viewed the caves with trepidation that bordered on fear. Even now, flashbacks of hiding there haunted him. The families hid from the soldiers in those hills. Others didn't make it. Sometimes the sound of screaming and visions of smoke filled his dreams. However, the nightmares occurred less often these days. Angus dismounted and climbed the stairs, passing the point where Dougal was murdered. He believed the man was killed.

The truth dawned on Angus as he stared at the distant hills. The only way to release his childhood demons was to face them head-on and put them behind him. He must go. He knew it. To start fresh, he must put the past behind him. This was why he had come.

Angus sat on the stone staircase, not noticing the damp seeping through his breeches. When he was up there before, he had been so focused on Dougal's death that he hadn't felt the pull of the caves. Now, in his mind, the wisps of smoke curled up through the newly budding trees. He thought he smelled the burning homes.

Curled in the cave, his mother had tried to keep Fiona from crying. Their people knew the animal tracks up the hills, but the soldiers had thought they looked too steep and didn't examine them closely. That simple fact had saved the lives of many. In the aftermath, Eileen's determination helped them rebuild their homes and village.

Angus did not know how long he had sat on the cold steps. But if he was going to move on, he couldn't leave without visiting the cave. The stone chilled his legs, and he rose and peered over the wall at the hill. Trees grew thickly around the base but thinned out, with heather and gorse covering the bald tops. Rock formations dotted the cliffs, but to someone unfamiliar with the land, the caves were easily missed, hidden in the crevices. Angus felt them. He knew they were there.

Angus ducked his head as he stepped through the low doorway, then stopped short, startled to see Hamish standing by his horse, patiently waiting.

"Ye need to go," he said.

Angus wondered how long his cousin had been waiting. "Where?"

"The cave. We've all visited them over time, each of us returning to theirs as they were ready. Ye need to face it."

Angus was surprised at this. "Ye too? He asked.

"Aye, eventually." Hamish nodded.

"I've avoided them my whole life."

"Would ye like me to go with ye?"

"Nay, this is something I must do on my own."

Angus approached on foot, pausing at the base. Unlike the small, sure-footed garrons, this horse could not climb the steep slope.

"I think I will need some time afterward. Would ye take Luath? I'll see ye back at the house later."

Angus straightened his shoulders and took a deep breath. He approached the slope one step at a time, his stride growing shorter as he drew near.

"Funny, the hills aren't as tall or steep as I remember," he mumbled. He had considered them mountains before, but these seemed small after the peaks he climbed in Pennsylvania. Or were these the imaginings of a six-year-old boy?

Halfway up the hill, Angus realized he did not have a torch. Oh, well, he did not intend to go far inside. He would step inside the opening and be done with it. Or so he thought. But curiosity overtook him once he reached the gap between the vertical stones. Over the years, rockslides had shifted the shape of the hill, and a portion above had fallen. It was after midday now, and sunlight filled the entrance.

Angus stepped between the stones. Before him, he saw the small chamber where his gran had peered out, listening. Just beyond was the flat rock where his mother had comforted Fiona. His wee sister was only two years old at the time. Further back was the chamber where Angus hid, trying to escape the screams of the people below.

His gaze drifted in that direction, and his eye followed the rays of sunlight that pierced the space. He saw something. Angus initially thought it was just a fallen stone, but it looked like a man's boot. He wondered why someone would leave their boots here when they had to walk over rocks to return down the hill. He ducked his head and moved closer to retrieve it.

Revulsion filled him as he bent to pick it up. It took a moment for his mind to accept what his eyes saw; a leg was attached to the boot. But it was a leg made of bone. Still stooping over, Angus dropped to his knees as his eyes beheld the skeleton stretched before him. *Who was this? And how long has he been here?* The fabric of his clothing was shredded, and the bones were picked clean, most likely by the small rodents he heard scurrying about deeper in the cave. Angus crawled along the floor of the cave to get a closer look.

The man was sprawled face down on the floor, or so it appeared to Angus. The collapse of the roof had crushed the skull. Angus looked up, but as his gaze returned to the body, he saw an arrow shaft stuck in the ribs. Someone killed him. The collapse must have occurred later. *What was he doing in here? And why was he killed?* Angus immediately began making mental notes. He rocked back on his heels, and a shaft of light lit the pickaxe in the man's left hand.

"A prospector?" Angus said aloud. "Here? There's no gold in these hills." However, that may explain why he was killed. "Was it robbery? Was someone with ye when ye found something?" He asked the bones.

Receiving no answer, Angus sat back, hugging his arms around his legs. He memorized things as they were so he could keep them in mind. It was obvious these bones had been here for a while. So this time, they could not accuse him of this death. Angus could do nothing for the man now except go for help to remove the body and bury him properly.

# CHAPTER 10

Angus' brows were drawn, his forehead creased, and he mumbled as he exited the path. His contemplation was abruptly interrupted when he heard Luath nicker at him. He was so engrossed in his thoughts he had not seen Hamish waiting with the horses.

"Ah, good. Ye are here." Angus wore a grim expression.

"I thought ye might be mad at me for waiting after ye said ye'd see me later," Hamish said in surprise. "Are ye all right?"

"I am. But there is someone up there who is not."

"Is someone hurt? Did they fall? Can I help?" Hamish started toward the path. Angus grabbed his arm, stopping him as he tried to pass.

"Nay. There is nothing to be done for him now."

Hamish stopped short as Angus' words sank in, and understanding showed on his face. Slipping from Angus' grasp, he limped up the path toward the cave. Angus followed his cousin back up the hill with a sigh.

Angus caught up with Hamish near the mouth of the cave. Both men gasped for air after their run upward. In the time it took Angus to go down the hill and return, the sun sank lower in the sky, its rays reaching further into the inner chamber.

"Ye get around well with that leg," Angus panted.

"Aye, when I have to."

"I've been curious about what happened. If ye don't mind my asking." He said as they entered the cave.

"I took a tumble years ago running from the soldiers. It must have been a few years after ye left. Soldiers chased Archie and me through the hills when I tripped and stumbled over the edge. I broke my leg in four places, and it never healed quite right."

"Oh, sounds painful." Angus winced at the thought.

Hamish turned to enter and ducked to a crawl, dragging his stiff leg as he went deeper into the interior. Angus stood above average height, but Hamish topped him by four inches. He allowed the big man to get inside before following. They sat in silence, staring at the remains.

"Why?" Hamish asked, pointing at the arrow. "And who is it?"

Angus noticed the light growing dim. "We better head down while we can still see. I don't fancy making my way down in the dark."

Hamish agreed. "There is nothing we can do tonight. Looks like he's been here a while. Let's get Archie and Geordie and come back tomorrow. And we'll need to let Catriona know. 'Tis her land." He looked at Angus as if watching his reaction as he said the words.

"Aye. 'Tis. Don't worry; the land is hers. I'll not lay claim to it."

Hamish sighed in relief as they started down.

The evening was growing dark by the time they reached the manor. Catriona crossed to the stables, hands on her hips, when she heard the men ride in through the gate.

"Well, what sort of outing have the two o' ye been on today?" she asked, her voice a mixture of concern and anger. They left early that morning without a word to anyone, and now evening was drawing in on them.

"Sorry," Hamish said. "I didna mean to worry ye. Angus needed to make his peace as ye ken we all have. I followed him to the caves."

A bit of tension left Catriona at this. Her mother had given birth to her nine months after the tragedy, so she had never gone up there. But she'd heard the stories over the years. Those who survived each came to terms with their pain in their own way, even her mother.

"I see. Ye might have let someone know ye were going." She looked at each sternly. "Well, ye are back now. Hopefully, supper is not burnt. When ye finish with the horses, come inside and eat."

Catriona watched them as they ate. They were both quiet and picked at their food. There was something they weren't telling her.

"All right, what is it?" She finally asked, setting her spoon down.

Hamish looked at Angus first and then replied. "Ye know we went to the hills so Angus could come to terms with the cave." Catriona nodded.

"Well, there is a dead man in there." Hamish blurted out.

Catriona gasped. "Who?"

Angus picked up the tale with a little more tact. "It's a skeleton, actually. I'd say it's been there for years, so it's hard to tell. The bones were picked clean."

"Well, thank ye for letting me eat my meal first," Catriona stated. Her face was pale. The men looked chagrined. "Any idea who it is? Or how he died?"

"I don't know who, but he was shot in the back with an arrow," Hamish told her.

"An arrow?" Catriona turned to him.

"Aye. We thought we'd take a couple of men with us tomorrow, probably Geordie and Archie, and go back for him with the wagon," Hamish told her.

"I don't know if there's enough of his clothing for anyone to recognize. Besides, I wouldn't imagine it would differ from anyone else's. Though his boots are there," Angus said.

"That may help," Catriona said, but she did not sound encouraging. "By all means, take Geordie and Archie. And ye might need a bit o' canvas to put the bones in to carry down. Ye won't get a wagon up the hill."

"There is one thing I noticed," Angus said as he mulled it over. "He was corrie fistit. He held a pickaxe in his left hand."

"Pickaxe?" Catriona's usually ruddy complexion went pale white as she looked at Hamish. What is going on? First Dougal, and now a man with a pickaxe shot by an arrow? She should probably let Sergeant Wolfe know about it. He'd most likely find out, anyway. That was the last thing she wanted.

Angus mulled this over as he lay in bed that night. Was there any significance to the pickaxe? While there were coal and lead mines in other parts of the country, he didn't think there were any nearby. And that wasn't something someone would go prospecting for, anyway. As he tried to sleep, he decided to ask Hamish in the morning. But after that look Hamish exchanged with Catriona, Angus wondered if he would get an answer. There was something else going on here. He rose and paced about the room, running his finger along the surface of the small writing desk as he went. The inkwell sitting on top was full. He ran his hand over the back of the sturdy oak chair. No Chippendale curves here. Angus preferred this simple style.

He suddenly felt the need to write to his friends. Liam? Or Little Hawk? He decided on Liam, as it would be shorter. His letter to Little

Hawk would require more time. He opened the drawer, pulled out a few sheets of rough paper, and sat down.

*My friend,*

*Life here is sure full of ups and downs. Little Hawk won't have my letter yet, but I recently travelled north to Durham County with Jeremiah to work with his former teacher, Mr. Burton. They credited my time on the survey as my apprenticeship, and I now have my license!*

*There was nothing for me in London, so I headed north to my old home in Scotland. I remembered there was nothing left here. But I arrived to find a cousin working the land as a farm. As ye know, I'm no farmer. I hope she believes I am not here to challenge her for it. That is not my desire. So I have some thinking to do on where I will go from here.*

*But it seems death follows my footsteps as I found a body when I arrived. The man would have likely fallen at my feet if I had not dawdled a bit on my ride. I think I have proven my innocence to those at the manor, but a few steal glances at me, and I believe hold me suspect.*

*Today I visited the old cave; you'll know the one. I thought it would help to face my demons afore moving on. Instead, I found a skeleton lying in the cave with an arrow in its back. At least no one can accuse me of that man's death.*

*I cling to Clever Otter's words that I will again get through it all if I remain true to myself.*

*My love to Maire and the family and especially to you, my friend,*

*Angus*

*16 April 1769*

Elspeth was clearing the table the following morning when Angus entered. "Hamish is in the stables with Geordie and Archie. He would like ye to join him there," she told him as she placed scones back on the table.

"Thank ye," he told her. "Where would I be able to post a letter?"

"I will take it. Catriona also has some letters to go out, and my lad will be going to town later today."

Angus thanked her again, grabbed a scone from the platter, and hurried to find Hamish. As he passed the blacksmith, he saw Iain quickly drop a piece of hot metal into the sand bucket near his foot. At first, Angus thought little of it. But the way the man surreptitiously watched him caught Angus' attention.

"Good morning," he called out with a smile on his face.

Iain nodded but said nothing. *What an unfriendly sort,* Angus thought.

After he passed, Angus glanced over his shoulder and watched the blacksmith pull the hot metal from the sand with his tongs. Though a few paces beyond the forge, Angus was pretty sure it was the head of a pickaxe. He knew the man created farming tools but couldn't think of a use for that on a farm.

He entered the stables just as the men finished harnessing a small cart. Hamish tossed in two lengths of canvas material.

"Morning. Saddle up, and we'll ride out," he said.

Angus nodded and, within moments, sat astride Luath, ready to go. Archie seemed friendly enough earlier but would not look at Angus now.

This puzzled him, and once they were on the trail, Angus sped up to ride alongside Hamish.

"I am sensing a distinctly unfriendly attitude this morning."

Hamish rode on in silence for a few moments. He shifted in his saddle and glanced behind him, where Archie rode alongside Geordie's cart. Turning to Angus, he sighed.

"It depends on how long those bones have been there," he said. "Archie's brother disappeared about five years ago without a word. There was talk that he'd run off with a young lass from another clan. Archie never forgave him for not saying goodbye."

"And now this body turns up, and he thinks it may be his brother." Angus understood.

"Aye. You and I think it has been there a while," Hamish said. "It may be best if he and I go up alone first. He may recognize the boots."

"Did his brother favor the left hand?" Angus asked. When Hamish nodded, he continued. "What would he be doing up in the cave with a pickaxe? Find any gold here ye aren't telling me about?" Angus grinned, but Hamish did not laugh.

Angus shrugged when Hamish did not reply. "Well, we don't know yet if it is him."

They continued in silence until they reached the base of the hill beneath the cave. Angus dismounted and hobbled the horses in a thick patch of new grass. Hamish and Archie slowly made their way up the path. Geordie remained silently perched on the wagon seat while Angus plopped down on the rock where Hamish had waited for him the day before.

"It's a wonder no one found the body afore," Angus said.

"Not really," Geordie replied. "Most people have made their peace and don't need to go there anymore. The place is haunted."

"Haunted?"

"The spirits of the dead villagers roam these hills. Besides, few of us ever enter the caves. I only peeked into the opening of the one where my family hid, and though I was ten, I remember that day."

"I was six," Angus admitted. "I remember the smoke. And the screams."

"So does Archie. He was a bit older than ye, maybe eight." Geordie looked up the hill. "Hamish too. It took him longer than the rest to face his demons. A couple of years after ye and your gran left, Eileen, Catriona's mam, moved into the old kitchen. Soon, she began fixing the place, maybe ten years back. Then the soldiers came again. They threatened to burn the place, and the people would've lost everything again. Hamish taunted them and lured them away. He nearly died when he fell off that cliff."

"And that is when he broke his leg?"

"Aye. No one thought Hamish would survive. Catriona was about twelve back then. But she idolized him for saving her mam."

"Hamish told me he fell running from the soldiers, but it seems he didn't tell me the whole story."

"Nay, he wouldn't." Geordie paused. "I understand your need to go up there. But I don't know how Archie will react if that is his brother, Niall, ye found." Geordie grew silent.

Angus thought about all of this as they waited. No wonder Hamish and Catriona had such a tight bond; he'd saved her home. Part of him hoped it was not Archie's brother he'd found, but maybe it was better if it was. At least the family would have answers. He didn't know how he could help with this. He would focus on Dougal's murder.

The sun was high overhead when Hamish and Archie returned. Hamish wore a grim expression, the corners of his mouth turned down, but it was Archie's face that identified the dead man above. It was his brother. Archie's face was deathly white, with no trace of the freckles that usually dotted his cheekbones. His eyes were red-rimmed, and Angus knew he'd been crying. He rose but said nothing as the pair stepped from the trees.

Geordie hopped down from his perch on the wagon but did not approach. Archie stopped when he reached the bottom of the hill, seeming not to know what to do. Hamish nodded at Geordie and Angus, but it was unnecessary. They knew it was Niall.

"It was the boots," Hamish told them.

"Why?" Archie wailed. "And all these years, I hated him for leaving me. But he didn't. Oh, Niall, I am sorry." His knees buckled beneath him as he collapsed to the ground. "What was he doing up there? Why would anyone kill him?"

"I dinna ken." Hamish shook his head. "Any thoughts, Geordie?" The other man offered no suggestions.

Archie looked up at them. "He was afraid o' them caves and believed the stories folk told about the spirits o' the dead hauntin' them. He wouldna go there willingly, nor on his own. It doesna make sense."

Geordie helped Archie to his feet without a word and led him over to the wagon. Angus grabbed the canvas from the back and indicated for Hamish to follow him.

"Ye got it in ye to go back up? Let's give him a moment to grieve," he said.

Hamish bent and rubbed his knee. "Aye." He followed Angus up the path.

Reaching the cave, Angus spread the canvases flat just outside the entrance. "If I crawl in and hand them out to ye, could ye pack the bones in these?"

Hamish agreed. "Better than crawling back inside." He rubbed his leg.

Angus slowly and gently brought the bones out a few at a time, handing them reverently to Hamish. It seemed a few were missing, and Angus brushed his hands over the soil, ensuring he left none behind. He picked up the arrow shaft and the man's boots. But as Angus reached to grab the pickaxe, he noticed scratches on the floor. Archie must have been hacking at the rock when he was shot. The coloring was different. Angus poked at it. The ground was soft, not hard like rock. Had Niall buried something there and come to retrieve it? Or was he in there hiding something? When he dug his fingers into the ground, Angus noticed the cave floor was spongy in that corner. But if he had been burying something, they would never know. Most likely, whoever shot him took it away. As Angus crawled out of the cave, he studied the pickaxe. He would ask Catriona and Hamish tonight.

Folding the corners of the canvas tightly, they each grabbed a bundle and made their way down the slope. Archie uttered an anguished cry as they gently placed their bundles in the cart. Geordie gripped his shoulder. "Ye'll ride back with me."

Angus fetched the horses. The cart lurched initially; then, under Geordie's steady hand, they rolled toward the path. Hamish and Angus mounted and led Archie's horse, staying a respectful distance behind on the slow return to the manor.

Catriona rushed out to meet them when they approached along the valley. It seemed to take an eternity to reach the gate. She knew by their faces that it was Archie's brother before they entered. A young girl at the time of his disappearance, she barely remembered what Niall looked like. A dashing young man running off with a lassie sounded so romantic. These days, she knew such dreams did not come true. She approached the cart and offered Archie a hand.

"Come inside," she invited him sympathetically.

Archie declined. "Kind o' ye, ma'am, but I must take my brother home. Mam and da will want to know."

"If there is anything I can do for ye and your family, just ask," she told him. "And give them my condolences."

"Thank ye, ma'am," he replied. Several others approached to offer their sympathies.

While Archie was distracted, Catriona approached the others. "Do ye think he has been there all this time?" She peered under the canvas and studied the smooth white bones before picking up the arrow shaft.

"So it appears," Hamish answered. "Animals did a fair job cleaning the bones, but I doubt these have been touched for years. It surprised me when Archie identified him. Niall was terrified o' those caves and refused to go near them. When we were about thirteen, we lured him up the hill. A few o' the lads hid and made scary noises. Niall ran home screaming and was found later under his bed. Never went up there again."

Catriona frowned at him. "And this?" She held up the shaft of the arrow. No one answered her. Taking charge, she turned to Elspeth's son, Alan.

"Go into Kingussie and inform Sergeant Wolfe what has happened. But tell him that his presence is not required." She ordered the lad as she tapped the arrow on her hand.

"Aye, ma'am." The lad sped off. Catriona spun on her heel and entered the house. She avoided looking at Angus. As he entered the gate, the wrinkled brow on his forehead told her he had questions. And she had yet to decide if she trusted him enough to answer them. She had doubts that he merely came north to see his old home.

⸻

As the men returned from the stable, they passed the smithy. Angus remembered Iain hiding the pickaxe he was making as Angus walked past that morning.

"Hamish, have people found gold or something in these hills? I'm serious this time."

"Not that I know of. Why do ye ask?"

"I was just curious why Iain was making a pickaxe."

Hamish stopped and stared at Angus. "Are ye sure? What use would that be on a farm?"

"Well, that's what I wondered. But that's two I've seen in two days. Niall was obviously digging in that cave, somewhere he would never go. Or so everyone says." He thought about it. "Or was that a story to keep folk away?"

"And ye are sure Iain was making a pickaxe?" Hamish looked puzzled. "I could use a new axe for chopping wood, but that would hardly do the trick. Moving rocks, maybe, but we got other tools for that."

"Aye, and he obviously didn't want me to see it. He dropped it in his sand bucket when he saw me coming and stood watching until I was well past. When I peeked back at him, he was pulling it out. I got the feeling he didn't want anyone to see it. We've known each other a long time, and being as ye are Catriona's steward, I thought ye ought to know."

Hamish turned away toward the manor but not before Angus saw the grim expression on his face, his jaw firmly set.

On entering the manor, Angus went straight to his room. He was covered in dust from the cave and desired nothing more than to wash his hands and face and think. To his surprise, a basin of hot water sat on the chest, and he took his time while he scrubbed, letting his mind run free.

*Nobody mentioned the axe Niall carried or seemed curious—even Hamish. And Catriona examined the arrow, ignoring the axe.* Angus pondered this as he sat on the bed. Comparing the two events, Angus could see no connection between this man's death years earlier and Dougal's recent demise. Besides both men being murdered, he could not determine any apparent connections. One was an older man shoved from the tower; the other was a young man shot in the back while digging in a cave.

Subconsciously, he fingered the bear claw at his neck. *The man was digging—the pickaxe. There has to be some significance to that.* First, it was odd to find it in the man's hand, but he would not have thought further about it had Catriona not responded the way she did at the mention of it. She started in her chair and immediately exchanged a glance with Hamish. But that had nothing to do with Dougal's death, so he put it to the back of his mind. That one was more pressing, and he needed to remove any doubts about his involvement.

The sun was still shining as Angus looked out of the window. *Luath.* He would groom his horse. It was soothing to himself, as well as the animal.

# CHAPTER II

THE FOLLOWING MORNING, SERGEANT Wolfe, accompanied by two soldiers, entered the gate. Finished with breakfast, Angus walked toward the stable. He shielded the sun from his eyes and saw the men riding toward him.

"There he is." The sergeant pointed. "Grab him!"

The two soldiers slid from their horses and raced toward Angus, pinning his arms. Not realizing they were after him, he had turned in the direction the sergeant had pointed, wondering who they were after. Now, as they grabbed his arms, he struggled to free himself.

"What is this?" He shouted. "What are ye doing?"

Sergeant Wolfe dismounted and approached. "We are arresting ye for the murders."

"What!" Angus twisted to be free, but one soldier pulled his arm painfully behind his back, preventing Angus from moving. "I've done nothing."

"Ye lied to me. Lord Shelton's nephew, indeed! You show up, and two men are killed. I don't believe those are coincidences."

"What is going on?" Catriona shouted as she came outside, Hamish hot on her heels.

"I came to your assistance, as requested, my lady," Sergeant Wolfe bowed to her.

"Oh, knock it off," she scolded him. "I didn't ask ye to come to arrest my cousin."

"The lad said there'd been another murder, and ye requested my help. I was out yesterday and only got the message this morning. I came to help as soon as I could." He sidled closer to her, a smile on his face.

"That is not what my message was. I merely wanted to inform ye of a death. I need no help. Now, let Angus go." Her face was livid; her hands were on her hips. She glared at him. Angus noticed the fire in her eyes. The sergeant should be careful.

At her glare, the sergeant nodded to his men. They released Angus. As he started to come after Sergeant Wolfe, Catriona raised her hand.

"We found a body up in the hills yesterday, Sergeant. But it was a skeleton. He'd been dead for years. We've identified who he was. So there was no need for all the fuss."

Sergeant Wolfe looked back and forth between Angus and Catriona before apologizing. "I'm sorry, ma'am. I only meant to help. Ye know ye can call on me whenever ye need me."

"Aye. I'll remember. But for now, I don't need your help. I think ye should go. Ye've been informed of Niall's death, which I am bound to do." She held out her hand.

The sergeant shook her hand and turned to leave. Angus stepped toward him, but Catriona put a restraining hand on his arm.

As they left, Angus hollered after them. "And Lord Shelton IS my uncle."

Father Michael, the priest, arrived late on Tuesday afternoon. Catriona offered him a small chamber for the night and discussed prayer rites for the deceased. Over dinner, the priest both shared and gathered the latest gossip. Most of the more remote communities received their news this way each month when a clergyman arrived for mass.

Practicing the Catholic faith had been banned following the Jacobite rising. However, many were still observant, and itinerant priests made the rounds returning to each district every month or so, where they performed marriage and death rites and held mass. The monasteries, such as the one nearby where Angus had studied, no longer existed. These days, the monks lived in small cells and did what good works they could for their people.

Their small chapel was perched on the back edge of the property. Thomas, the Verger, lived in a small cottage nearby. To the unobservant, the chapel appeared as if it had not been used in over twenty years. So far, none of the soldiers had bothered to look inside to see how well Thomas maintained it.

A small group gathered for the mass the following day. Angus, Catriona, and Hamish took their seats in the front row. Just as the bell rang ten, Callum strode in as if he were the laird of the manor. He stopped at the end of the row where Catriona sat on the aisle. Hamish sat next to her with Angus beside him. Callum stared at her, gesturing they should slide over to make space for him. Catriona remained where she was at first but ultimately moved. Angus knew Callum would not give in until she made space for him, and she would not want to create a scene. Hamish turned to Angus and shrugged. The bench was crowded with three men plus Catriona. Angus moved to the next row beside a woman with two small boys.

The woman smiled at Angus and made room for him. Sitting behind the others, Angus chuckled to himself. Callum sat self-righteously upright as if he belonged there. Angus swore he could hear Catriona grinding her teeth when she inched closer to Hamish. Hamish bristled; the hair on his neck stood up like a male cat about to pounce. This could be an entertaining service, Angus thought.

At that point, the priest came down the aisle. The service was long but straightforward, bidding the people to love each other as God loved them. Angus thought about Sundays in the colonies as the priest's voice droned on. Charles Mason was an ardent Anglican who believed strongly in the Sabbath as a day of rest. Mr. Mason sometimes reviewed the results of the previous night's observations of the stars, claiming that was not work. But the men had the day off, and services were held to respect each man's religion.

Soon, the service ended, and Angus followed the others outside, where people gathered to chat. No recent births or marriages had occurred, but the priest had agreed to hold a blessing for the deceased the following day before leaving for the next village.

Niall's family did not wish to hold a wake, with him being dead for so long, but at Catriona's urging, they agreed to have a small gathering at the hall that evening. The women hurried home to bake and prepare food. The men grabbed their whisky, cider, and beer.

As Catriona hurried past the farm buildings, Callum caught up with her.

"Lady, may I beg a room from ye for the night? I wish to attend the evening's events, and it is a fair distance to ride home afterward."

Catriona groaned. The last thing she wanted was for Callum to stay the night. She had so much to do to prepare for the festivities, small though they would be. But highland courtesy prevailed, and Catriona consented.

"Aye, I believe I can find a room, though it will not be of the standard to which ye are accustomed," she said. Angus now lived in the room Callum had stayed in before.

"Thank ye, Lady," he bent his knee and lowered his head in a bow.

"Oh, stop it with the Lady. My name is Catriona."

"Ye could be a lady if ye reconsider my offer." He took her hand.

Catriona jerked it away. "Offer? Is that what ye call it? I merely remember ye saying I would be better off with ye living in Kingussie."

"Well, ye would," he protested as they reached the hall. "I have much to offer."

Catriona opened the door herself before he could reach in front of her and do it. "Hamish!" She called out as she stepped inside.

When he stepped from his chamber, she said, "Callum needs a bed for the night. Please see he is taken care of while I prepare for the gathering."

Callum scowled. Hamish's jaw dropped, but he did as he was bid.

"Follow me." He led Callum down the hall.

Catriona went into the office and slammed the door behind her. She needed to put an end to this. She had no interest in Callum or Sergeant Wolfe. Why would they not listen?

Angus watched the local people arrive that evening. There were fewer folks this time, but each brought items of food or drink. As they gathered, some chatted with Catriona first; others paid their respects to Archie and his parents before joining their friends. The village men gathered around the long table which held the beverages. This room had not been used for entertainment in over forty years. Now there had been two wakes in a week. These hardy folk made do with what they had. There would be no pipes tonight, but there would be plenty of music and dancing to the rousing tunes of the fiddler.

The wake stretched into the wee hours of the morning. The pretty, petite redhead Angus danced with before was not there this evening, but a willowy blonde openly flirted with him. He partnered with her for two reels and then with a few other lasses. But Angus didn't feel like dancing. His thoughts focused on the recent events.

He poured two mugs of cider and joined Archie on the bench. Niall had been one of the boys who teased and played tricks on him as a child, but Angus still sympathized with the family for their loss. He had questions, but this was not the time to ask them.

Angus' head throbbed the following day as he made his way toward the office, where Catriona sat at the table with her head in her hands. A steaming cup of tea sat before her.

"Were ye up all night?" he asked.

"Almost," she answered, raising her head. "Hamish stayed on when I could not. I believe there are a few still sleeping in there." She pointed toward the larger room adjacent. "I imagine Callum Dubh stayed late as well."

Elspeth slipped in quietly with more tea and some boiled eggs. "I'll bring ye some bread and jam." She, too, seemed a little rough around the edges.

"Well, I have to say these wakes are a wee bit different from the dinner parties at Shelton House." Angus chuckled. "And a lot more fun." He had enjoyed himself, especially at the first one, and mused over the gaiety considering the occasion. The Highlanders viewed it as a celebration of the deceased's life, much as the Indians had. Fond memories of Little Hawk filled his thoughts.

"Ye are smiling. Meet someone special last night?" She teased. Angus had danced with several of the local lasses, including the blonde.

"Nay," Angus blushed. "Just thinking about a friend. She was one of the Indians I met in Pennsylvania. I have often been struck by the similarities between her tribe and the clans. Last night, for example, they, too, honored their dead with a celebration. It's different from ours but with the same idea. I saw nothing like that in the somber events in London."

"Ye've mentioned that afore. I'd like to know more about your friends," Catriona said. A thump came from behind Angus. "Speaking of the dead..."

Angus turned to see Hamish stumbling in the doorway, his light brown hair tangled in knots streaming over his shoulders, his face white. "Is there any tea?" He staggered across the room and collapsed in the chair.

"Good thing those are sturdy," Angus said as the man's bulk hit the seat. The MacKay clan was known for their size. Most men were over six feet tall. Even women, such as Catriona, nearly matched the height of the men.

Hamish drank the cup of tea and rested his head on the table. Angus' stomach growled, and he reached for the eggs. He slathered two slices of bread with butter and raspberry jam and devoured them. Two more cups of tea, and Angus felt like himself again.

Catriona sipped her tea but declined offers of food. Hamish rested his head on the table and snored. Catriona smiled at Angus as her head slowly dropped onto her arms on the table.

As he roused them later, Angus looked down at his shirt. It had a stain on the front, but his waistcoat would cover it. His other shirt was in worse shape. However, he had attended a funeral in his working clothes in the colonies. So be it.

"It's time to go to the chapel," he said as he poked Hamish. But after the service, they needed to sit down and discuss the murders.

Most of the village gathered again at the chapel that morning for the prayers. Many looked rough around the edges after the previous evening. Once again, Catriona, Hamish, and Angus sat in the front row. On the opposite side sat Archie and his parents. And once again, just before the service began, Callum entered and moved to join Catriona. This time, however, she did not budge.

"We represent Dougal's family today," she told him, refusing to make room.

"Not him." Callum pointed at Angus.

"Aye. Angus lived in this house when his grandfather held it. Dougal's father was their steward." Catriona held her ground.

"Fine." Callum was making a public scene this time, and he soon backed down and sat in the row behind them.

Angus peered down the row at Catriona and saw the smile curving the corners of Hamish's mouth. If Catriona married, he hoped it would be Hamish. They were good for each other. And whether they were ready to admit it, Angus sensed they loved each other. He understood Catriona was afraid of losing her land if she married, but Angus knew Hamish would never take it from her but work it with her.

The priest began the service, invoking prayers and the familiar words of the blessing for the dead. Archie stood up and spoke of his brother while Hamish shared memories of Dougal Og, his friend. He knew him better than any of the others.

Angus sat quietly, remembering Dougal Mòr, a quiet, efficient man who helped Angus' mother when they lived in the small corner of their destroyed home. He and his son, Dougal Og, hunted for them and found supplies and items to make their living quarters more bearable. Dougal Mòr scrounged up blankets, straw mattresses, and wooden plates and cups for the family. As most of the area had been burned, Angus remembered his gran wondering where he found those items. But she would never ask. Dougal Mòr was a soft-spoken man, and Angus had thought of him as a gentle giant and often followed him around. As Angus recalled, his son was much like him.

Angus began to study the other people while listening to the speakers. Would any of them have cause to kill? There was an undercurrent here of something he was not being told. Well, it was time for them to tell him.

Catriona said her farewells quickly while Angus lingered, talking with Geordie and Archie. They watched Callum mount his horse and leave.

"He'll never win," Geordie commented, watching him. "Even if there wasna someone else already here, she'd never accept him." Archie agreed and crinkled his eyes in what Angus assumed was a wink. They expected her to marry Hamish.

Catriona stormed out as they approached the house and threw an object on the blacksmith's fire. She cursed as Angus hurried toward her. Geordie and Archie followed.

"What was that?" Angus asked. "Is everything okay?"

"Someone put a charm on my bed. And I think I know who."

Hamish stepped from the stable, "Well, 't wasna me."

"Nor me," Angus said. "A love charm?"

"Aye. With lavender and ribbons," Catriona spat out the words. She clenched her fist. "Well, who else could it have been?"

"Anyone. There were many people in the house last night," Hamish paused. "Including someone who just saddled his horse and left."

Catriona stomped her foot. "That man better not have entered my chamber!" She shook her fist in the direction Callum had ridden.

"I guess ye have to give him credit for trying," Archie said.

"Well, I don't," Hamish snapped.

"Nor do I." Catriona stormed to the house. Hamish followed.

# CHAPTER 12

N OW WAS NOT THE time for questions. Angus wasn't sure whether to go for a walk or take Luath for a ride. But the house was the last place he wanted to be right now. He knew there was something they were not telling him, and it was sending in his mind directions he did not wish to consider. Did they trust him? Angus hoped a ride on the moors would clear his head.

Luath stomped his front hoof in excitement when Angus entered the stable. They had not gone out yesterday, and the horse was eager for a run. One of the farm's large brown dogs trotted at Angus' heels. He seemed keen to be out on the meadows above the farm. Angus quickly saddled Luath and rode off, the dog following.

The radiant sun shone in the sky, casting its warmth across the wildflowers dancing in the breeze on the hillside. Amongst the grasses, Angus noticed the droopy stems and bright color of bluebells dotting the field through which he rode. The dog still trotted alongside. Gran had told him stories of these fairy flowers of spring. On a whim, he dismounted and led the horse along, looking for the rare white ones. Gran claimed the fairies touched the petals of those blossoms. Angus shook his head, his logical mind at war with his belief in the mystical, especially here in his homeland. Over time, he learned it was possible to accept both. Little

Hawk certainly believed in the powers that existed in nature. Her voice filled his head as he fondly remembered conversations similar to those he had with his grandmother.

Not seeing any white ones today, he remounted and continued. It was early in the season, and he may yet find some. As they rode off, the dog sneezed. Pigs, Angus knew, hated these flowers. The local farmers referred to them as Fuath-mhuc or hated-by-pigs. Maybe those intelligent creatures sensed the fairies in their midst. *Perhaps the dog did too?*

The lower meadow stretched below them over the hill and through a narrow valley, where a large flock of sheep grazed in the grass. Angus looked around for the shepherd and soon spotted a young lad perched on a massive stone projecting through the soil. His dog lay beside him, soaking up the sunlight. The manor dog gave a soft woof, and the shepherd's dog trotted to greet them. Angus approached slowly, not wanting to spook the animals.

"Hello," the young lad sat up, obviously happy at a chance to relieve the boredom of his job. His dog sniffed Angus, then stood nose-to-nose with the dog from the manor. Both wagged their tails happily.

"My name is Fergus," the boy informed him.

"I'm Angus, and this is Luath," he said, pointing to the horse.

"Is he fast?" the boy asked.

"Aye," Angus nodded, not surprised Fergus knew the name. Gaelic peppered the speech of many in the region; Angus doubted English was spoken by choice. The boy appeared to be twelve or thirteen, lean and gawky, not yet grown into his man's body. His clothing hung loosely on his thin frame, and his trousers had grown short. His unkempt sandy hair blew freely in the wind, and a lock fell over his left eye.

"Anything interesting out here?" Angus asked, hoping for some gossip.

The boy laughed and gestured at the meadow, "Here?" The lad was right. He wouldn't see anything here.

"These look like Dunface sheep," Angus commented.

"Oh, aye, the best wool there is," Fergus replied proudly.

"I agree. We raised the Dunface as well when I was a lad."

Fergus looked curiously at Angus. "Ye did? Do ye live around here?"

"I did until I was almost seventeen, though it's been twelve years since I left."

"Then ye know yer sheep." The lad sat back, satisfied. "There be some folk bringing in the Black Face, but my mam doesna like the feel o' their wool. Too coarse, she says."

Angus agreed, "My gran loved the feel of Dunface wool. Nice seat ye have there." He climbed up next to the lad on the large, sun-warmed stone. "May I join ye?"

Fergus nodded, and Angus scrambled up onto the rock. Sitting down, he reclined against the smooth surface, stretching his legs in the sun. How often had he done this as a boy on a warm spring morning? Angus wondered. Sometimes, he had joined the local shepherds moving their flocks to different meadows. He might still learn something from this shepherd.

"Aye, the giant of Torvean Hill threw this stone back in the days when ogres and trolls lived in these hills," Fergus answered matter-of-factly. "He and the giant from Dunain threw their stone hammers in a contest, but ye'd know that story bein' from here."

Angus suppressed a grin and crossed his legs, "Isn't this a bit out of his usual territory, nearer to Inverness?" He had heard such stories before.

"Ach, nay," the lad replied. He sat up. "Giants have a fearsome stride. Their legs are so long, 'twas a mere two-day walk."

This time Angus did smile as he did the math. They were forty miles from Torvean Hill. Twenty miles a day? But he would let Fergus have his dreams and said, "Oh, aye. A giant could easily cover that distance."

Satisfied, Fergus reclined back again on the rock.

Angus spent most of the morning with Fergus and shared the scones he snatched from the tray Elspeth left on the table.

"Did ye hear about the murders?" Fergus asked eagerly.

"Aye, I found the bodies," Angus told him.

Fergus looked wide-eyed at him. "Oh. Were ye at the wake?" The lad asked as he nibbled on the scone. "My mam wouldna let me go, seeing how the lambs are coming."

"Aye, I was. Dougal Og worked for my grandfather."

The boy sat up, alarmed. "Ye are from the manor?" He ran his fingers through his hair.

"I was, but I left many years ago, dinna fash yerself." Angus watched as the boy slowly relaxed though he still looked warily up at him.

"All right, then," he said after a few moments. "Tha sin math." The lad settled back on the rock. Angus wondered. *Is everything well?*

"I was hoping you might help me. I'm sure ye observe things as ye sit here."

Fergus appeared to ponder this. "Not so much out here, but I wondered if the old man found what he was looking for afore he died."

"Who? Dougal Og?" Angus turned to look at him. "What do ye mean?"

"He came to see my gran. He wanted to find something and thought she could help," Fergus answered.

"Your gran?"

"Aye, Morag. She has the sight. Many folks come to see if she can help 'em."

Angus bolted upright at this. Could this have anything to do with Dougal's death?

"We were sorry to hear he fell. The lady from the manor came too, a couple of times."

"From the manor? Which lady?"

"The mistress. She came once afore the old man and again after he came."

"Tall for a woman? Red hair?" Angus held his breath, waiting for an answer.

"Aye, with eyes the green of the meadow grasses," Fergus replied.

"Catriona." Angus considered this development. "Do ye know what she was asking of your gran?" He paused, then asked, "Or what Dougal Og wanted?"

"Nay. We ain't supposed to listen. I was helpin' my gran move her loom when the old man arrived, and he started talking afore I left. He wanted her to help find somethin' important. I guess he lost somethin' valuable to him."

Was that why Dougal was in the tower? "Were ye around when Catriona came?"

"I saw her comin' up the lane. Hard to miss her." Fergus blushed.

Angus stretched back out on the rock again, mulling this over. What was Dougal looking for? And why did Catriona visit the seer? Did these visits have anything to do with his death?

"Ye know, ye look an awful lot like her. With your coloring and all. Ye even have the same eyes."

"Like meadow grasses?" Angus teased him.

Fergus blushed again and turned away.

"Do ye think I could meet your gran?"

"Did ye lose somethin' too? Ye dinna look like ye need love charms."

"Nay, I'd just like to meet her." Angus chuckled.

"Oh, well, that's okay then," Fergus swiped at the hair that hung over his eye. "She might make ye pay."

"That's fine," Angus told him.

"Tomorrow morning, I move this flock to the croft land so the ewes can be nearby for the lambing. Can ye come then?"

"I could," Angus replied. He knew the seer could not tell him the reason for their visits, but he knew from Gran there were other ways of finding out information if you asked the right questions. Excitement built as he hoped he might finally get some answers.

"Ye could help me if ye like or just meet me there," Fergus said hopefully.

Angus smiled. "I'll meet ye here, and we can work them together. Sun up?"

"Aye," said Fergus. He pointed up the hill. "I'll be in the hut up there for the night. Just give me a holler when ye get here." He grinned from ear to ear as he walked with Angus over to where Luath grazed the nice, new grass.

Angus mounted. "See ye in the morning." He rode off toward the manor. When he glanced over his shoulder, Fergus was still watching him. Angus waved.

Angus couldn't decide how to broach the subject. Catriona hadn't told him she had visited the seer. Then again, it wasn't any of his business. Or was it? She claimed not to believe in coincidences. Well, he didn't either and thought it odd she visited the old woman at the same time as Dougal, and now he was dead. He had been murdered. Was Catriona in danger?

Angus briefly thought about talking to Hamish but pushed that notion aside. Hamish was utterly loyal to her, and whether he was ready to admit it, Angus knew Hamish was in love with her.

Back at the stable, Angus brushed Luath's glossy coat and filled his feeding trough with oats. The water bucket was empty, and Angus shook his head. The young groom hadn't refilled it. Angus grabbed the handle and headed toward the well.

As he crossed the threshold of the open door, he heard voices murmuring and paused. Gaelic. Though it was many years since he had spoken his native tongue, Angus still understood the language. The men spoke in low voices, almost whispering. He could barely make out the words. Angus remained behind the open door and listened.

"We'll do it next week when I've finished the axes," one man said. Angus recognized the voice as Iain, the burly blacksmith. "I'll put off the one for the man in Kingussie as long as I can."

The men planned to meet outside the back gate once given the signal. But where they were going or what they were up to, Angus had no clue. He remained motionless behind the door, hoping to hear more. He figured they were looking for treasure and not planning to use the axes for something too terrible to imagine.

The breeze blew the open door into his arm, and he dropped the bucket. The men abruptly stopped talking. Angus strode out as if he was just leaving the barn and had hit the door on his exit. He scooped the bucket up by the handle and proceeded to the well.

Duncan, one of the villagers, greeted him. "Lovely day, eh?" The man spoke to him in English as he pretended to be merely passing by. The other men joined in, following suit.

"Aye, 'tis," Angus replied, noting the switch of language. This was interesting. He grew up here, but they did not remember he spoke Gaelic.

He would keep it that way for now. And he'd keep his eyes and ears open. Until he had some questions answered, he'd keep this to himself. He was slowly gathering the pieces.

"Where were ye off to today?" Catriona asked Angus over supper that night. Elspeth entered and served the rabbit stew before Angus answered.

"I went off on a ride." Here was his opening. After she left, he let the conversation flow, hoping he could steer it in the right direction. That would determine how much he told her.

"Anywhere in particular?" Catriona asked.

"Just through the hillsides. I love spring when the Fairy Flowers bloom." This comment elicited no response from either of the others. "Though I saw no white ones."

"Might be a wee bit early in the season yet," Catriona responded. "I remember searching for the fairies when I was a girl." Hamish merely grunted.

Realizing at least she might believe in the old ways, Angus continued, 'tis lambing season just now, and I ran into a young shepherd laddie."

Hamish smiled. "So, 'tis. I've not worked sheep in many a year." He patted his leg.

"Lad named Fergus," Angus said, watching their reactions. There was none. "He has a flock o' the Dunface." He approached the question slowly, still wondering whether they trusted him. "My gran loved their wool."

"Good stock, fine wool," Hamish offered. "Used to tend 'em as a lad."

"He claims his gran has the sight. I know my gran had it." He casually brought the spoon to his lips and blew on the hot stew. "I met a native seer while I was in the colonies. Do folk here still believe?" Angus asked innocently, watching Catriona as she choked on her soup.

She brought her napkin to her mouth and said, "I imagine some do; there are those that still practice the old ways." She grabbed her wine glass and took a big swig.

"Ye all right?" Hamish rose to pat her on the back.

"Aye, I'm fine. Sit down." She brushed a lock of hair back from her face and picked up her spoon. Angus noticed her hand tremble.

There had been no reaction from Hamish. Catriona stared down into her bowl, her face almost as pale as the napkin she brought to her mouth. *So,* thought Angus, *there is a story here.* This piqued his curiosity and his desire to unravel the threads.

"Have either of ye ever visited a seer?" Angus pressed.

Hamish scoffed, but Catriona excused herself and left, leaving his questions unanswered.

Later that night, as he lay in bed, another thought struck him like a lightning bolt now that he focused on Catriona. Fergus told him Dougal was searching for something. And so was Niall, with a pickaxe in hand. And Iain was making those in secret. *Were the deaths related even though they occurred years apart? What were the two men looking for? The cave, the tower? And where were the men going with pickaxes?* These may be uncomfortable questions, but they needed to be asked. Catriona knew something. And most likely, Hamish did, too. Breakfast was going to be interesting.

# CHAPTER 13

ANGUS WAS DISAPPOINTED TO find no one awake when he reached the dining room the following morning, though it was probably best since he wanted to meet Fergus on time. Elspeth had placed hard-boiled eggs and scones on the table. Angus grabbed a couple of each and crammed them into his pockets. Then he slipped out into the dawn light. The sun was cresting the hill, and there was a nip in the air.

Thankful for his warm greatcoat, Angus rummaged through his saddlebag and pulled on a pair of thick leather gloves. He would need these this morning, though he hoped it would warm up once the sun reached him. He quickly saddled Luath and rode through the gate. The brown dog opened an eye but snuggled further into the straw. The heavy dew glistened like frost, but it was not cold enough to freeze the previous night. Still, he pulled his greatcoat tighter. Angus wore the old pair of trousers he brought. He had questioned his decision to bring them but was thankful now that he had. He wished he'd also brought the hunting frock he wore in the colonies. That would be more suited for today's work.

Luath enjoyed the cool morning weather, though Angus hoped it would warm up by midday. They trotted through the meadow, listening to the songbirds. Angus heard the hoot of an owl slowly circling above the forest. Soon, the shepherd's hut came into view. Fergus stepped outside and stretched as they neared.

"Ye're on time," he said to Angus. "Being a gentleman, I didna know if ye'd be awake so early."

"I'm no gentleman," Angus retorted. But as he spoke, he looked down at his horse and the quality of its saddle. He imagined he must look that way to a shepherd boy. "Let's get to work."

Angus dismounted and clipped a long rope to Luath's bridle. He grabbed a stick, nearly as long as his own height, and balanced it between his hands. It would do. Fergus whistled at the dog, who immediately recaptured a stray sheep. With them grouped tightly together, Angus and Fergus slowly strolled behind the sheep through the valley. Once or twice, one of the curly beasts meandered off, but Fergus or Angus quickly forced it back in line with the others. The dog nipped at the heels of any that thought of straying. Angus used his stick for walking, never needing it to corral the docile animals.

They crossed through the valley and into the meadow above the small cluster of homes, each on their own croft land. This was the tricky part, ensuring the flock stayed tight. Once one headed off, others would follow. But they seemed to know there was sweet grass below, and they headed tamely down the slope. The sun was now high in the sky, and Angus removed his outer coat and gloves, packing them in the saddlebag.

The men finally relaxed once they corralled the animals in the fenced paddock where the ewes had easy access to the covered barn. A thatched cottage of stone stood before them. The small building was constructed in two sections and contained a door on each side, the butt, and the ben. A thin woman with scraggly light brown hair slipping below her cap came from the smaller section to meet them. That was the butt end where the family lived and slept.

"Allo, Fergus. And who might this be with ye?" she asked.

"This is my new friend Angus. He is visitin' up at the manor and said he'd be pleased to help me." He turned to Angus. "This is my mam."

Angus nodded at the woman. She smiled. "Pleased to meet ye. My name is Sarah; please come into the house. I can offer ye a simple fare and some tea. I know my Fergus is starving." She tousled her son's hair. Sarah led the way to the door on the larger side, the ben end, and disappeared. Ducking under the doorway, Angus noticed the soot staining the walls and understood why the old butt and ben houses were often called blackhouses. He'd never been inside one before.

Sarah returned and placed a wooden plate on the table with thick slabs of brown bread and slices of cheese. A crock of butter sat next to it.

"How did ye meet my son?" she asked.

"I was riding yesterday and came across him tending the sheep. We raised Dunface when I was a lad. But that was some time ago." Angus smiled at her.

"He wants to meet Gran," Fergus piped up in explanation.

Sarah's head snapped around, and she cocked an eyebrow at him. "Why would ye want to do that?" she asked.

He looked back and forth between Fergus and his mother before replying, "I heard Dougal Og came here afore he died. And I was curious. My gran had the sight as well."

"Well, in that case, ye know she willna tell ye anything," Sarah replied.

Angus nodded. "Aye, but he's been killed. I don't think it was an accident. I hoped she might listen to me and provide something I could use."

"Mebbe," Sarah mulled it over as she spoke. "Sometimes, she has helped. Ye can ask. Finish yer tea, and I will lead ye to see her."

"Thank ye, ma'am." Well, at least he would see her.

Once they finished, Sarah showed them to another blackhouse across the garden. Bright yellow curtains hung in the window of the ben where she received the folk who came for her help. Sarah knocked on the door.

"It's me, Mam, with a guest. Is anyone with ye?" Sarah asked.

"Nay. Enter," a voice responded.

Angus stooped to enter the low doorway. On a chair in front of the fire sat an older woman who rose to greet them. Her bright eyes contrasted with her wrinkled face.

"I am Morag," she said, "how may I help ye?" She nodded at Sarah, who retreated.

Angus studied the woman before him as she pointed to a chair near the fire. Her voice defied her appearance, full, rich, and surprisingly strong, coming from such a petite, fragile-looking woman. She wore no cap over her disheveled gray curls. Angus dutifully sat as she resumed her seat.

"Angus, ma'am," he answered. "My gran had the sight. And well, I need some help with a rather sticky situation, and I hoped ye might offer some advice."

"Aye, I ken who ye are," she stared him directly in the eye. "Ye have the bloodline running strong in ye. And I knew yer gran well. She was a dear friend."

"Ye knew her?"

"Aye, and 'twas sorry the way things befell her family."

"She raised me on her own 'til I was sixteen," Angus said once again, feeling that sense of loss.

"I imagine ye are here about Dougal Og," she said.

"Aye." Though he spent his youth with Gran, it never ceased to surprise him how clearly these women saw things. Clever Otter, the native wise woman he met in the colonies, had been the same. She had told him to be true to himself, and all would be well. She had been right.

"Ye ken he came to see me?" At Angus' nod, she continued. "Then ye also ken I canna tell ye our conversation."

Angus nodded again. "I understand that, but I hoped ye might see something to guide me in the right direction. Ye see, I don't believe his death was an accident."

"Well, I can tell ye that much. T'was not. Nor was Niall's, but I suspect ye ken that since there was an arrow in his back."

"Ye know about that?" Angus gasped in surprise.

"It only appeared to me recently, probably because ye were on yer way to the cave. I dinna always get to choose what I see or when I see it."

"Aye. Gran said the same. It often bothered her."

"Yes, that's the hard part, ye see. Ye wish ye could help the families in their grief or prevent things yet to happen." She stared into the fire, and Angus patiently waited for her to speak again.

"Ye are correct that Dougal Og was seeking something, as are many folks of late. Niall, too, though he didna ken what he sought. He was in the wrong place. Dougal Og knew, though, and he was correct though he didna believe it. I canna say more." She paused and focused on Angus, her stare boring into him. "But ye should beware the watcher in the woods who shows false." With the words spoken, Morag leaned back in her chair and closed her eyes. That was all he would learn today, though a shiver ran down his spine.

*Well, that was no help,* Angus thought to himself. The watcher in the woods? That meant nothing to him. He rose to leave, depositing several copper pennies on the small table between them. Morag said nothing as he turned to go.

However, as he opened the door to leave, she said, "ye will travel great distances." And with that, she turned back to the fire.

"Or maybe I already have," he muttered, disappointed as he approached Sarah's home. Hadn't he been a great distance to the colonies? He tapped on the door and thanked her.

"Ye helped my son. That is thanks enough for me," she said kindly.

Pensive, Angus mounted Luath and turned toward the manor. He had not gotten far when he remembered Catriona saying she often felt like someone was watching her. Then, he recalled that feeling he had when they rode back from the broch that day after examining the site of Dougal's death. Angus swore he heard a horse matching pace with them in the woods. *The watcher in the woods...* Angus thought about warning Catriona and urged Luath to go faster.

One of the stable lads came to take the horse as they approached. When Angus entered the house, he met Hamish in the entryway, a scowl on his face.

"What's the matter? Where's Catriona?" Angus asked.

"In there." Hamish pointed at the dining room. "And *he's* with her." He scowled.

"And ye just stand out here?" Angus crossed the hall and knocked.

"Come in," Catriona said.

Angus entered to find Catriona standing by the fire and Callum beside her. There was relief on Catriona's face and the glare of controlled anger on Callum's.

"Angus, welcome. I am glad ye are back and just in time for supper." She paused as she took in his rumpled, dirty appearance. Catriona wrinkled her nose.

"Ye stink. Go clean up and come back to join us. And send Hamish in if ye see him." She smiled at him as she stepped away from the fireplace toward the sideboard. "I will pour us all some wine."

Angus stepped back into the hallway where Hamish paced. "Ye are to go inside." When Hamish didn't move, Angus hissed at him. "Stand up for yourself, man. I think she does not wish to be alone with that one."

"Oh," Hamish responded with a smile. "Well, that is a good thing, then." He rushed to the door, stopping to straighten his waistcoat and run a hand through his wavy hair before entering the room.

*Well, that is interesting,* Angus thought as he entered his chamber to change clothes. It meant he could not speak to Catriona right away as he hoped, but at least she was safe for the time being.

The water in the basin was cold, but Angus splashed it on his face and scrubbed at his hands. He pulled on the nice, white linen shirt he had brought with him. *I might as well make myself presentable for our guest.* Angus grinned as he pulled on his clean breeches and a waistcoat in deep forest green. Now he was glad he'd brought different clothing.

As he entered the dining room, Angus knew this must not have been a planned dinner. Otherwise, Catriona would have set up the formal room next door to entertain someone of Callum's station. The grain had been moved to the fields for the wakes, and the space sat empty. The former family dining room was a workspace now, not a place for entertaining. A settee and chair sat in front of the fireplace. The table where they usually ate was shoved to one side. Otherwise, the room contained a sizable desk, a small bookcase, and crates full of farm implements. Bags of seed were stacked in one corner.

Catriona crossed the room to greet him and handed him a glass of wine. "Thank ye," she whispered to him. Angus made a show of greeting her with a peck on the cheek.

"I need to talk to ye," he whispered back.

She gave him an imperceptible nod and turned back to playing the hostess. She introduced the men, "Callum, I don't believe ye properly met Angus before. Angus, Callum Campbell, his estate is near Kingussie."

Callum stood glaring. Angus stepped toward him and held his hand; he would at least show some manners. "I don't believe we were formally introduced." He smirked.

Callum rigidly stuck out his hand, but his grip was feeble. Angus' dislike of the man increased. Angus greeted his cousin, who stood stiffly by the fire.

"Ye were off early," Hamish said to Angus once seated at the table.

"Aye. Remember that shepherd I mentioned? He was bringing his flock down to the croft for lambing. I decided to help him. It's been a while since I worked sheep on the moors."

Callum scoffed. "A gentleman working sheep? Did ye find any more dead bodies?"

Angus clenched his fist in his lap. Catriona stiffened.

"What? Ye think he killed them?" Hamish burst out.

"Ridiculous," Catriona scoffed. "Besides, he was in the colonies when Niall was killed. I think that clears him of any wrongdoing there."

"But what about Dougal?" Callum pressed the issue.

"Nay. I don't believe he did it." Catriona shook her head and poured more wine.

A notion struck Angus. "I thought ye agreed that Dougal's death was an accident?" He watched Callum as his dark countenance paled. His hand clenched the glass tightly as he sat it on the table.

At that moment, Alan, Elspeth's son, entered carrying a large tray containing roast chicken with carrots and parsnips. As they ate, Callum bragged about his estate and manor house with all its luxuries. But Angus could not ignore Callum's reaction to the offhand comment. He wondered if Callum knew more than he admitted. But he shook it off. What was his motive in killing either man?

Angus glanced at Catriona and had the odd notion that she was counting the bags of seeds in the corner while she ate. He smiled to himself. No one else bothered to make conversation. They finished their meal with slices of lemon cake and cups of coffee.

Their larger meal was typically eaten at midday, with only a light supper in the evening. But when Callum arrived earlier, Catriona asked Elspeth if she could delay the meal. Neither Hamish nor Angus had been around, and she had no desire to be alone with Callum. Highland hospitality dictated Catriona provide for her guest, and a room was prepared for Callum to spend the night. Hamish tilted his head at Angus, who immediately understood the message. They would ensure Catriona was safe from any advances this man may have planned.

"I have an early start tomorrow, so Callum, I must bid ye safe journey. I shall not see ye in the morning." Catriona rose and held out her hand. "Hamish will show ye to your room."

Disappointment on his face, Callum rose and took her hand. "Ma'am." As she released his grip, he added, "Anything I can help you with in the morning?"

"Nay. Thank ye." Catriona left.

Neither man wanted to talk with Callum, nor it appeared he with them after Catriona went to bed. Soon they rose, and Hamish showed their guest to his room.

Hamish woke Angus in the middle of the night for his shift, watching Catriona's door. He told him Callum had quietly slipped into the hall once but retreated immediately when he saw Hamish sitting in the chair.

"What do ye think of his comment about Dougal's death?" Angus whispered as they stood at the door to his room.

"Not much. Why? A few people are starting to ask questions about it."

"I just wondered," Angus replied. "Do others think I was involved? Or did I place too much on it? Or is Callum involved?"

" I can't see he had a motive for Dougal, or Niall, for that matter." Hamish left for bed.

They did not expect to see Callum again, and all was quiet on Angus' watch. As he thought about it, Angus decided Hamish was probably right.

After a few hours, Hamish returned to the hallway. "I canna sleep. Not with that man under the same roof. Go to bed."

"Are ye sure?" Angus asked. "I'm willing to finish my time out here."

"Aye. No use both of us being up all night." Angus returned to his room. Exhausted from the day before, he slept later than he intended.

Elspeth heard Angus and brought him a steaming pot of tea and scones. Alone in the room, Angus opted to sit on the settee in front of the fire rather than at the table. He was staring into the flames when Hamish entered. He grabbed a cup and joined his cousin at the fire, stretching his long legs before him.

"Is he gone?" Angus asked Hamish.

"Callum? Yep, he left a while ago. Catriona went into the fields at dawn with Geordie. She wanted to avoid seeing him this morning." Hamish stared into the fire.

"Ye need to tell her," Angus said.

"Tell her what?" Hamish asked though Angus knew he understood him.

"How ye feel."

Hamish looked down at his hands. "Aye. But I'm afraid she'll not feel the same way, and I'd rather keep what I have than lose it all. I couldna stay if she didna want me."

Angus had noticed the looks Catriona gave Hamish since he arrived but said instead, "I feel she will need your protection. I saw Morag yesterday."

"The seer? Ye?" Hamish looked at him. "Ach, your gran had the sight, did she not?" He waited for Angus to continue.

"She warned me to beware the watcher in the woods. I am not sure what she meant, but I know Catriona sometimes claims she feels a presence. And that day we rode back from the ruin, I swore someone was riding alongside us, watching."

Hamish sat, absorbing this information while sipping his tea. "Is that what ye wanted to tell her last night when ye returned? And ye know who was here."

" I don't think Morag meant Callum, but I wanted to tell her to be careful." He rose. "I should talk to Archie. I think he has finally forgiven me for finding his brother's body, and I'd like to see what he remembers from back then."

# CHAPTER 14

A FTER SPENDING SEVERAL HOURS splitting logs with Archie, Angus brushed the sweat from his eyes. Chopping wood was hard labor, but it felt good on his muscles. He had been idle far too long. Angus climbed aboard the cart after loading the last logs onto the wagon. Archie urged the team toward home and the fresh hay in the barn with a click of his tongue.

"Thank ye for yer help," Archie said to him.

"No problem," Angus replied. "But I fear I will feel it tomorrow." His effort to get Archie to remember the events of five years ago had been of little use. Angus considered mentioning the conversation he'd overheard but figured he would not get an answer. And maybe it was not yet time to admit to understanding Gaelic. He might learn more without arousing suspicion.

Angus hopped down to open the wide wooden gate behind the manor when they heard a scream. Angus hot-footed it toward the house as Hamish burst from the stable. Both of them reached the door at the same time. It was open, and Angus let Hamish go first. As the cousins entered, they heard Catriona swear. She came out of the room, her face red, her hands on her hips. She scowled at the men.

"Catriona, what is it?" Hamish caught his breath. He grimaced as he slowed down and put weight on his leg.

Angus stepped around him to Catriona, checking for any evidence of a wound.

"Have either of ye been in there?" She pointed at the office. Her finger shook with rage.

Angus shook his head, "not since breakfast this morning. I've been chopping wood with Archie up in the woods."

"I was at the widow's cottage repairing the thatch after that storm the other night." Hamish shook his head, saying, "I just got back."

"Well, someone has been in there," Catriona informed them, leading the way into the room. "My ledgers are open. Someone has been looking at my accounts."

"Open? So? Ye were working on them when I left for the widow's," Hamish replied.

"I was," Catriona admitted. "But I was going over the current entries, and I finished those. Now, the book is open to last month, to the total valuation I did of the estate."

"But who would look at that? Can everyone here read?" Angus asked.

"Some, but not many," Hamish answered. He pushed past Catriona into the room.

"Who else has been here?" Angus asked. "What about Callum? Didn't ye say ye saw him leave this morning?" He glanced at Hamish.

"Aye, he did," Hamish answered. "Besides, ye were in here after Angus and I left." He turned to Catriona.

Elspeth entered and heard the last of their conversation. "That sergeant was here earlier, maybe an hour ago."

They turned to her. "Wolfe?" asked Hamish.

"Aye," the cook answered, "but I don't believe he came inside. My lad, Alan, told him the mistress was away." We thought he left.

"Did anyone see Callum leave?" Catriona asked.

"I did. And his horse was gone when I left for the village. Did Alan see Sergeant Wolfe leave?" Hamish asked.

Elspeth shook her head. "I think he did."

Angus turned to Catriona. "Is this what ye meant by strange happenings?"

"Not quite," she answered. "Those were more of a feeling that someone was there, not tangible proof."

The next day, Catriona was buried under heaps of yellow blossoms. Their overpowering aroma filled the air. She raised her head, her coppery locks shining above the flowers as she watched Angus enter. The last day of April was the eve of Beltane.

"Beltane," he said. "I enjoyed the May Day celebrations in the colonies, but they were nothing like Beltane in the highlands. Do ye need any help?" he asked.

Catriona was stringing flowers together with twine. The women had gathered primrose, rowan, hawthorn, gorse, hazel, and marigolds that morning.

"Nay, I will do this," she gestured at the mountain of yellow before her. "But Hamish may need help with the wood for tonight's fire."

"I can do that," he said. The kitchen door opened, and the smell of bannocks baking competed with the sweet scent of the flowers as Elspeth entered the room.

"Oh, those smell good! I love oatcakes!" Angus sniffed the air loudly.

"Thank ye, Angus," the cook smiled at him. She turned to Catriona. "I've put Alan to work on the caudle. Let's hope he doesn't make a muck of it." The mixture of eggs, butter, oatmeal, and milk was simple to prepare and would simmer over the bonfire that evening.

Angus laughed. "I'll be out o' your way then and go help Hamish."

Catriona returned to stringing the blossoms. But she was worried. She had ignored the first few times it had felt like someone had been in her home, claiming it was just her imagination. But lately, odd noises and rustling had become more frequent. Morag had warned her of danger ahead. And someone had been in here, looking at her books. Then there were the murders. She sighed. "Chin up, girl," she told herself, "this day is for your people."

Cleaned up after the day's chores, the household members gathered in the courtyard just before dark and waited for Catriona to come out of the house. As the head of the household, she ensured all hearth fires were extinguished, and no candles were lit. They would light these in the morning with the torches from the Beltane fire, bringing the hope of prosperity for the summer.

When Catriona joined them, Elspeth and her daughter, Ailsa, helped her place the bundles of May flowers around all the doors and windows. Then the unorthodox family sang songs and laughed on their way toward the small hill where they would light the bonfire. The stacks of wood Hamish, Angus, Archie, and Geordie had chopped sat in neat rows nearby. Nine different trees were represented in the piles.

The herders, with their cattle, were already there. A few shepherds were also present, with their rams representing their flock while the ewes minded their lambs. After exchanging greetings, Catriona stepped forward.

"Blessing to all," she chanted in Gaelic, then recited the words of the age-old blessing.

> *Everything within my dwelling or in my possession,*
> *All kine and crops, all flocks and corn,*
> *From Hallow Eve to Beltane Eve,*
> *With goodly progress and gentle blessing,*
> *From sea to sea, and every river mouth,*
> *From wave to wave, and base of waterfall.*

Hamish stepped forward and approached the fire carrying nine logs in his arms.

"We have the nine sacred trees tonight," he said as he held up the first log. "Rowan, the wizard's tree." He placed it on the pile and then added one log at a time, as he named them. "Briar that burns so keen and green. Oak, the mighty giver of heat. Alder, the battle witch. Holly to burn dry. Elder to burn the armies of the sìth. Birch to burn constant. Aspen to burn late. Yew, the most sacred to the feast."

Then, taking the lit cord Angus held, Hamish ignited the bonfire. The men fanned the sparks, igniting the logs. The villagers watched in reverence as the flames flickered.

Once the wood was fully engulfed in the blaze and smoke spiraled through the air, the herders and the shepherds led their animals three times sunwise around the bonfire, ensuring they led them through the smoke. This provided protection to see them healthy and productive through the summer. Before the men escorted their beasts back to their fields, the people took their turn around the flames, receiving the blessing of health.

To one side of the blaze, Alan stirred the caudle. When the men returned from the barns, Catriona poured the mixture into a large jug. She dribbled a little on the ground as she spoke to appease the spirits. "One bit to protect the horses. One for the sheep. One for the cattle. One for chickens." Turning the other way, she added drops for the predators, the fox and the eagle, so that they not harm the sheep and chickens. After she finished, the people filled their cups and toasted good health and fortune.

The final piece of the ritual was the sharing of the bannock. Several women passed around baskets full of sliced oatcakes, one containing a slice marked with charcoal from the fire. Whoever drew this portion would be the symbolic sacrifice for the year. Angus was somewhat concerned to see Iain, the blacksmith, receive the honor. To appease the spirits, he would wear a crown of flowers for the night and be the butt of their jokes.

"I'm always glad when that isn't me," Hamish said to Angus and Catriona.

"Aye, me too," Angus replied. Catriona nodded. She looked around, ensuring everyone was enjoying themselves. She wore a brave smile on her face.

Soon, the fiddler players tuned up, and the dancing began. The men kept the fire burning brightly for the rest of the night. Catriona, Hamish, and Angus joined the festivities but had anyone looked; their smiles were not as broad as usual.

Angus spun away from a young lass and thanked her for the dance as the musicians took a break. He grabbed a cup of beer and gulped it down. Whew! He needed to catch his breath. Behind him, Angus overheard the conversation of three men. He recognized the voice of Iain.

"I am almost finished. But that man from Kingussie is trying to move in on our business. We need to act soon." The other men agreed with him and then dispersed. Not sure what to make of their conversation, Angus pulled up a stump and sat by the fire. Though they spoke in Gaelic, he understood their words. *What was this business Iain mentioned? Was Callum the man from Kingussie?*

Toward morning, the woodpile grew low, and they tossed the stumps people had been sitting on into the flames. Angus stepped away from the heat and gazed up at the stars. During his time with Charles Mason in the colonies, he learned about the constellations. Dawn approached, and he knew he should see the Pleiades, or the Seven Sisters, appear on the horizon soon. Their arrival on this day heralded the coming of summer. He peered at the sky as Hamish and Catriona joined him.

"See them yet?" Catriona asked.

"I don't," Hamish replied.

"Aye, there they are, just there on the horizon," Angus pointed. Once the stars appeared, the three cousins linked arms and watched the sunrise.

The dancing finally broke up; the fire was reduced to glowing coals. As the sun rose, the young girls gathered the morning dew from the grass and rubbed it on their faces to keep them looking youthful as they grew older.

"Well, it's time," Catriona said to the two men as she yawned. "Let's head home for some sleep." She handed each of them a torch soaked in fat. They dipped them into the dying embers to light their way. Once at the house, they ignited the home fires again from the sacred bonfire.

After grabbing a few hours of sleep, Angus entered the office around midday. His head throbbed. The fire in the hearth no longer roared from the embers of the Beltane fire and was reduced to coals. Angus poured a cup of tea from the kettle and set it on the mantle as he bent to add wood to the fire. When he picked up the logs to toss them in, one slipped from his grasp, hitting the floor with a thump. Hamish, asleep on the sofa, was startled awake. He struggled to sit up.

"Ach, 'tis ye," he growled. "Can ye keep the racket down?" He sat peering up at Angus, his eyes squinting in the light.

"Rough night?" Angus teased though he was not in much better condition.

"Is there tea?" He grunted. Angus nodded, going to the table to pour another cup.

"Catriona awake yet?" Hamish asked.

"Haven't seen her, but I just rose myself."

Sipping their tea, the two men sat in silence for several minutes. But Angus had questions after overhearing the conversations around the bonfire, and now was as good a time as any, despite Catriona not being present. But he'd known Hamish since childhood.

"We need to talk," Angus told Hamish as he related the conversation he had overheard. Hamish squinted at him, and Angus continued.

"I told ye I had seen Morag. Did ye know Dougal Og went to see her? He was seeking something and sought her advice. As ye know, she could not tell me what he asked of her, but she confirmed quite a few people are hunting for something here, and several have visited her for guidance. Know anything about this?"

Hamish leaned forward, then rocked back again as if trying to decide. Eventually, he shifted in his seat, turning to face Angus.

"Dougal Og and a few others were present when his father died. They were hunting illegally in the woods, and the soldiers chased them. Though they escaped up in the hills, Dougal Mòr was shot."

Angus sucked in a deep breath. "I didn't know. I assumed he died naturally, as he was old when I left."

Hamish continued. "He died in a cave near where ye found Niall. I believe Niall may have been one of the men with them that day, but I wasn't there."

When Hamish paused, Angus leaned closer, "and?"

Hamish rose and paced. "Well, if Iain is making pickaxes as ye say, I guess this isn't a secret anymore, so I will tell ye. When Dougal Mòr died, he mentioned that the MacKay family held a secret treasure they brought with them when they moved here from Nairn. Since he was the old Laird's steward, people believed the tale. Now some think the Templar gold is hidden here on the manor."

Angus was angry at the news. "Why didn't ye mention this afore?"

Hamish shrugged. "Well, it's never been found. Honestly, I didn't believe the tale. I don't think Catriona does either." They heard a horse entering the gate, and Hamish struggled to his feet to see who was there.

*The Templars*. It was Angus' turn to pace as he remembered discovering Finlay, his father's brother, in Pennsylvania. Everyone thought he'd been killed in battle with the others. But, he had had a secret too, in the form of a brooch, a large pin. Finlay claimed it was a relic of the Templars. He had given it to Angus since his father would have inherited the secret treasure. Angus said nothing as he decided this was something he should tell Catriona first. But he wanted time to think. *Was this behind the murders?* Angus headed to the stable to ride Luath and contemplate the matter.

Angus had promised Catriona to stay and help solve the murders. Unfortunately, he felt all too experienced at that. When he solved these, he would go. He wanted to leave. Angus had no desire to claim his rights to the manor. He needed to make sure she understood that.

The stones of the ruin appeared through the trees. The possibility of danger slipped his mind as he was drawn toward the tower. Angus' thoughts drifted to Finlay, his uncle. Since he was a child, Angus assumed his father's younger brother had been killed in the battle. No one had seen him since. But soldiers had captured Finlay and taken him prisoner. His uncle had spent seven years in an English prison believing his family was slaughtered. Upon his release, he escaped to the colonies and made a new life there.

The two men met in the colonies when Finlay recognized Angus as the spitting image of his dead brother, Alasdair. Finlay told Angus the secret of the brooch and how the Templars fled to Scotland. Refusing to disband, many fled north into Nairn and Moray, the former MacKay clan lands of the MacKays. They pieced out their relics amongst local chieftains to be held in trust until the Order rose again. The MacKays had received a brooch in the shape of a ruby red cross, which Finlay had retrieved. Now Angus held that trust.

Angus dismounted and wandered up the stairs. He gazed out over the meadow. Finlay had settled on a farm there. He had married and raised a family and was a successful trader. Angus remembered the hours they spent over the years catching up with each other at his uncle's farmhouse.

*Eileen!* The name popped into Angus' head. Finlay confessed he had handfasted with a local woman named Eileen the night he left for the battle. *Click.* Angus jumped to his feet as the pieces dropped into place. Catriona's mother's name was Eileen. It all fits. Catriona's height. The red hair. The green eyes. As green as the meadow grasses, he remembered Fergus calling them and smiled. The mark of the clan was strong. Angus was surprised no one had noticed. Maybe they had, and that was why they willingly followed her. *Catriona was Finlay's daughter. And his first cousin.* With that thought, Angus leaped to his feet, flew down the stairs, and, mounting Luath, raced toward the manor.

# CHAPTER 15

THERE IT WAS AGAIN, that rustle in the undergrowth. At first, Angus thought it was an animal, but it paralleled his path too perfectly. The soughing sound must be the murmur of the wind, he decided. Angus slowed, peering into the heavy vegetation beyond the trees. Whenever he stopped, he heard nothing, but the swishing sound returned when he clicked the reins, and Luath started forward again. There was someone there—*the watcher in the woods. Morag.* He'd pushed the seer's warning to the back of his mind until now. Angus felt a chill down his spine and decided to hightail it home. He gave the horse a swift kick. The animal, alert to the danger, sped up, and raced along the path.

Angus heard a twang as they hurtled past a thinning in the undergrowth. Then a sharp pain caused him to gasp. Looking down in panic, he saw the shaft of an arrow stuck in his riding coat and realized it had grazed the meat of his left arm just above the elbow. Though it barely scratched the skin, it burned like fire. Luath sensed something was wrong and galloped faster toward the gate, just visible as they came over the rise. *Who shot me? Why? Have I gotten too close to the killer?* Angus' heart pounded as panic set in, and he struggled to stay in the saddle.

"Ma'am," the stable lad shouted as he burst into the house through the front door. Catriona rose to scold him until she realized something was wrong.

"What has happened?" she asked as she stepped into the entry hall.

"Angus has been shot! Come quickly."

Hamish took the stairs two at a time as he came charging down. Without a glance at Catriona, he raced through the door. But she was quick, running just behind. Seeing the lad returning to the stable, they followed him. Inside, Angus was sitting on a barrel, offering Luath a slice of apple. He looked up as they entered.

"Are ye okay?" Hamish bellowed.

"What happened?" Catriona asked, rushing to Angus' side.

Both slowed and looked at Angus, who rose. Catriona saw how pale his face was and that he appeared shaken.

"Hush, I just got him settled." His left arm hung limply at his side. Angus scratched the horse's muzzle, and the tall gray rubbed his head against Angus' shoulder.

"Someone tried to kill me with this." Angus reached over to the barrel and picked up the arrow. Hamish's jaw dropped; Catriona paled as she saw the blood on his sleeve."Where are ye hurt?" she scanned his face and grabbed his sleeve. She spied a hole near his elbow.

Angus pulled his arm away, "I'm fine. 'Tis a scratch."

But Hamish was having none of it and grabbed his sleeve, jerking the riding coat from his shoulder. "Let me have a look," he demanded. Angus winced as he pulled the coat off and slid his shirt sleeve up his arm.

Catriona frowned, her lips drawn tight. What was happening? This hit too close to home. Her hands shook as she reached for his arm, where bright red blood covered the white linen of his shirt.

Angus jerked his arm free. "I tell ye, 'tis only a scratch. There's more damage to my shirt and coat than to me. But we need to talk. I think this means we are on to somebody." He waved the arrow. "What have we missed?"

"Who did this to ye?" Catriona was surprised at her concern over this man she had not trusted only a few weeks ago. Did one of *her* people do this to him? Why?

Angus nodded at the stable lad. "Can ye give him a good rub down, please?" The youth nodded and removed the saddle.

Angus turned back to his cousins, "let's go inside. I could use a wee dram."

Catriona took him by the arm and led him to the well. She hoisted up a bucket of water and scrubbed the wound on his arm. After she examined it, she ordered him inside. "Now, ye can have that whisky."

Angus grabbed the bottle and a glass and poured the potent amber liquid. He threw back his head, swallowing a large gulp before turning to the others. It was time to talk. He sat down on the settee. Catriona snatched the bottle and took a swig straight from it without bothering to get a glass.

Hamish pulled a chair closer to Angus and peered at him. "All right, who do ye think shot ye?" He looked down at Angus' arm as Catriona dabbed it with a whisky-soaked cloth. Angus flinched as she patted the wound.

"Ouch!" Turning to Hamish, he continued, "after ye and I spoke, I needed to think a bit, so I went for a ride. I do my best thinking in the woods. But coming back, I had that sensation of someone following me."

Catriona paused and let go of his arm. "And it wasn't the wind in the trees this time," he said as he looked her in the eye.

"As ye know, I feel that way often, as if someone is watching me," she said, meeting his stare. "But why ye?"

"Aye, 'twas nothing obvious, just a feeling, a murmur amongst the trees. At first, I put it off as the wind. Then I remembered Morag's mention of the watcher in the woods." He paused as Catriona gasped and sat heavily in the chair opposite. "So I slowed, and the sound slowed as well. And when I stopped, it stopped. I knew it was not the wind. Not being armed, I decided to get out of there. But when I neared the clearing, I heard a twang, and then..." he glanced down at his arm.

Hamish shook his head, "ye know, all these years, I have ignored Morag's talk of someone watching from the woods, though I know many folks believe it. But I'd not heard any mention of it in years. Until lately, that is. There have been more stories recently, but no one has ever seen anything, much less been shot. I'm sorry I didna pay attention afore. Maybe I should have listened to ye."

"What brought on this need to think? What were ye talking about?" Catriona asked suspiciously, looking back and forth between the two men. "What aren't ye telling me?"

"Angus went to see Morag," Hamish told her. Catriona stiffened. Hamish rose and crossed to lean on the mantle. "He heard Dougal Og had been to see her and thought she might provide a clue to the man's death."

"But she can't tell ye anything. Can she?" Catriona said nervously and rose from her seat to pace.

"Nay," answered Angus. "She can't. I knew that from Gran, but I still hoped she might give me something to go on, a hint, maybe."

"And?" Catriona asked when Angus paused.

"All she did was confirm my suspicion that he was searching for something."

Relaxing, Catriona returned to her seat as Angus continued. "She also hinted others were doing the same. So, this morning, I forced it out of Hamish, who told me about Dougal Mòr's confession. That the MacKays have a secret treasure," Angus said.

He saw Catriona and Hamish exchange glances and watched Hamish nod at her as he said, "it's no secret anymore." His expression was grim, the corners of his mouth turned down. Catriona turned to Angus and waited for him to continue.

"And now, I have a confession to make to ye. Dougal Mòr was right," Angus said.

"What?" Stunned at this, Catriona leaped to her feet. "What do ye mean?" Both of them stared at Angus. Catriona clenched her jaw; her face was livid, and red splotches appeared on her cheeks, covering her freckles. "Tell me. Now."

"I think ye both had better sit down." Angus rose and checked the door to the hallway before crossing the room to ensure no one was listening from the kitchen.

"Elspeth has gone to the village, her children with her," Catriona said as she returned to her chair. "Tell me," she commanded.

Hamish slowly sank back into his chair. Angus cleared his throat and sat on the settee.

"I know what they are looking for and where it is. But there is something ye need to know first." He reached across and took Catriona's hand. Hamish started to rise, but Angus stilled him with a shake of his head.

"While in the colonies, a man followed me wherever I went. Not knowing who he was, I assumed he was the one sabotaging our survey.

But he was watching me, trying to figure out how to tell me he was my father's brother."

"Finlay?" Hamish gulped. "But he's dead. Isn't he?"

"He was taken prisoner," Angus answered. "He tried to fight the soldiers off, but they overpowered him. The English held him captive for seven years. When he was finally released, he tried to return home, but soldiers chased him again when he drew near. He had no desire to return to prison, so he fled to the colonies, believing he was the last of the clan."

Angus shifted in his chair to look Catriona square in the eye. "Before he snuck off to join the others in the battle, he handfasted with a local lass. It's been five years since we spoke of it, and I had forgotten. But her name was Eileen. Looking at ye, your coloring and all, I believe Finlay might be your father."

Catriona gasped and jerked her hand away. Hamish reached for her other hand. "Lass, are ye okay?" All the color had drained from her face.

"Why didna he come for us?" She stammered in a whisper.

"He didna know about ye. Finlay returned for Eileen but was told the clan was dead and the village was deserted. He nearly died trying to see for himself and was almost recaptured. He was devastated, felt he had nowhere to go."

"So, he lives in the colonies now?" Her color was returning to her face.

"Aye, in Pennsylvania. He's a farmer, like ye." Angus smiled at her. "I think he'd be proud o' what ye've done here."

Catriona was shaken, but Angus saw her efforts to pull herself together. "Ye said Dougal Mòr's deathbed confession was true. What did ye mean by that?"

"The Templars left a relic with the Mackay clan. But it's not a hoard of gold. It is a cross-shaped brooch set with red rubies. They were to hold it in trust until the Order returned. They hid several items among the clans for safekeeping."

Angus sighed and shifted in his seat. "I believe Dougal Og had gone to retrieve the brooch when he was killed. Why he went for it now? I don't know. As my grandfather's steward, his father, Dougal Mòr, would have known of its existence and location. I think he had told his son. But when Dougal Og looked, it wasn't there."

"Hidden in the tower..." Hamish finished the sentence.

"And this Finlay, my father," Catriona stumbled over the word, "he has it?"

Angus nodded. "He did." At their look, he continued. "I'm the son of the eldest son, Finlay claimed it should have been my father's, and he insisted I take it."

"And ye have it with ye?" Hamish asked. He smiled at Catriona.

"Nay, but I know where it is." Angus watched the exchange between them and saw their eyes light up at this news.

"Ah, so that is why ye are so willing to let me keep the land? Ye have the treasure." Catriona burst out, an accusatory gleam in her eye.

"Nay!" Angus shouted at her, leaping to his feet. "It is to be held in trust for the Order's return. And if ye both consider it a treasure to be spent, I will keep its location to myself. But I believe that is what the murderer is after. And I think I may have gotten a bit too close." With that, he stormed from the room and slammed the door behind him.

Disappointment flooded Angus as he entered his chamber. He grabbed his frock coat and pulled it over his bloodstained shirt. Angus began gathering his belongings. He did not know where to go but would not stay here. He was not welcome. If they did not trust him before, now things would be worse. All they wanted was the treasure, like everyone else. His hands shook as he tried to pack his things, and in frustration, Angus threw it all on the bed and stormed from the room and out the front door.

*How could Catriona think that of me? And Hamish? He said nothing.* "I thought they were my friends, my family," Angus said to the horse as he threw the saddle onto Luath's back. Refreshed from their earlier ride, the horse was eager to run. No one came out to stop them. It was early evening but not yet dark as the days lengthened.

Angus rode hard, the horse enjoying the free rein he was given as they raced up and over the hills. The peak of Ben MacDuibh loomed large on the distant horizon in the setting sun, the upland moors stretching out in front of them. Once clear of the manor's lands, Angus finally noticed how low the sun was on the horizon. It would be dark soon. He should turn around.

As they topped the subsequent rise, he saw the hut where he'd met Fergus that day when he helped him herd the sheep.

"Well, Luath, it looks like we have traveled further than I thought." He reached forward and scratched the horse between the ears. They stood on the hill and watched the sunset. "I think the hut will do us for tonight." He had no desire to return to the manor and face Catriona and Hamish, much less find his way back in the dark. He'd slept rougher than this in the mountains in western Pennsylvania.

He tied the horse to a tree outside the shack and removed his saddle. Angus found an old bucket on a hook inside. He dipped it into the nearby stream and placed it near Luath. Laying the horse blanket on the ground inside, Angus dropped down, laying his head on the saddle as a pillow. His stomach growled, and he realized he had eaten little that day, but he did not feel hungry.

His mind was awash with thoughts. *Where shall I go?* Returning to his original plan of seeking work in Edinburgh came to mind. Mr. Burton thought there might be opportunities for him there. And Angus hadn't explored the city at all on his way north. But he would need to fetch his belongings first, especially his certificate, and then find work.

And his letters, he remembered as he drifted off to sleep. However, in the back of his mind, Angus knew he would not leave until he solved the murders. Otherwise, they would plague him, and he loathed leaving the task unfinished.

# CHAPTER 16

When he awoke, Angus rolled over on the firm ground, momentarily forgetting where he was. He stretched his stiff back. Despite the hard-packed soil, he had slept well and felt refreshed until he remembered why he was there. Outside the hut, it was a glorious morning. Sunshine streamed over the horizon, bathing the hillside in light. After splashing the brisk stream water on his face, he mounted Luath and sat staring up at the peaks of Ben MacDuibh. Angus knew he should return to the manor, but he felt the mountain drawing him upward. Before leaving the area for the final time, he needed to conquer the summit as he had the cave. The peak, however, did not inspire the same anxiety, only curiosity. He looked forward to the view from the heights. He pushed the fear of someone following him away. No one knew where he was.

A well-worn track led the way up the slopes, twisting and turning, eventually breaking free of the treeline. Though narrow, someone used the path regularly, Angus noticed. When they neared the summit, Luath's ears twitched. Angus made out a small hut perched on a massive outcropping above them. *Why is that there?* The trees were well below them now. No one tended sheep this high, even in the summer when they grazed in the upper meadows. Nothing but scrub grasses and gorse covered the moorland at this elevation.

A man emerged from the hut as they came into view and called out a greeting. His brown robes identified him as a monk. The man shaded his eyes from the sun as they drew near. Angus slid from his saddle, keeping ahold of Luath's reins.

"Good day, brother," he greeted the man.

The monk stood gaping at him. "Angus? Wee Angus?" He peered up at him. "Aye, 'tis ye. Look how ye've grown!"

Though the monk had grown a long gray beard and wrinkles creased his cheeks, Angus knew that voice. "Brother Thomas!" He hurried toward him and clasped the man's hand tightly. Angus spent many years studying with this monk, learning mathematics and science. He owed him much.

"Aye. Welcome to my home." He heartily returned the handshake and then clasped Angus on the shoulder.

"What happened? How did ye end up here?" Angus asked.

"When they destroyed the monastery, we monks scattered. Each of us going his own way. I felt the need to be closer to our Lord and remained in the area. Ye can't get much closer to Him than up here." He grinned and gestured out over the valley below. Angus saw he was missing several teeth.

"Aye, I met one of the itinerant priests at the chapel," Angus told him.

"That would be Father Michael," the monk replied. "He keeps me up on the news below whether or not I desire to hear it. Though he has not been lately, so I didna hear o' your return." He gestured at two large smooth stones near the hut. "Sit, please. Join me in some mead and tell me your story."

Angus obliged. After removing the saddle from his horse and allowing him to graze freely, he shrugged off his frock coat and plopped down on a stone in the sunshine.

Brother Thomas eyed the bloodstain on Angus' sleeve but patiently waited until he was ready to speak of it.

"Last word I had o' ye was from your uncle some years back. He'd been keeping me abreast of your education in the south. I heard ye left London for the colonies. But 'tis harder to find me here, so letters are few and far between these days. And now, here ye are." The monk clapped Angus on the shoulder. "Good to see ye, lad."

"Aye, it was an adventure. I learned so much. And I met so many people."

Angus felt the anxiety melt away. They spent an enjoyable after-noon in the sunshine discussing Angus' adventures from London to the colonies and back to London. Several times Brother Thomas stopped him to ask questions about their work and the people he met.

"But then, I returned to London when our task was completed." Angus ended with the recent events at the manor. The bottle of mead was empty now. They finished the plate of bread and cheese Brother Thomas had brought out long before.

"That's quite a tale, lad. I always knew ye'd go far in this world," he said to Angus. "And yet, I feel ye have more adventures ahead.

"I recently earned my surveyor's license and hope to pursue that now," Angus added.

"Congratulations. I assume ye will not stay at the manor after this."

Angus shook his head. "Nay. I dinna feel I can. 'Tis not my home anymore. Deep inside, I think I'd already made that decision. But I had to go."

"The murders? Do ye have any inkling who committed those foul deeds?"

"Nay. But I'm sure it has to do with the 'treasure,' as they call it. Though now it seems everyone knows about it, though few were present when Dougal Mòr made his declaration from his deathbed."

"And ye know where it is, and 'tis better kept that way. And far from here, I hope?"

"Aye. And I'll not tell anyone."

Brother Thomas raised his hand, "I don't wish to know. 'Tis better that way. But I suppose ye are correct in not saying anything. If everyone knows, it makes everyone a suspect."

Angus gave him a grim smile. "True. However, I can't believe it of anyone at the manor or the village. I don't know if Sergeant Wolfe is in on it or if he merely visits to see Catriona. But Callum Campbell also comes wooing, and I don't trust that man. Though I'm not positive whether he knows about the *secret*." And yet, he suddenly realized a man in Kingussie had ordered a pickaxe from Iain. Was that Campbell? Did he know? "And there is the blacksmith, Iain, and his gang. Are they trying to keep me from finding out about it?"

"Of course, ye understand this means ye are in danger should word get out that ye know where it is. I'm guessing that's how ye came by your wound." He pointed at Angus' arm. "Do ye trust your cousins?" Brother Thomas asked.

Angus nodded. Despite his wild thoughts the day before, he trusted them, especially Hamish. He felt bad about running away. "Aye, I do. Was this someone trying to scare me off?" He raised his arm and lowered it again.

Where will ye go?" The monk asked after a while.

"Edinburgh? Maybe Glasgow. If I can find work as a surveyor, I'll be fine."

"An interesting career, I'd say. And one I think suits ye. This has been an enjoyable day, the best I've had in a long time. I rarely receive visitors." The monk's tone was thoughtful. "Ye'll not make it back down this late, Angus. There's room to stay the night, that fine horse too. And I've some root vegetables and a fresh rabbit if ye'd like some stew."

"That sounds delicious. The view ye have is magnificent. I'd always meant to climb to the summit." Angus rose, staring out over the valley. The river below meandered through the trees, glistening in the late afternoon sunshine. Though the peak was visible in the distance from the manor, Angus could not make out that structure from where he stood. The village, situated in a clearing in the trees far below, was just visible if ye knew where to look. The smaller crests of the range faded into the mist in the distance to either side.

"Aye. A suitable place for prayer and contemplation," the monk replied.

As dusk settled, the men moved closer to the fire. Brother Thomas emerged from his hut with another bottle of mead. Angus relaxed.

Crunch. Pause. Crunch. Someone was walking across the small stones on top of the mountain. Angus peered into the mist. The footsteps grew closer. Angus watched the grayness part like a curtain as it swirled about him. Before him, a man appeared, but this was not just any man. He stood twice Angus' height, and no colors existed beyond the varying shades of gray of the man himself.

*Am Fear Liath Mòr—the Great Gray Man.* Angus felt no fear of him, only a sense of his presence. The man tilted his head to the side as he studied Angus, then just before the mists enclosed him again, he nodded and smiled. Then he disappeared.

Angus rolled over on the hard ground and woke with a start. Thank goodness, it was only a dream. Gran had told him stories in his youth of the man of the mountain. He was sure she meant to frighten him off, and it had worked then. So why had he dreamed of him now?

Angus looked across the cabin at the monk's cot. Brother Thomas offered it to Angus the night before, but he refused. "I slept many a night on the ground in the colonies," he had explained. Now the cot lay empty.

Footsteps sounded outside, and Luath nickered as Angus heard the monk give him fresh water. Angus sat up, placing his hand on top of a small stone.

"Ow." Angus rubbed his palm and looked down to find a highly polished stone lying on the blanket. It was smooth as he rolled it about in his hand. He liked the feel of it and took it with him as he stepped outside the hut.

"G' morning," Brother Thomas greeted him. "I've got the fire lit. Come, warm yourself. It's chilly in the morning here, but it will warm up when the sun is higher. Do ye like eggs? I keep a few chickens."

"Sounds perfect," Angus said and squinted in the sun's rays. Looking down at the stone in his hand, he studied it, wondering how it became so polished up here. Light and dark gray swirled about it, with one side almost black, but the other held a vein of rosy quartz. The stone was beautiful and warm.

"Is this yours?" Angus asked Brother Thomas as he held the stone out to him.

The monk looked at it in surprise. "Nay. I believe that is meant for ye."

"Meant for me?"

"Few have seen the gray man, but some who do occasionally find stones like that. Though I never found one." The monk shrugged and returned to his cooking.

"Then, ye've seen him?" Angus asked.

"Aye, once or twice, though 'twas more like a vision than a real man."

Angus nodded. "I thought it was a dream. So, ye think he left this for me? What does it mean?"

"I don't know. I suppose it will reveal itself to ye in time."

Angus shrugged at the cryptic message. He accepted a mug of tea from the monk and sipped as he stared at the view.

After breaking their fast, Angus saddled Luath. "I must go. I need to return and make amends and try to help Catriona. But I am so glad I decided to climb up here. It's been good to see you again, Brother."

"Aye, for me too. Don't be a stranger if ye remain in these parts. Come visit," the monk clapped him on the shoulder. "And if ye don't, keep in touch. I get the odd letter now and then through Father Michael."

"I will. Thank ye for listening." Angus mounted.

"And be careful chasing that killer," the monk added. When Angus turned back suddenly, Brother Thomas said, "Ye know ye'll solve this before ye move on."

Angus nodded and promised to let his old friend know if he identified the murderer and where he ended up once he settled. Angus made his way back to the manor. He did not look forward to returning.

As he descended the peak, Angus began planning his departure. He gazed out over the scrubby moorland and rode down into the trees. He decided to allow a week for one more attempt at finding out what happened to Dougal Og and Niall, and then he would go. Despite the years between the deaths, Angus believed they were connected. And once he laid it out, Hamish had agreed with him. Both men were searching for something, and now that Angus knew about the dying man's confession, he believed he had the why. Now to find the who.

There would be work in Edinburgh. Angus was sure of that; the city was experiencing new growth. The manor was no longer his home, and he would always be in the way. He still wasn't sure Catriona trusted him, not entirely anyway. And Hamish, the only one who stood up for him in his youth, now felt threatened by him. But Angus suspected he was merely jealous, though there was nothing to be jealous of; he had no designs on Catriona or the lairdship.

Little Hawk had been much in his mind lately. When an inept sheriff accused Angus of the murders of two men in the colonies, she had been there to discuss theories with him. The native helped him prove his innocence, as well as that of her people. And when Angus strayed too far down the wrong path, she brought him back, primarily where his uncle, Finlay, had been concerned. Angus had suspected that man of all the wrongdoing; the murders, the sabotage, everything from the start. But through it all, Little Hawk steadfastly refused to believe it, and she had been correct. Angus missed her and her sharp mind and wished she were here. He would write to her when he returned.

# CHAPTER 17

CATRIONA STEPPED FROM A small shed when Angus rode in through the gate. She sighed in relief. She'd been more worried than she realized.

"Oh, thank God! Ye are back," she said as she hurried toward him. A small part of her wanted to scold him for disappearing like that but knew she was partly to blame. All Catriona felt now was gratitude that he was safe. She looked him up and down as he dismounted.

"I am so sorry." Angus approached her, looking uncertain of his welcome.

"Nay, 'tis I who am sorry. Hamish, too. We misjudged ye." She looked around. "I am not sure where he is right now, but we should let him know ye are back."

"Aye. And we need to start looking closely at what has happened."

"I agree. It's been in my mind, too. I'd like to hear your thoughts."

"And I yours. I had a friend in the colonies that helped solve the murders there. Sometimes, it is good to work together."

Catriona smiled at him and started toward the house. "Let me find Hamish."

Angus led Luath into the barn and removed his saddle. He gave the horse fresh oats, and when Catriona did not return, he sat down to polish the saddle. Catriona's warm welcome took a load off of his mind. Maybe they could work together.

"Have ye seen Hamish today?" Angus heard Catriona asking people as she passed the stable. Lost in contemplation, he jumped when she entered.

"Can't find him?" Angus asked and laid the polishing cloth aside. "His horse is here." He pointed at the large black, peacefully munching hay two stalls away.

"I woke early and have been outside ever since," she replied. "Well, tell him to come into the office if ye see him. I'll be there the rest of the day, and we can talk then," she said. Angus nodded in response, then rose to hang the saddle on the peg on the wall. Catriona stopped as if she wished to say more, then turned on her heel and left.

Later that afternoon, Angus entered the back door and walked toward his chamber. Ailsa, Elspeth's daughter, ran down the passage after him.

"Ye have some letters that came by the post," she called out to him. "Mam sent me to give them to ye."

Angus turned. "Thank ye," he said, taking the two envelopes she held out. As she skipped off toward the back door, he saw one was from Little Hawk. Angus had been on his way to his chamber to write to her, and he smiled at the coincidence. He'd thought about sending one earlier but didn't know what to say. Angus turned the other one over, noting in surprise that it was from Joel Bailey, one of the colonial surveyors employed to help define the border. He stood in the corridor wondering why Mr. Bailey would write to him or how he knew where to address it. Liam or Little Hawk must have given him the details. Looking down, he saw his uncle had forwarded both letters from London. He recognized Lord John's precise lettering on the envelopes. Angus had sent word of his whereabouts upon arrival. Mr. Bailey's letter was crumpled and worn after its long journey. He would read that one first.

Angus pulled out the small knife in his pouch, but Catriona stepped from her chamber before he could slit the envelope open. She was chewing on her lower lip and looked distracted. When she glanced up at him, her eyes reflected her concern. She barely acknowledged his presence as she closed the chamber door and walked down the corridor toward her office.

"Catriona?" Angus shoved the letters into his pouch and stepped into her path. "Ye all right? Is something wrong?"

Startled, she noticed him for the first time. "I canna find Hamish anywhere. And no one has seen him at all today. It's unlike him to take off like this. I'm worried."

"No one has seen him? When did ye see him last?"

"Last night. I went to bed early; he was still sitting in front of the fire." Catriona bit her lip. Angus knew she was fighting off the tears that tried to spill down her freckled cheeks. "Elspeth thinks he was here this morning, but she didna see him. A cup of tea was on the table, but it was only half-finished. And a half-eaten scone, crumbs scattered across the table." She peered up at him. "Why didn't he finish them?"

He took her by the arm and gently guided her into the office.

"Oh, Angus, where is he?" The dam broke, and the tears burst free, flowing down her face. Angus was unsure what to do. She'd always seemed so strong, so confident. The events of late must be wearing on her.

Angus reached out and put an arm around her shoulders, comforting her as she sobbed. He remembered doing the same for his other cousin, Rose when her husband treated her poorly. He dug around in his waistcoat pocket for his handkerchief.

They did not hear the soft footsteps from the hallway until Elspeth announced Lord Callum's wish to speak with Catriona.

Callum cleared his throat as he pushed past Elspeth into the room. Catriona pulled away from Angus.

"Ah, so this is the way of things, is it? I had thought ye were partial to the lame one." Callum sneered.

"Hamish isn't lame," Catriona defended him. "He has a slight limp."

She straightened her skirt. "What can I do for ye, Callum?" Ever the hostess, she led him toward the table where Elspeth placed a teapot, and the dainty cups were only used when they had guests. Callum glared at Angus, who noticed a slight smile curve his lips.

"Ye can go read your letters, Angus. I'm fine now." She turned and thanked Elspeth.

Angus reached for the doorknob but paused. He did not like that smile on Callum's face—a smile of triumph. Angus glanced at the pair as Callum held the chair out for Catriona. Callum leaned over her protectively as she sat as if to comfort her, his hand brushed her shoulder, and his dark hair swept down against her bright red tresses.

Angus hesitated, then closed the door and crossed the hall to his chamber. While he was concerned about Catriona, she was safe here in the house, wasn't she? He wanted to read his letters. When he pulled them from his pouch, where he had shoved them moments before, the stone from the mountain fell onto the floor. He retrieved it, subconsciously rolling it in his hand. Black and red. Black and red. Angus remembered Callum's dark hair sweeping down over Catriona's red. *The hair!* Was the stone telling him she was in danger? His mind clicked. He looked down longingly at the letters in his hand, but instead tossed them on the bed and returned to the office.

Rather than enter, he paused momentarily before slipping into the adjacent old dining room. There was a connecting door, which was now sealed shut. Angus knew from childhood that he could hide in the small private room and listen to the parties in the larger one. Would it be possible to do it from the reverse? Could he hear them? He crept near the adjoining door to test it.

"But don't ye see? By marrying me, we'd have the largest property in this part of Scotland," Callum said.

But Catriona was not listening. She picked a fingernail, worried about Hamish. She'd asked Archie to find Geordie and others and search for him. Hamish's horse was in the stable, so he hadn't gone far. Was he lying injured somewhere?

"Callum, I appreciate your offer, but I dinna have time to discuss this now," Catriona said. She rose, crossed to the desk on the other side of the table, and shuffled through some papers. She could handle herself.

"What can be more important than marrying me?"

"I dinna love ye, for one thing."

"But many marriages have nothing to do with love but alliances," Callum countered. "We could return this estate to its former status."

"Well, I am happy with what I have. I dinna need any alliances, as ye call them."

"But I think ye do," Callum started before Catriona cut him off.

"I said nay, and that is my final answer." Catriona stood, her hands on her hips, her green eyes flaring. "And now, I will see ye out. I have other things to deal with at the moment."

"Can I help?" He would not go easily, she knew.

"Nay. Just go, please."

---

Angus remained hidden until he heard the front door slam. It had taken several minutes. Angus waited in agony before he felt safe to emerge. He imagined Callum was lingering in the hallway, trying to devise a reason to return to the room. As Angus cracked open the door, he didn't hear the soft footsteps of Catriona coming from the office.

"Are ye all right?" He asked her as he stepped from the dining room into the hallway, meeting up with her.

"Ye? What? Did ye hear it all?" she asked, startled by his appearance.

"Aye." He nodded in answer. "I used to listen through that doorway as a child. I wanted to make sure ye were all right."

Her eyes flared. "Does anyone else know ye can do that?"

"I don't believe so," he said as he thought it over. "Probably not. No one else, other than ye, has lived here since then. I don't think Hamish would. Besides, I doubt both rooms have been used at the same time for someone to find out ye can hear through the door."

They entered the office when Catriona turned suddenly and leaned against him. She dropped her head on his shoulder. Angus froze, startled by her reaction, his arm outstretched before slowly bending his right arm and patting her shoulder.

"Are ye all right, lass?"

"Oh, Angus! Where is Hamish? I need him right now." She sighed deeply.

"We'll find him." Angus brought his other arm around her shoulder to comfort her. "He has to be around here someplace." A new thought dawned on him as he wondered where Hamish had gone. He gently pushed her back to look into her face. "Ye love him, don't ye?"

"I do," Catriona replied without hesitating as she looked at him. She stepped back and straightened her skirt. "Now, if I could just wipe that smile off Callum's face. He assumes I will accept him. He won't take no for an answer." Her feistiness was back.

"Does he know how ye feel about Hamish?"

"I don't think so," she said softly. "Angus, ye don't think he had anything to do with Hamish's disappearance?"

"Nay," he began, then paused. "But I don't know the man well. What do ye think? Would he go that far? Especially if he thought Hamish was in his way?" He hadn't considered that. "I keep expecting Hamish to show up."

"It isna like Hamish to be gone this long without telling me where he is going. The thing is, he didna take his horse or a cart. I'm worried he's lying injured somewhere, but the men I sent out earlier didna find him anywhere." Catriona breathed deeply, "I need to get some work done." She crossed to her desk and sat down.

Angus watched her for a moment. He understood her fears. His friend Little Hawk had been taken during the survey. Was it happening all over again? Had Hamish been taken?

He crossed toward her. "I don't know if ye believe in omens, but I think ye need to beware of Callum."

He held out his hand, showed her the red and black stone, and explained how he had come by it and what he thought the colors meant.

She looked up at him wide-eyed. "My mam had one of those stones. It differed from that one, more red and yellow. She said it was given to her mother. Maybe I should have asked her more about it. And paid more attention to Morag's warnings, as well."

Red and black. Red and black. Angus rolled the stone in his left hand, stroking Luath's neck with the other. His gran believed in paying attention to the omens. So did Little Hawk. In fact, she was given her name because of her ability to see things and understand the big picture as a hawk does. Did this stone come from Am Fear Liath Mòr, as Brother Thomas believed? He sliced the apple and ate a bite, feeding the rest to the horse. "This is a sign. It must be, but what does it mean? It connects Catriona and Callum, I'm sure."

Luath knickered in answer. "Aye, big fella. I suspect it means Callum is somehow involved. If he's pressing his suit with her, he'd want Hamish out o' the way. He's the black to Catriona's red." Angus turned to go. "But what would *he* have to do with Dougal or Niall?"

The afternoon wore on, and Angus wondered if he should be out with the others searching for Hamish. It was a large property; Hamish could be anywhere. He'd have taken his horse or a cart if he'd gone to the village. Maybe he got a ride. Angus stepped outside. It was growing dark. He couldn't look for Hamish now, but Angus could keep Catriona safe. That was something he could do.

He remembered the letters tossed on the bed. Angus peeked into the office and saw Catriona bent over her desk, staring at the ledgers. It wasn't time for supper, so he decided not to disturb her. There was time to read them. Both letters were addressed to his uncle's home in London and had taken over two months to arrive. Angus wanted to take his time over Little Hawk's message. Why would Joel Bailey write? He prayed it was not bad news.

Suddenly worried it might be, he rushed to his room and tore open the envelope from the surveyor first. Inside was a single sheet of paper.

*1 March 1769*

*Greetings Angus,*

*I hope this finds you well. I'm sure it surprises you to hear from me, but I hope it is acceptable to write you. Liam tells me you may no longer be in London, so I hope this somehow finds its way into your hands. I recently received a letter from Jeremiah Dixon written before you headed north. He mentioned his intent to see you receive a surveyor's license from Mr. Burton. I recall he often spoke of him around the fire in the evening. I hope to hear that his plan came to fruition and you have obtained your license. May I be so bold as to implore you to return here? I am able at present to offer you a position with me as a surveyor. There is much growth here, with more and more folk arriving daily. Many are from other parts of the continent, with more Germans coming with each tide. I can't keep up with all the work. As competent as you are, you most likely have found employment, but I would be grateful if you considered my offer. I am often away, but please reply soonest. My wife will ensure I receive it.*

*I eagerly await your reply,*

*Your friend,*

*Joel*

Angus sat still, stunned, the letter in his hand. It was written over two months ago, but to make it here so soon, his uncle had received his message that he was in Scotland and sent it directly to Kingussie. This was the answer to his prayers. But could he do it? Could he return? Set up life in Pennsylvania? He had his savings from the survey and some money left from his work with Mr. Burton. He'd have to sell Luath. That saddened him, but he'd ensure he had a good home.

"It's where I truly wish to be," he said to himself. He knew it. "How could I not do this?"

His mind began planning as he vaulted from the bed and sat at the desk. But as he picked up the quill to write, he thought of Catriona and Hamish and laid it back down. *I will find Hamish, solve the murders, and then go.* He knew they would understand, as would his uncle in London. But first, he would write to Mr. Bailey and accept the offer.

*Greetings to ye, Joel.*

*I will admit your letter has caught me off guard. At present, I am in Scotland on the old estate we talked about on those long nights around the fire. My cousins run it now as a farm, and I believe I am in their way. I received my certification through Mr. Burton, and I feel honored to receive your offer and gratefully accept. I was considering going to Edinburgh to seek employment in the field, and your kindness is most timely. Before departing for Philadelphia, I must return to London to my uncle's house to attend to some business. I will send this reply to begin its journey and post details as I tie up my obligations here and in England. Please give my greetings to all our acquaintances.*

*With my deepest thanks,*

*Angus*

*15 May 1769*

As he thought of those acquaintances, Angus leaped from the chair, knocking it over in his haste to grab Little Hawk's letter from the bed. As he opened the envelope, two daffodil flowers dropped to the floor. He retrieved them and held them to his nose. Though pressed in the pages of the letter, he detected a trace of their musky scent.

*Angus, my friend,*

*It is the beginning of March, and Liam arrived this morning at Bryan's farm on his way home from Philadelphia with your letter in hand. Oh, how we grieve for ye. We all hoped for a bright future when ye left. Martha Bryan and I held hands at the kitchen table and prayed to the spirits we each worship that ye have had a change of fortune and are in a better place today. I enclose the daffodils, one from each of us, as a symbol of hope and new beginnings with our desires that these find ye safe and happy.*

*I hope to receive a letter from you soon since I've not received one from ye since the first one telling of your arrival, but I hope that ye have not forgotten us and that one will arrive soon.*

*Please know that we hold you in our hearts and keep in touch.*

*Your friend always,*

*Little Hawk*

Angus paled as he sank down on the bed, clutching the letter. He had not expected Liam to share his news of failure, especially with Little Hawk. His gaze returned to the letter as he raised the flowers to his nose again.

"Of course." He reread it. "This is from March, so she would not have received the letter I wrote in April by then." He rose and paced the room, talking to himself.

"But she would surely know about his license now. Mr. Dixon had written to Mr. Bailey. And that was before I knew anything about his plans, the sneaky devil. She probably knows of Mr. Bailey's offer, too." News like that would spread like wildfire in an area where gossip was exchanged like money. Angus smiled; he hoped she knew. He would write to her and send it along with the other letter first thing in the morning.

Things were looking up, and he believed Hamish would walk in the door any moment. Luath would enjoy a ride down to Kingussie. That would speed the process along. The post to the more remote areas such as this was sporadic, but the coach passed through that town daily.

*My dearest friend,*

*I hope by now you have received my letter from January. By the time you receive this one, you will have read my next one informing you I am a fully certified surveyor! I hope you don't mind if I pat myself on the back a bit. I know how news spreads there, so you probably know that Joel Bailey has offered me a position working with him. I am sending my acceptance to him today as well. There are some loose ends to tie up here in Scotland before I leave, but I will tell you about that when I see you. I hope to reach Philadelphia before the autumn. I must return to my uncle's home in London first. Most of my belongings are there, what few I possess. And that gentleman has been so kind to me; I could not depart without saying goodbye to him, my aunt, and my cousin, Rose.*

*I look forward to my return,*

*Angus*

*15 May 1769*

# CHAPTER 18

T HE SOUND OF A door slamming woke Angus from peaceful
dreams the following morning. Then Catriona cursed. Reality
returned. Angus stumbled out of bed, grabbed his breeches, and pulled
them on beneath the linen shirt he wore to bed.

He left his room. "What is going on?"

Catriona was on her way into the office when she turned toward him.
She scowled.

"This!" She held out a tiny cushion of purple fabric, violet ribbons
draping over her fingers. As he approached, he smelled lavender.

"A charm? Again?" He winked. "Is Hamish back?"

Catriona froze. "Nay. He isn't." She threw the charm at Angus. "And
that's not funny." She spun on her heel toward the office.

"Catriona, I didn't leave this," he picked up the tiny pillow and followed her. She slammed the door behind her, the force of it causing the
door to bounce open.

Angus knew he was in trouble now. But if Hamish had not returned,
who left the charm? He followed Catriona into the room.

"I'm sorry," he said as he entered. "I assumed..."

"Nay, he isna back, and I am more worried than ever. Geordie took
some men to search again." She dropped onto the sofa.

"I'll help too. But let's talk this through first. This is the second time someone has left ye a love charm. At first, I was convinced it was from Hamish." Angus sat next to her.

"Aye, so was I. Or I hoped it was." She blushed. "But it occurred to me later when I thought about it that Callum was here that night too. He was gone before I found it, so I dismissed that idea." She grabbed the charm from Angus and threw it into the fire. "This time, it was under the other pillow. Does that mean that man went into my chamber? He was here yesterday."

"I think he's the one leaving them. Ye've mentioned afore ye suspect someone is spying on ye. Has Callum been here those times, too?"

Catriona rose and paced the room. "Some of them, aye. Maybe? He was here after the wake. And he showed up for dinner that one day, which was odd. Why?"

"Just curious, really. But, the man seems to spend a fair bit o' time here. I figured he was just wooing ye." Angus looked at her. "But that sergeant comes around here almost as often."

"Well, I ain't interested in either of them." She sat back down. "There's been talk about someone in the woods following people and watching them. I've felt it. Ye've noticed it, and ye were shot. Folk tales, mostly of the gray man. I never believed in them until ye were shot with that arrow."

"Oh, he never comes down from the mountain," Angus told her. When she cocked her head and looked at him, he realized what he had said. "Brother Thomas, the hermit up there told me." He finished quickly. Or had the gray man spoken to him?

"Well, I guess the folk around here will be glad to hear that," she smiled grimly. "But ye have felt it, as well."

Angus nodded.

"What is going on? And where is Hamish? He's never been gone overnight afore." The smile left her face. "And then there are the murders." Her eyes widened.

"Well... let's focus on Hamish right now," Angus stuttered. "I'd like to talk with the men and see what they found in their searches yesterday. Try to trace his footsteps if I can. As ye know from the tower, his imprint is unique."

"I think they covered most o' the ground yesterday," Catriona said. "But go ahead. Fresh eyes might be good. I keep hoping he'll walk in the door."

Angus hadn't been overly concerned the day before, as Hamish often did odd jobs for people, but not overnight. He nodded.

After an hour of questioning the few men he saw, Angus entered the stable again. None of the lads there remembered seeing Hamish. Angus was hopeful, but he'd asked them yesterday. Luath softly whinnied. "Not now, laddie," he said, "we'll take a ride later."

As he passed along the windows, he watched Iain, the blacksmith, gesture to Geordie. Both men glanced around before approaching each other. When they neared the stable where Angus stood, he ducked out of sight between that window and the next, hoping the men did not see him. Their behavior was secretive. Iain spoke first.

"The axes are ready. We can start our search soon," Iain told Geordie in a low voice.

"But what about that *other one*?" Geordie asked.

"That man can come himself to pick it up. I dinna deliver."

The morning light cast the men's shadows on the inner wall of the stable. Angus watched as the shorter man's image nodded towards the manor house as he answered. That would be Geordie.

"Aye. And with herself here, I dinna imagine it would be any inconvenience to him to come for it in person," Geordie answered, confirming Angus' supposition.

So, Iain had made tools for the men. They were indeed looking for the suspected gold. This seemed to remove them from his suspicions that they had more nefarious intentions. But Iain made one for someone else, too. Someone that did not live here, and Iain would not deliver it. Angus' heart skipped a beat. It *was* for Callum. It had to be. He knew the blacksmith was working on one for a man in Kingussie, which meant Callum had heard about the gold everyone believed was here. Angus waited in silence until the men moved away from the window. Then he exited through the back door and approached the house as if coming from the opposite direction.

As he passed Geordie, he saw him hitching up his wagon. "Heading somewhere?" Angus asked in a forced, friendly tone. He believed he had a better chance of getting the truth from Geordie than Iain.

"Aye, down to Kingussie for supplies for Catriona."

"Can ye wait a moment? I have letters to post."

Geordie nodded, "I'll be about ten minutes."

Angus hurried inside, looking for Catriona. She sat staring at the ledgers on her desk, but he suspected she was not working. He told her of the conversation he had overheard.

"So, all of my men are aware of the deathbed confession? Is that what ye mean?"

"Aye. We already knew it wasn't a secret anymore, but I'd like to ride down to Kingussie with Geordie. He might know more than he realizes about Hamish and maybe Callum. At least, I hope so. I'm sure the *other man* Iain referred to is Callum."

"Are ye saying Callum has ordered a pickaxe from my blacksmith?" When Angus nodded, she continued. "Go ahead. Especially if ye think he has information about Hamish."

"Archie is heading to the village later, and I think ye should go with him. Ye know, safety in numbers. I won't leave ye here alone. Promise?"

Catriona protested but, at his look, nodded. Angus ran to retrieve his letters and joined Geordie as he climbed into the wagon. Geordie reached out to take the envelopes.

"It's a nice day; I think I will ride along if ye don't mind," Angus said. He climbed onto the seat next to him without giving Geordie a chance to say otherwise.

Geordie guided the wagon down the hill, expertly navigating the steeper portions and the narrow sections through the trees. At first, the two men rode in silence, then Angus tried to engage Geordie in idle chit-chat about the weather, the farm, and wondering where Hamish might be. Geordie initially said little but expressed concern over the missing man. He seemed genuine, and Angus decided he knew nothing about Hamish's disappearance. After a while, they came out of the trees above the Ruthven Barracks. The castle was formerly the home of the Comyns, but it had sat in ruins until the English soldiers built a fortress on the site to suppress the local rebellion.

"Ever been there?" Geordie asked Angus, pointing at the roofless structures.

"Nay. I never came down to Kingussie much. My gran claimed the ruin is cursed."

"I believe it. Pretty spooky place." Geordie replied. "Anybody with any sense stays away from there. My pa and my grandpa were there when the Prince's men blew up the buildings, destroying them so the soldiers couldna use them to imprison our clansmen."

"So, your family were among those that fled Culloden?"

"Aye. They waited inside there for the Prince's order to continue the fight. But when word came, it was for each man to seek his own safety. So they decided to blow it up."

"Gran used to tell me stories of the Wolf of Badenoch. She claimed his ghost still walks the grounds."

Geordie shivered. "Aye, I heard the same tale. An evil man as there ever was. He stole the cathedral's treasure at Elgin and burned the building to the ground. They say he is buried in the undercroft, though some believe he is at Dunkeld Cathedral. But as he died playing chess with the devil here in Ruthven, I dinna believe he is buried in that sacred ground. Most o' his castle was destroyed after his death. It sat unused until the English built the barracks. But, even five hundred years later, no one dares enter the castle ruins underneath."

As they passed the site coming down the hill, Angus watched Geordie cross himself. When they neared it, however, Angus saw the distinct signs of a path around the back of the mound. It looked fresh.

"Then who made that?" he asked Geordie.

"I dinna ken." The man paled and clicked his tongue at the horse to hurry past the hillock, not looking at the trail leading away from them.

Angus reached over and snatched the reins, and the wagon rolled to a stop. It was time for the truth. Most likely, Geordie was in it for the gold. Angus didn't suspect him of anything more sinister. And he could defend himself against the smaller man.

"I know something is up, and ye will tell me about it afore we go any further."

"I dinna ken what ye mean." Geordie refused to look at Angus.

"I overheard ye with Iain."

Geordie gasped and turned to him, reaching for the reins. "Ye understand the Gaelic?" He paused. "Aye, ye would, wouldn't ye?"

"I grew up here." Angus kept control of the reins and continued, "So explain to me why men on a farm need pickaxes. Does Catriona or Hamish know what ye are up to?"

Resigned, Geordie admitted that almost everyone knew about Dougal Mòr's last words. "Niall heard about it and searched near the caves close to where Dougal Mòr died. He told me Dougal claimed there was gold hidden somewhere. But shortly afterward, Niall disappeared. Some thought he'd run off with the gold, but Archie insisted 'twas not true. If Niall had found gold, he would've shared it with his family. So, the family put the word out that he ran off with a lassie. Right after, the villagers began noticing strange things, like being followed whenever they left their homes or went to the fields."

Angus nodded. "Catriona said as much. She claimed some of the folk believe it is Am Fear Liath Mòr."

Geordie smiled, "That's ridiculous. I never believed that. It's all to do with the treasure. But I sometimes feel I am being watched when driving my cart and making deliveries. 'Tis why I let ye come with me today. Ye look like ye'd be good in a fight," he paused. Turning on the bench to face Angus, he said, "But isn't that the true reason ye came home? To look for the gold? Your family would know about it."

Angus shook his head. "Aye, they did, but I only recently learned of it. But that's not why I came home." He didn't think Geordie believed him.

"Shall we continue?" Geordie asked after a moment's consideration. He held his hands out for the reins.

After a long pause, Angus said, "Not just yet—this path. Ye say no one comes here? Then why is that there? And they're fresh." He pointed a few yards down the path. Geordie saw the horse droppings visible from where they sat. They were recent.

Eyes wide, Geordie shook his head. "Ye ain't thinkin' o' goin' up there? Are ye?"

"Aye. I am. I'd like it if ye come with me. Just in case. Safety in numbers, you know." Angus turned the cart along the path until it ended at the base of the mound. Angus brought the horse to a stop and sat looking up at the old fortress for a moment. "Ye coming?"

"Nay. I'll wait here," Geordie said as he remained on the seat when Angus jumped down. "I ain't too pleased about meetin' the ghost of the Wolf."

# CHAPTER 19

"I DINNA THINK ANY wolf made these." Angus pointed at the hoofprints in front of them. Then he indicated a man's footprints winding up the steep slope. Angus gazed up at Geordie, still sitting on the bench. His shoulders were rigid, and he held the reins tightly. His knuckles were white. Geordie looked ready to flee.

"If someone wanted to avoid being seen, they would use this back entrance on the mound. Otherwise, why not use the old roadway to the main gate?" Angus asked.

Curiosity overcame Geordie now, and he hopped down to look more closely at the prints in the soil. "And they were draggin' somethin'. Look." He pointed at the grass.

Angus had already noticed the flattened grass and smiled as Geordie pointed, his finger following the trail up the hill. Angus was relieved when Geordie jumped down; he didn't relish going alone.

"Do ye think it was a body?" Geordie's voice trembled.

"Hamish!" Angus exclaimed. The men looked at each other and sprinted up the hill toward the building.

At the top, however, the earth was hard-packed, and they lost the trail. One building stood apart from the other two. It took only a moment for Angus to see there was nothing there; the roof was gone, and only partial walls remained. Across a stretch of grass were two more substantial buildings flanked by towers rising above a crumbling wall. The gate was missing, and Angus crossed the courtyard and entered. Geordie sighed and followed him.

There was a hush about the place, but it wasn't scary, not to Angus. Geordie remained at the gate. As Angus entered the compound, a gust of wind blew through, creating a whistling sound through the holes where glass once filled the windows. Three rows of empty openings looked out onto the courtyard from each structure. The roof above and the floors inside were gone. The buildings were open to the sky. There was no place to hide anything here.

Angus inspected each edifice to no avail, while Geordie went only as far as the central court until Angus returned moments later. His brows were drawn together in disappointment.

"I didna find anything," he told Geordie. "I was sure someone dragged Hamish up that hill, but there's nothing here but stone walls. What made those tracks?"

Geordie shrugged. "And that noise? It is just the wind, right?"

Angus smiled, "Aye, 'tis only the wind. This place is too open, even for ghosts."

"Well, that's all right, then." Geordie relaxed.

"Now, where did we lose the marks?" Angus wondered aloud.

Geordie pointed through the gate to where they crested the top of the mound. "Over there, beyond the first building."

Returning to where they reached the top of the hill, Angus studied the ground and saw the grass was trampled down along the outer wall. The marks ran behind it along the crest of the rise. In their haste to search the buildings, they walked right past them.

"Did ye say the Wolf was buried in an undercroft? Where is that?" Angus rushed to the edge of the knoll. His gaze followed the trampled grass. It was not much of a path, but someone recently made those impressions. The imprint curved around and stopped in the middle of the incline below where they stood.

"I ain't going down there," Geordie whined as Angus started down the slope. Angus motioned to him to be quiet. But as they reached the broken door into the undercroft, they realized there was no need. No one seemed to be around; until they heard a low moan.

"Hamish," Angus called. The moan echoed from inside.

"I ain't goin' in there. That's not the wind. 'Tis the Wolf," Geordie's hand trembled as he grabbed Angus' arm.

"Well, I'm going. Hamish'd do the same for me," Angus said as he shook him off and entered. Lining the central passage carved into the stone were chambers branching off each side of the arched walkway. These spaces once stored supplies when this was the Lord of Badenoch's castle. The doors to the first set of compartments were missing. The groaning bounced off the stone; it was hard to tell where it originated. Angus peered into a few more as he made his way along the corridor, moving further into the dark depths. Wooden doors still hung on the openings there.

"Hamish?" he called again. The sound was closer now.

The hinges creaked as Angus entered two more rooms. However, a wooden peg through a rusty metal hasp kept the third one closed. When he removed the peg, the door swung inward.

A hoarse whisper moaned, "I am here."

Angus felt his way across the rocky floor with his foot as he moved toward the sound. It was much darker the further he entered the chamber, but he could make out the shape of something large in the corner. He hadn't brought a candle or lantern.

"Hamish? It's Angus. Are ye okay?"

"My head feels as if it will explode. But the rest of me seems all right."

Feeling his way, Angus reached out, his hand brushing Hamish's shoulder. He then ran it lightly up over the man's head. There was a considerable lump just above his right ear. Hamish's thick hair was matted and sticky from what must have been blood.

"Help me sit up," Hamish whispered. He swayed, nearly losing consciousness as Angus slid his arm behind him to help. Eventually, Angus maneuvered him upright against the wall.

"We need to get ye out of here afore anyone returns. Who did this to ye?" Even before Hamish could answer, Angus knew it was Callum. He wanted Hamish out of his way.

"I was drinking my tea when I saw a shadow at the window, but when I went outside to look around, I didn't see anything. I went to the well and raised the pail to wash the sleep from my face, and someone caught me off guard. But I didna see them. Later, when I roused, someone was dragging me up a hill. But I lost my senses again and woke up here, though I'm not rightly sure where here is."

"The undercroft beneath Ruthven," Angus answered.

Hamish swore. "I never would've guessed that. It's so damp and dark I thought I was in one o' the caves. Later ye have to tell me how ye found me. But I canna think straight right now. I'm just glad ye did." Hamish paused and slumped back against the stone. "Angus, it was Callum. I roused a bit as he dragged me along. He's going to force Catriona to marry him."

"Aye. We know. He was at the house yesterday. She found another charm under the pillow on her bed."

Hamish choked at that and immediately regretted it. "Help me up, and let's get out o' here. We've got to stop him."

"Aye, we will. But Catriona's safe. I suggested she go to the village today. Archie and a couple of herdsmen will be with her." He hoped she had listened to him and gone with Archie. "I've Geordie with me. And his wagon. Let's get ye out of here if ye can manage it."

"Not much choice, is there?" He groaned in pain as Angus helped him to his knees and gradually to his feet. "Ugh, I've other parts hurting now that I'm moving."

"Aye, he drug ye over the stones. I imagine ye've got some nice bruises." Angus slid underneath Hamish's arm, taking some of his weight. "Be careful of the low ceiling in here," he warned.

As they neared the opening, they heard Geordie. "Come on, Angus; I heard the Wolf." Hamish moaned as they came up the stairs. "Ah, 'tis only ye." He collapsed in relief.

"Hey, I'm the one who's injured here," Hamish said, groaning again when he stumbled on the uneven ground. Angus and Geordie helped him slowly down the hill to the cart. It took both of them to heft him up into it as he grew more unsteady on his feet the further they walked down the hill.

"I'll take ye back home and then come back down to Kingussie," Geordie said as he climbed onto the bench and picked up the reins.

"I would like to make sure Catriona is safe," Hamish told them. His face was pale in the light, and Angus could see a fair amount of blood congealed on the side of his head.

Catriona walked out of the storage shed as the wagon entered the gate that afternoon. She brushed her hair back from her face and stood, afraid to approach. They were back too soon to have completed their errands in the town. Angus waved at her and jumped off the seat before Geordie halted in the courtyard.

"He's here," he hollered at her. "We found him. A little sore, but safe."

Catriona's heart pounded in her chest. Hitching up her skirt, she dashed toward the men. At first, she did not see Hamish hidden under the canvas they used to cushion him and make him comfortable.

"Where was he? What happened?" The questions gushed from her as she caught her breath. Catriona scrambled into the wagon and pulled the canvas off Hamish, who moaned in pain. She barely listened to Angus' explanation of finding Hamish in the undercroft, nor how he got there or who had done this. She ran her hands frantically up and down Hamish's arms and legs.

"Where are ye hurt?" she asked in concern, then noticed the blood matting his hair above his ear. Hamish looked up at her and smiled, bringing her back to earth, and she heard Angus' comments.

"Wait a minute. Callum?" She stopped and looked at Angus.

Angus nodded. "He wanted to get Hamish out of the way so he could marry ye."

Catriona's eyes grew wide at that. "I didn't take him seriously. I never dreamed he would go that far."

"He planned to claim the laird's right," Hamish told them.

"But that was abolished generations ago."

"Not according to him," Hamish replied. He groaned in pain as he tried to sit but flopped back against the bags of grain in the wagon instead.

"Other than your head, are ye hurt?" she asked him, concerned.

"Nay, just my head. Did ye worry about me? Even a bit?"

"Well, if it's only your head, that's all right." She let out a sigh, shaking her head. Her face broadened into a wide smile. "It's good to see ye back, Hamish."

Hamish reached up and took her hand. "I was afraid I'd never see ye again."

Catriona's eyes teared up in happiness. "Well, then, I guess ye oughta marry me so I can keep a better eye on ye," she said, leaning over him.

"Keep an eye on me? Hey, aren't ye supposed to be in the village?" Hamish looked at Angus.

Catriona had the decency to look guilty when Angus glared at her.

Hamish scrambled into a seated position to say something but swooned from the sudden motion and collapsed against the side of the wagon.

"Well, I didna expect that for an answer," Catriona said to Angus. "Help me get inside."

Angus helped Catriona put Hamish to bed. She refused to leave his side the rest of the day and ordered Elspeth to serve their supper in his bed chamber. Hamish ate little, propped up on the pillows, though he sipped some broth.

After a while, Angus slipped out of the room, leaving them alone together. He nibbled on his food as he sat on the sofa, staring into the fire. His thoughts began to piece the events together. Shortly after, Catriona entered.

"He's asleep. But I want to thank ye for finding him and bringing him back to me."

"I'm just glad I did. I wanted to look for Hamish, but he wasn't in any place I would have thought. It was a last-minute decision to ride down with Geordie." He set his empty plate on the side table and stretched his legs. "I decided to see if he knew anything. I hadn't expected the day to turn out as it did."

"Did ye learn anything?" She joined him on the sofa.

"How long have ye known about what Dougal Mòr said?"

"My mam told me afore she died three years ago. Neither of us put much stock in it. We figured if there had been a treasure around here, it was long gone. Mam believed Dougal Mòr might have been a bit confused. He was old by then, and it had been almost twenty years since the old laird was killed."

"I think all the events here stem from what he said that day. Geordie told me Niall knew about it. That's why he was up there on the hill. Dougal Mòr died in a cave, and my family hid in one nearby. He must have thought he'd strike it rich, as he was afraid of those caverns. But someone caught him. Afterward, I think they realized he hadn't found anything, which may be why they left the body, thinking no one would ever find it."

"And ye said Dougal Og was looking for something as well. So the deaths are connected, aren't they?" She asked flatly. Suddenly, she sat bolt upright and turned to Angus. "It all fits, doesn't it? Ye've worked it out as well. Being followed. Spied upon. Someone believed there was gold to be found."

"Aye, the watcher in the woods... Morag warned me to be careful. She said he'd show false." Angus nodded at her.

"I saw Morag too," Catriona confessed sheepishly. "Not for the treasure but for the feeling that someone was always watching me. She told me trouble would arrive from an unexpected source. And then ye walked in days later."

"And ye suspected me," Angus said.

"Aye," she admitted.

She blushed. "I went to Morag a second time, but that was to see if I had any future with Hamish. She beat around the bush with her premonitions of finding satisfaction. I guess that's an answer." They sat staring into the fire.

"But no one knew exactly what they were looking for. I overheard the men. Some think the family secret is gold in the ground, and others believe it is the fabled Templar hoard." Angus said eventually.

When Catriona looked up at him, a question on her face, he sheepishly admitted he still understood the Gaelic. She smiled. "Was Dougal Og correct, then? Was the brooch hidden in the old tower?"

"Finlay didn't say, just that he sent a man to retrieve it from his family's home, so *he* must have known where it was. He wanted to keep it safe. But aye, I believe that must be where it was. He didn't know of your existence when he gave it to me and believed your mother had died."

"Well, I dinna want it. I thought about what ye said afore. We hold it in trust; it is not ours to spend. So keep it wherever it is, and dinna tell me."

"Are ye sure? Someone should know about it."

Realization flickered across her face. "Ye know who it is, don't ye?" She placed her hand on his arm. "Including the murders, not just who took Hamish. Tell me the truth, now."

"Aye. I do. It's the only logical answer. Since Callum ordered a pickaxe, he knew about Dougal's dying words. He's after the Templar gold. And I believe he is the one watching your people; whether he is doing it himself or paying someone to spy for him, I don't know."

"And that is why he is so insistent upon marrying me...." Catriona pondered this as the door slammed open, and Hamish staggered in.

"Nay. Ye asked me to marry ye; I'm holding ye to your word," he said as he collapsed headlong onto the floor.

# CHAPTER 20

The following day, Angus rose once again to a commotion in the entry hall. The sun was barely visible on the horizon. He heard Elspeth screaming at someone, telling them they could not barge in like this. He pulled his breeches beneath his linen shirt and dashed barefoot from his room.

Callum was attempting to force his way past the cook toward the private chambers.

"I must see your mistress," he demanded.

"Why? What is so pressing?" Angus asked. "Can I help ye?"

Catriona entered through the back door. "I thought I heard someone arrive. Callum, what are ye doing here so early?"

"I came to warn ye," he crossed toward her. Angus followed. "There's a dangerous man around, and ye need my help. I have considerable resources to bring to bear on the matter."

"Oh?" She retorted. "And who may this dangerous man be?"

"Hamish MacKay," he told her. "He attacked me on the road. He was like a madman."

"Hamish, eh?" Angus asked. "Why would he attack ye?" He hoped that gentleman would stay in his room and not barge in on this scene.

"I don't know. He was crazed. I hit him over the head and barely escaped with my life."

Right on cue, Hamish stepped from his chamber, clad in only his linen shirt, hanging to his knees. "Well, one part o' that is right. Ye hit me over the head afore ye locked me up beneath the barracks."

"I would never do such a thing!" Callum turned to Catriona, imploring her. "How could ye believe that o' me?"

"Well, the fact I found him locked up there might be part of it," Angus said. He leaned over to Alan, Elspeth's son, and whispered in his ear. The lad sprinted out the door.

"Well, I didn't want him to hurt anyone else until I could get to the local magistrate," Callum stammered.

"But ye came here instead," Angus pointed out. "I don't see the sergeant, either."

"Let's go into the office and discuss this," Catriona ordered the men. They followed her into the room. "Now, to begin with, why do ye think Hamish would attack ye?" She leaned back against the mantle, facing them. She gestured to Angus to close the door.

"I don't know, but I think he's jealous that we are to marry."

"I never accepted ye, Callum. In fact, I told ye no, several times."

"But in time, you'd have changed your mind." He protested. "Ye know we are meant to be together."

Angus cut her off before Catriona could protest and strode to the mantle beside her. "So, the fact that ye are looking for the gold has nothing to do with it," he said calmly.

Callum sputtered. "Gold? What are ye talking about?" He approached them.

"Don't play innocent with us," Angus said. "Catriona knows what ye are up to, and 'tis nothing to do with Hamish. Ye needed him out of the way so ye could move in on her."

"Well, I never." He implored Catriona. "Ye know our love is real."

Catriona slapped his face. "No, it is not."

Hamish snorted at that, then grabbed his head and groaned. He dropped heavily onto the sofa. "Then why did she ask me to marry her?" he asked.

All the color drained from Callum's face. "Nay! In your dreams." He spat at Hamish, but his voice quivered as he turned to Catriona. "My Lady, how can ye believe this nonsense?"

Catriona crossed to Hamish and sat down next to him. "It was Angus here that put the pieces together. Ye knew what Dougal Mòr said as he lay dying. Ye were there, and ye knew about the *secret*." Angus knew she was bluffing, but the look on Callum's face confirmed that he had indeed been present.

"Someone has been spying on the people here at the manor and those in the village. But it isn't Am Fear Liath Mòr, is it, Callum? Was it ye that shot me?" Angus watched as the man blanched even further ashen. "And ye also knew what Niall was up to, didn't ye?"

Before he could protest, Alan returned with Iain. "How may I assist ye, ma'am?" The burly blacksmith asked. He fiddled with his cap in his hands as he stared nervously at the floor.

"I need your answer, Iain, and ye'll not be in trouble for telling the truth. Did this man commission ye to make a pickaxe for him?" Catriona gestured toward Callum.

Iain looked back and forth between them for a moment. He toyed with his cap in his hands. "Aye, ma'am, he did. He asked me to make one like I made for Niall." He stared at his feet. "Some o' the men and

I were planning to look for the gold Dougal mentioned. So I asked Mr. Campbell if he was also looking for gold. He said no, but his face told me otherwise. And besides, how else would he know about Niall's pickaxe? Then he offered me well above the usual rate; otherwise, I wouldna have done it."

Alan leaned over and whispered in his mother's ear. Elspeth turned abruptly toward her son, grabbing his arm. "Ye tell Miss Catriona that right now."

"I saw Lord Campbell following Dougal Og around afore he fell from the tower. The funny thing, though, was that the boots he was wearing didn't fit so well. They were way too big, and he stumbled a couple o' times. I thought it was funny."

"No! The lad is lying." Callum edged his way toward the door.

"And why would he make up something like that?" Angus asked, ready to pounce should the man try to leave.

Callum turned to Catriona and pleaded with her not to listen to the lies, but she merely shook her head. Callum picked up one of the side chairs and launched it at Angus, who neatly sidestepped it and gave chase as Callum raced from the room and out of the front door.

He would not have gotten far as, at that very moment, Sergeant Wolfe and one of his men entered the courtyard. Archie stood behind them.

"Excuse us, ma'am; I don't wish to intrude. I was making my rounds to say hello and heard voices raised. Is everything all right?"

"These men attacked me, Sir." Callum stopped and straightened his frock coat.

"Is that true, Ma'am," the sergeant asked Catriona. He doffed his cap at her.

"Nay, 'tis not," she replied. Callum stepped back as she answered, ready to turn and run through the gate. But Angus was ready. As Callum turned to run, Angus quickly stepped in his path. Callum threw a punch, but Angus grabbed his arm and twisted it up behind his back in one swift movement. Callum screamed in pain.

Sergeant Wolfe frowned. "Can someone explain to me what is going on?"

A crowd gathered in the courtyard as word spread that something was happening at the big house. Catriona noticed and led those involved inside. She sat on the sofa and took Hamish's hand while Angus led the sergeant to the table and offered him a seat. Sergeant Wolfe nodded to his soldier to keep an eye on Callum, who looked around the room.

Catriona motioned to Angus. "It's your story to tell," she said, "please." She leaned against Hamish.

"I thought the events began with the death of Dougal Og when I arrived," Angus began. He stood, blocking the path to the kitchen door. "But the story goes back much further, to when Callum learned of a treasure belonging to the MacKay's. Along with everyone else, he believed there was gold buried here somewhere. Young Niall MacKay was shot in the back while searching for it in the caves. Dougal Og was thrown from the tower when he went to retrieve the item. He was the only one who knew what it was and where it was. Though he didn't know it had already been removed."

Callum and Sergeant Wolfe had been staring at the clasped hands on Catriona's lap. At this, however, they looked at Angus.

"So, the gold does exist," Callum sneered.

The sergeant indicated for Angus to continue, "Go on."

"There is no gold," he informed them. Catriona realized he wasn't sure how much to say when he paused. She nodded for him to continue. "Not in the way most people think. A brooch belonging to the Templars was hidden here at the manor for a time. The MacKays in Nairn were one of the clans charged with caring for their artifacts until the Order rose again."

Everyone in the room let out a gasp. Callum sputtered, "That's it? A lousy brooch?"

"Aye. After Culloden, my uncle retrieved it and took it with him when he sailed to the colonies. But it was here until then."

"Ye have it, then! Sergeant, arrest this thief!" Callum shouted.

"There is no theft. With my father's death, his brother had a right to it."

"Finlay is alive?" Elspeth grabbed the back of the chair in shock. She looked at Angus, who nodded, then stared at Catriona as she collapsed on the chair.

"Who is Finlay?" Sergeant Wolfe asked.

Elspeth looked up at him, "The laird's younger son. He handfasted with Eileen afore he left for the battle. He never returned. We thought he died with the others. Eileen was my older sister and Catriona's mother. I'm the only one who knew." She looked at Catriona, "I'm sorry, lass, your mother swore me to secrecy. She was embarrassed when she turned up with child. It was easier to let people think her husband was one of many killed in the battle." She turned to the others. "He was well above her station, ye see."

Catriona slowly rose and crossed to Elspeth. She put her arms around her. "No wonder ye took such good care of me." Tears flowed down her face as tenderness filled her.

"Finlay was captured and imprisoned for seven years," Angus explained to Elspeth. "I met him in the colonies, where he fled when he was released. He tried to come back but was chased off by soldiers. They told him Eileen was dead."

"Well, what about me?" Callum demanded. "I never wanted the gold. I just didn't want her to have it. She wouldn't need me then, and I needed her to need me."

Catriona turned on him. "Ye don't get it, do ye? I was never interested in any treasure."

Callum persisted. "So, are ye going to release me?"

Sergeant Wolfe looked at Catriona. She thought for a moment before she answered. "Well, I would charge him in the deaths of Niall and Dougal Og. And for attacking Hamish and leaving him to die in Ruthven barracks." She smiled at Hamish.

"So Dougal's death was not a fall, then?" Sergeant Wolfe cocked an eyebrow and turned to Angus, who looked chagrined.

"He lied for me," Catriona said.

Hamish rose. "And he wore my boots so that I would be blamed." He glared at Callum.

"I believe Callum was trying to bribe Dougal into pleading his case with Catriona. I suspect Dougal did not realize Callum had followed him that day when he went to the secret hiding place in the ruin," Angus explained.

"All right, I followed him to speak with him," Callum admitted. "He couldn't see that Catriona loved me. And he wouldn't listen. We fought. He fell. I didn't kill him."

"That is not how it happened," Catriona interrupted. She knew Angus wouldn't mind if she finished the story. "I think Callum was planning to do some harm to him if he didn't get his way. Otherwise, why wear

Hamish's boots? Dougal probably thought he was there to convince him. But he would not have wanted Callum to know why he was really there."

"He was acting all crazy. I didn't know what to think," Calum protested. "It was odd. I slipped in behind him and saw him count up thirteen steps, and then he counted up twelve courses in the stonework and followed that line across to the stairs. He sat down where that row of stones met with the steps."

Angus threw back his head and laughed. "I always wondered why my father thought the year 1312 was so important. Why did I need to know the year the Templars disbanded? The Templar brooch was 13 steps up and then up 12 courses of stone and across to where it met the steps. How clever."

Everyone stared at Angus as the importance of the date dawned on them. With a glance from Sergeant Wolfe, the soldier bound Callum's hands behind his back.

"Can I help ye with anything else, my lady?" he asked Catriona. "For ye, I'll forgive *him* for lying to me. And for withholding information." He glared at Angus.

"I thank ye, Sir. There are other lesser charges, such as scaring my folk into thinking they were always being watched. Ye know how superstitious folk can be. But nay, I think ye have enough. Oh, and he shot Angus, too."

The sergeant turned to him, but Angus assured him he was fine.

"I only meant to scare him," Callum admitted.

"But that pales to what he did to Niall and Dougal. I must tell their families and hope it brings them some peace." Catriona said. "Hamish too." She squeezed his hand.

The sergeant and his man grabbed Callum between them and proceeded outside.

Once everyone else finally left that night, Catriona sat with her feet up, finally relaxed. She sipped a glass of sherry as she listened quietly to Angus. He told them his intentions to work for Mr. Bailey in the colonies. She expressed her regrets at his departure but understood there was nothing for him here. She realized she would miss him. Thanks to him, her people need no longer fear the watcher in the woods. They were safe now.

As Catriona sat at her desk, Angus entered the office three days later. His bags were packed. Hamish had purchased Luath, having had an eye on him since Angus arrived. Callum was locked up. However, his quarters in the basement of the magistrate's house as he awaited trial were more comfortable than Hamish's had been in the undercroft. Despite it all, Catriona felt a little sorry that the man might hang for his crimes.

She looked up from the ledgers as Angus entered. "I am so glad I met ye," she told him as she rose from the chair. "Ye know we'll both miss ye."

"And I ye," he replied. "Letters take a while back and forth, but I promise to write."

"Ye better." Catriona gave him a hug and a peck on the cheek.

Hamish entered and took in the scene. But he smiled at them both. "I'll miss ye too, Angus. But I am pleased to see ye turned out all right. When ye spent so much time with those monks, I had ye figured for the church. Ye have too many brains for that life. I'll take good care o' the horse. He's a beauty." He grinned.

Watching Hamish give his cousin a bear hug, Catriona felt a pang of sorrow. She would miss Angus. But she knew he'd be happier in the colonies.

Angus turned and took both of their hands. "I know ye will take better care of the family's heritage than I would. It is left in good hands."

"But first, some business," Hamish said as he pulled a swatch of checkered fabric from his pouch. "I'd like the pair o' ye to come down to the broch with me."

Catriona's face lit in a smile. "Why, Hamish MacKay, are ye asking me to handfast with ye?" Her heart beat faster in her chest, and she felt breathless.

The big man blushed. "Aye. Who knows when the priest will be here again? Besides, I want Angus to be present."

Catriona and Hamish said their vows in front of the old tower while Angus bound their hands in the strip of MacKay tartan. Angus stood as witness and was so happy for them.

Afterward, the three strolled toward the horses, where Geordie waited in his cart. Several of the villagers heard the news and stood by, watching. Elspeth ran up and hugged them both. Then she turned and hugged Angus.

Catriona reached into her pocket and pulled out an envelope. "Would ye give this to my father when ye see him?" she asked Angus. "I'd like him to know of me. The ring inside this was my mother's." She handed him a small pouch.

Angus smiled at her and said, "Gladly." He hugged her tightly and then Hamish. He placed Catriona's hand in Hamish's and turned to go.

He would miss them, he knew. Angus climbed into the cart to set off on the trail toward Kingussie and his future.

# CAN YOU HELP OUT?

If you enjoyed the story, I kindly ask you to please leave a review at the point of purchase.
To follow my random history blog, please follow me and join my mailing list on the website for information on the continuation of Angus' story.


https://www.carolamorosi.com

# BOOKS BY THE AUTHOR

The MacKay Mysteries:

Death on the Line
Secret of the Old Tower
Sign of Nine Stripes

# AUTHOR'S NOTES

I drew heavily on historical events in *Death on the Line*, the first book. However, I delve into Scottish folklore, which has long fascinated me, in *Secret of the Old Tower*. However, I have thrown in a few historical references.

**The Act of Proscription** was enacted in the Highlands on 1 August 1746, following the Jacobite defeat at Culloden Moor the previous April. It replaced the 1716 Disarming Act but was more rigorously enforced. The primary intent was to deprive the Scots of their arms and render them defenseless. Nighttime searches under the watch of a constable often occurred. The lack of weapons rendered them unable to hunt for food, leaving only trapping and fishing for survival. The new act's secondary purpose was to deprive the Scots of their heritage by banning their dress and bagpipes. Children in schools were required to include prayers for the king and not be taught any seditious material. The first offense was six months of incarceration; the second meant transportation to a penal colony. This Act was not repealed until 1 July 1782. Over the years, there has been much discussion about their tartans being banned; however, most historians now believe the term 'dress' referred to the Highlander's clothing, the kilt, and not the fabric itself. Many period paintings show clothing such as shawls, skirts, and trewes (men's trousers) in these colorful fabrics.

**Ruthven Castle** was built in 1229 as the home of the Lords of Badenoch. Its most famous occupant was Alexander Stewart, more famously known as the Wolf of Badenoch. It continued to be the seat of the earls until it was severely damaged in 1689 during a Jacobite Rebellion. In 1721, the British government erected a fortress on the hilltop to subdue any further rebellion. Following the defeat at Culloden, roughly 3,000 Jacobites fled to the abandoned fort to await word from Prince Charles. When his message arrived four days later, it was "Let every man seek his own safety in the best way he can." Before departing, they blew up the fort so it could no longer be used against them.

**Wakes** – Vastly different from funerals today, a wake celebrated the deceased's life. The women washed the body, wrapped it in linen, and laid it out, sometimes for seven days. Initially, a window was left open for the soul to escape. The body was laid in a coffin or upon a sturdy board. Salt was placed on one side, representing the eternal soul, and soil on the other, the earth from whence one came. As the body was transported, keeners would sing the story of the deceased's life. Food, drink, and dancing followed in celebration. An Englishman in the 17th century wrote of the town bellman walking through the town, ringing a small bell, announcing a death, and inviting people to the wake.

**Beltane** – I remember May Day in school as a child. We strung flowers and danced around a Maypole. But Beltane in the Highlands was much different. It is one of the Celtic seasonal festivals and represents summer, the opposite of Samhain or winter. Imbolc represents the spring, and Lughnasadh the fall. I based the events in my story on 18th-century source material from people such as John Ramsey, an 18th-century Scottish writer who described the festival he attended as a guest. He was particularly interested in the bannocks and noted that the farmers cut holes in them and milked their cows through the opening. In his 1769 *A Tour of Scotland*, Thomas Pennant wrote about pouring the libation, or caudle, on the ground to bless their animals and adding a few drops to spare them from predators.

**Am Fear Liath Mor** — When I began looking for the setting for the second novel, I knew it had to have hills with caves and not be too far from Culloden. The village of Crosstown and the manor are fictitious, but I placed them in the Highlands above Kingussie. However, scanning maps and descriptions, I came across Ben MacDuibh (with various spellings), the 2nd highest peak in Scotland and the tallest in the Cairngorms. And I found this gem; the existence of The Great Gray Man on the mountain. Few have seen him, but many have heard footsteps and crunching sounds in the stones. He is described as standing over ten feet tall and shrouded in gray with long silver hair. Even as recently as 1925, reports abound, such as the one from Royal Geographical Society member J. Norman Collie: "I was returning from the cairn on the summit in a mist when I began to think I heard something other than merely the noise of my own footsteps. Every few steps I took I heard a crunch, and then another crunch, as if someone was walking after me but taking steps three or four times the length of my own. I said to myself, this is all nonsense. I listened and heard it again but could see nothing in the mist. As I walked on and the eerie crunch, crunch sounded behind me, I was seized with terror and took to my heels, staggering blindly among the boulders for four or five miles nearly down to Rothiemurchus Forest. Whatever you make of it, I do not know, but there is something very queer about the top of Ben Macdui, and I will not go back there again."

The Celts remain a superstitious people today, and I mean that in a positive manner. They believe in fairies, seers, and other explanations for the unknown or unexplainable. I tried to weave a bit of their culture into the story.

# MEET THE AUTHOR

## Carol Amorosi

**Author-Amateur Historian-Traveler-Celtic Enthusiast**

History permeates almost everything Carol enjoys, whether travel or volunteer work. Just ask her family! She enjoys gardening, especially learning about plants from the past and their culinary and medicinal uses.

Today, Carol and her husband, Dave, call Germany home, and she spends her time practicing German on their two cats and Widgit, the History Hound, who often joins them on their escapades.

Over the years, she has put her passion for history to good use as a volunteer and an interpreter spanning different periods from the Romans to the Middle Ages to the Revolutionary War, most recently as a member of the 7th Virginia Regiment.

Carol recently achieved a lifelong dream of participating in an archaeological dig when she joined the Melite Civitas Romana Project on Malta. During their tenure in Italy, Carol participated in the Pompeii Food & Drink Study, exploring the eating and drinking habits of the residents in 79 AD. While living on the Eastern Shore of Virginia, Carol volunteered as a docent conducting tours at Ker Place, a colonial home constructed in 1799.

Made in the USA
Middletown, DE
12 March 2024

50663178R00154